Infinite Choices

by

Jane Drager

Infinite Choices

Cover Art by *Debbie Taylor*

The Wild Rose Press, Inc.
PO Box 708
Adams Basin, NY 14410-0708
Visit us at www.thewildrosepress.com

Publishing History
First Crimson Rose Edition, 2015
Print ISBN 978-1-5092-0163-1
Digital ISBN 978-1-5092-0164-8

Published in the United States of America

He froze at the sight of her tear-stained face. "What happened?"

Moving her head, she motioned toward the patio since words wouldn't come from her clogged throat.

Mitch ran out, took one look at his father, and fire rose in his eyes. "Why aren't you working on him?" He grabbed the lifeless body and lowered him to the ground. "Call 911!"

She stared wide-eyed as he listened and felt for breaths. "Mitch, stop. He's gone."

"Not if I can help it. I've too much to tell him." He intertwined his fingers and positioned his palm over Jack's sternum. He pumped on the old man's chest. "Help me!"

"Mitch, please stop. Let him be. He doesn't want this."

"How the hell do you know what he wants? He's my father. Call 911, dammit!" He blew air into his father's mouth.

This is a dream. I'm still upstairs sleeping. She squared her shoulders and placed a hand on his shoulder. In her sternest doctor voice, she leaned down to force him to look up. "Mitch, enough. He wanted to go in peace. Please let him."

He shrugged off her hand. "Are you going to call 911?" He pumped harder, his speed fueled by his anger.

Ribs cracked, and she cringed. She grabbed his arm. "Mitch, stop!"

He pushed her away. "If you're not here to help, then get the hell out." Pumping with one hand, he used the other to reach into his pants pocket for his cell phone. He fumbled, caught it, and dialed. He glanced up at her with a glare. "Out! Get out of this house!"

Praise for Jane Drager

"SECRETS BY NECESSITY took me by surprise. I fell in love with the characters and experienced each and every emotion. The same goes for *ASK NOTHING IN RETURN.* Jane Drager's characters are real. The plots in both books grab you and hold your interest 'til the end."

~Peg G.

~*~

"Jane Drager's books, both *SECRETS BY NECESSITY* and *ASK NOTHING IN RETURN,* are exciting and packed with a true sense of adventure. I had a hard time putting them down because I wanted to find out what happened next."

~Margaret K.

~*~

"I liked both *SECRETS BY NECESSITY* and *ASK NOTHING IN RETURN.* The characters were real and the story lines gripped my attention. I kept reading because I wanted to find out how the stories ended. Jane is a very talented writer and her style of writing is interesting."

~Kathy R.

Dedication

To the Wild Rose Press, who took a chance
on an unknown writer
when no other publisher offered the time of day

Chapter One

Life was dull. Dull and mundane.

Carisa MacDowell repeated those words as she jogged, giving the latter emphasis on every curb jump. The syllables had a certain rhythm as she zipped through the streets of her Philadelphia neighborhood. At least twice a week, she took an afternoon jog to clear her head, and today was perfect with its cool autumn breeze to keep her sweat to a minimum.

As with her life, nothing happened around here either. The crimes so common in a large city avoided her neighborhood because of a great community watch. Just a bunch of old biddies with phones to their ears. Big deal, they had the occasional dog bite to report. A domestic. And yes, the buzz of the week, which had heated the phone lines; the cops had arrested the man three doors down for embezzlement. A sleazy fellow. Shifty eyes. Upturned nose with hair sticking out. Nobody liked him. Otherwise, nothing changed. Only the tree roots. They pushed the concrete sidewalks higher with each passing month. Soon, she'd be doing hurdles.

Oh, hell.

The phone call this morning had put her in a funk. A friend had called to brag about her upcoming trip to Rio de Janeiro with a man she'd met at a bar. Fun. Excitement. Adventure. Head-over-heels in love. The way life should be.

Well, la-dee-da. In a book maybe.

Jealousy without question. And why? Carisa had made a success of herself. She had a great profession, nice house, plenty of friends. Her job as an emergency room physician in a center city hospital kept her adrenalin going. Two years so far and everyday, something new, something to challenge a few dormant brain cells. Except for the knife and gunshot wounds. Those came in every shift. She'd stitched up more cuts in her short career than a seamstress working for a fashion designer.

No, her personal life made the dull and mundane list. She never met anyone worth a second look. Even when she socialized with friends at a bar, she yawned at the men who approached. Not like she wanted a pirate with a knife between his teeth. Just a man a little less humdrum. She wasn't asking too much, right?

Maybe all she needed was a good hobby.

"Hi, Carisa!"

Little Harriet Turner called from across the street. The cute little girl had dark curly hair bouncing on her head like loose springs. They surrounded a pudgy face, a kind of doll-like appearance straight out of the toy store. She sat on Mrs. Schubert's immaculate lawn with its precise edges and polished flamingoes. The old fuss-wart might slip into cardiac arrest when she spotted Harriet's butt cheeks imprinted in the grass.

Carisa preferred the dandelion look. The yellow flowers always gave her lawn the right touch of color. Little Harriet loved to come over and blow the white seedlings when they sprouted. Carisa had often joined her, and they'd have a blast. Consequently, she had the worst-looking lawn on the block. A regular dandelion garden. Carisa waved to Harriet and continued her pace.

Ouch. She should have worn her other sneakers. These had pounded the pavement one too many times and were hurting her feet. *Last run for sure. In the trash they go.*

While house-hunting last year, she had a stroke of luck. Not only was a great mortgage rate part of the package, but the house had sold for less than it was worth because of foreclosure. So what if she'd bought a townhouse where every unit resembled a cookie sheet cut-out? She owned it—at the end of the mortgage anyway.

"Oomph!" A man plowed into her. He shoved her across the pavement onto someone's front lawn, tangling his arms and legs with hers in a wide sprawl.

What the hell! Since when do we have elephants on the streets of Philadelphia?

She stared dazed at a gorgeous head of curly brown hair that smelled of sweat and shampoo. She tried pushing him off, but he was like an anvil on her chest, restricting her breaths to short ineffective puffs.

The man scrambled to his feet, muttering and cussing. "Sorry, ma'am. Hope I didn't hurt you."

Hurt me? I'm a frog under a tire!

And he was gone. Boom, like that. The way men always came and went in her life. She couldn't move. Her air, vision, and everything in between, gone. *Take a breath. Let it out. Repeat.* She stared at a clear autumn sky and counted stars.

"Are you all right?"

An old woman stuck her head into the sunlight.

She wore a pink jogging suit with matching

3

sweatbands around her wrists and forehead, like Mrs. Corolla down the block. After a few blinks to clear the stars, recognition registered. The face was indeed Mrs. Corolla. "I'm trying to figure out what happened." She palpated her sternum in case he'd separated it from the ribcage. *No flail chest from the anvil. A miracle in the making.* She rolled to a sitting position.

Mrs. Corolla took a leaf off Carisa's hair. "All I saw was two men running. One was chasing the other, but people run around here all the time. Like you. I never know who's doing what." She used a wrinkled hand to shield her eyes against the sun. "I don't see them anymore. The first one ran through the separated buildings. The second collided into you. He was pretty big. Are you hurt?"

Carisa rubbed the back of her neck to hear the vertebra snap, crackle, and pop. "I think he rearranged all my bones." Or crushed a few. Highly probable her internal organs had shifted into new territory. "I landed on my glenohumeral junction."

Mrs. Corolla blinked, and her mouth rounded into an "o."

"Shoulder joint." *May as well clarify for the old lady.* She rotated the cuff. *Maybe a slight displacement.*

"You doctors and your fancy words. Like a foreign language." She pointed to the grass. "I hate to give ya bad news, but you're on Willoughby's lawn. He doesn't like to clean up after his dog."

Aw, shit. Literally. She inspected her hands. A brown smudge. *Oh, dear.* She sniffed and made a face before wiping her hands on her pants.

"Maybe you should call the cops."

And tell them what? She had no idea who he was,

4

where he went, or where he came from. They collided, and he was gone.

A police car raced down the street, lights and siren full. A second police car followed. Both whipped around the corner, tires screeching, and disappeared.

"The cops must be after those two," Mrs. Corolla mused. "Maybe we'll see them on the six o'clock news."

"Maybe." Carisa wobbled to her feet.

Mrs. Corolla pinched the front of Carisa's sweatpants. "You got some red marks on you, dear. See?" She dropped her hand and pointed. "There's also dog poop on your butt."

Blood smeared the front of her pale blue sweat suit. A faint trace also soiled the pant leg. She refused to look at the back. "Not mine. The man was hemorrhag...bleeding." Not like she noticed. The extent of her description involved curly brown hair. And stars. Brown hair and stars.

"I've been meaning to ask you, can I pick some dandelions from your lawn next summer?"

Carisa stared at the old woman, not certain she heard right. Maybe she had some grass in her ears.

"Italians love that stuff, you know. Cooked or raw. Some people make wine. You don't use pesticides, do you?"

Carisa shook herself. "Okay, yes, of course. Pick all you want. It's completely organic."

"Thanks. Me and the mister haven't had a good dish of cooked dandelions since the new drug store paved over the neighborhood park. Sure, the Italian market sells them, but we like picking the leaves ourselves. Ever try them?"

"No, and I don't intend to start." Bad enough she was force-fed escarole as a child. Ugh.

"Ah, well. If you cook them right, they're not so bitter." She studied the surrounding lawns. "Too bad you don't have pokeweeds. I can't find them anywhere."

Carisa stared. "I don't even know what that is."

"Just another Italian dish. Are you gonna call the cops?"

"I don't know what to tell them, Mrs. Corolla. Did you get a good look at the man?"

"Not really. Big guy. Brown hair. That's it."

That was her account, too. She thanked her neighbor and headed for home, ignoring the untied shoelace dragging on the ground. She couldn't bend to tie it anyway.

By the time Carisa drove into work, she suffered from shooting daggers around her right rotator cuff. Not a good sign. A possible hairline crack. Either the scapula or ball of the humerus. Both had sustained the brunt of the man's weight, but the lawn softened the blow. Willoughby's poop-filled lawn. If she had fallen onto concrete, she'd be on a gurney by now.

A painkiller. That's what I need. One that wouldn't put her in a comatose state while she worked. Highly probable the impact squirted the bursa fluid straight to her chest cavity. The area needed a good ice pack, but she'd wasted enough time and was running late.

She entered Jefferson Hospital's busy emergency department to find chaos. Two orderlies struggled to restrain a wild man running naked through the waiting area. A cardiac code was in progress. An old man cried at the top of his lungs that he was dying and no one cared. *Same old, same old.* No matter what shift, chaos reigned. After slipping on a lab coat over her dress clothes of blouse and pants, she approached the charge nurse. "All right, give me the lowdown."

The nurse with her hair askew and cheeks flushed slammed on the computer keyboard only to watch the Enter key pop out of its slot. She held the key in her hand with a look of exasperation.

"Everything rolled in at once," she complained. "Dr. Bonner's running the code in trauma. Dr. Cirello is handling two cardiacs and one respiratory distress. Dr. Patel is in ortho setting a leg, and he has two more fractures waiting for him. We have three bowels, two head colds, and one wino sleeping like a baby in ENT." She pounded the Enter key back in place on the keyboard. "We need you first in bed four. Stab wound. A cop. Get him stitched and out so we can clear the waiting room of all the suits. They're wandering around acting like he's on life support and making the patients nervous."

Carisa chuckled. "I'll take care of him." She walked down the hall past several open doors with patients reaching out, as if they were the walking dead trying to grab her. One little lady was in the process of closing her door. With a raised hand, Carisa stopped her. "We keep the doors open, ma'am, unless a doctor or nurse is with you. Safety reasons."

Unless they were puking their guts out or using the bedpan. Even a big hospital like Jefferson afforded a patient some privacy. She stepped through the open door to bed four and paused to survey the scene.

The man on the gurney, stripped to the waist, had his back to the entrance. He rested on his side with a hand propped on one elbow to hold his head.

A quick visual assessment revealed a man with a broad muscular back that tapered to a slim waist where a large gauze pad covered his wound. No moaning or groaning so pain levels were tolerable. Skin color decent. No monitor was attached so no problems with heart rate or blood pressure. He rotated his head when she shut the door.

She froze. She had never gawked at her patients, male or female, but this man stopped her dead. His head of curly brown hair was a coincidence, right?

A slow smile spread onto his lips. "I'm glad to see I didn't hurt you."

Take it easy. She stiffened her back. She was here to help him, not kill him. "You didn't even stick around to see if you crushed me to death."

"I can see that I didn't."

Her heart pounded with fury at his lackadaisical tone. The increased pressure pulsed through her aching shoulder to egg her on. She wanted to strangle him or pinch his balls with forceps. Instead, she stepped back. "I can't stitch you."

He dropped the hand holding his head. "Why not?"

"Because I want to use the biggest needle we've got, that's why not." Or use a bottle of alcohol to pour on his wound so he could scream bloody murder.

His smile broadened. "You're even more beautiful when you're angry."

Just what she needed to start her shift—a flirty cop. Far too many men were flirty these days. Half of them were married. The other half...well, if she had taken them up on their offers, she wouldn't have a dull and mundane life to complain about. She'd be like her friend running off to Rio de Janeiro for a fling.

Carisa turned toward the sink to wash her hands. She needed cold water to ease the fury, but hospital water was tepid at best. Even after several minutes of scrubbing, she still wanted a big needle. And wire for sutures. *Yeah, great idea.* She faced him while drying her hands. "I apologize for the outburst."

"I'm a big boy, Doc. I can take whatever needle you use...I assume you're the doctor."

She forced herself to calm down. The ER was too busy to pass him off to another doctor. She approached the computer at the head of his bed to read his medical chart.

"Shouldn't you introduce yourself?" he asked.

She was doing everything wrong with this man. What happened to all her training? *Focus, girl, focus.* She should step out the door and start over. She extended her hand. "Dr. Carisa MacDowell."

"Nice name." He took her hand and squeezed. "I'm Mitch Montero."

"You're a cop?"

He still held her hand. "Lieutenant. Homicide. Philly PD. I'm sorry if I hurt you. I was chasing a murder suspect. I didn't see you until I whipped around the van."

She hadn't seen him, the other man, or the van. *Duh.*

"You should be more aware of your surroundings, Doc. Life is dangerous enough in this city."

Her grip tightened in his. She wasn't in the mood for a lecture from a man she wanted to thump...even if he was right. Instead, she forced her hand from his. "I'll keep that in mind. Did you catch the guy?"

"Two blocks later. I couldn't find you when I returned."

Her eyebrows shot upward. "You came back?"

"Of course, I came back." His gaze narrowed. "I don't make a habit of plowing down beautiful women."

The compliment rattled her. He said the words with a tone of annoyance, but the sincerity came through.

Just a flirty cop. Nothing more.

Her heart didn't listen. The vessel jumped around in her chest like a calisthenics workout. The man was distractingly handsome with warm brown eyes that surveyed with more than a casual interest. Cop eyes, clear and analytical, trained to see and evaluate before the next blink. His lips had a sensual fullness while the curls in his brown hair looked finger soft and tempting. If only the knife wound was in that curly mass so she could—

At that thought, she cleared her throat and turned back to the computer screen.

His medical record listed him as single, which had nothing to do with his injury, but a good doctor was thorough. No other pertinent medical history struck her except for a small scar on his left cheek. *Hopefully not too close to the curls.* She peeked only to lock onto his twinkling brown eyes.

Best to get this man out the door as soon as possible.

Distracted by his knowing look, she returned to the sink.

"You washed your hands already, Doc."

"Yes, but I shook your hand." If she had done that in the first place, she wouldn't need a second wash.

She slipped on a pair of latex gloves and removed

the gauze covering his wound. The slash covered a seven-inch section of his waist—not deep, but enough to make a mess of his clothes and require stitches. "You smeared blood all over me," she said while palpating the area. Nothing but hard muscle. *Nice.*

"Sorry, but I wasn't about to let the perp get away. I had him on suspicion of murder and assaulting a police officer. Not to mention resisting arrest. I wanted to beat him to a pulp, but I threw him in the back of a squad car. Then I returned to see if you were okay."

Commendable. Now, she was sorry she hadn't lain on the poop lawn longer.

She tore off her latex gloves and pointed to the head of the bed. "I need you to put your head on the pillow, Mr. Montero. Once I set up a surgical area, please keep still." She opened a surgical kit, slipped on the required sterile gloves to prevent infection, and then laid out the contents on a nearby tray. The sterile drape was next with the cutout hole positioned over his wound. Cleansing with the iodine solution took only a minute, but before starting with the sutures, she dragged a stool over with her foot to sit.

He lifted his head to see the contents on the tray. "You weren't kidding about the big needle."

"These aren't big. They're standard surgical size. Relax, Mr. Montero. You're already on a gurney. If you faint, I won't have to catch you."

He snorted as he flopped his head back onto the pillow. "I won't faint."

If she learned a few lessons in her ER career, she knew big men sometimes fainted. She also learned never try to catch them.

"How's the wound look?"

"You'll live." She filled a small syringe with a numbing agent and tapped the side to clear the bubbles.

"You're a good doctor. All I feel is a pinch."

"That's because I'm numbing the area. The pinch is the small needle included in the kit. I didn't start the good stuff yet." She leaned back as if admiring a work of art.

"How old are you?" he asked.

"Personal questions are prohibited between patient and doctor."

He half-rose, eyes wide. "Who the hell made that rule?"

"Me. Right now, in fact. Lay down. You're messing up my sterile area, and if you're trying to distract me, it won't work." *Although he is doing a damn good job.*

"Oh, I get it. You can ask personal questions, but when the tables are turned, you change the rules. I can find out, you know."

Why couldn't he be an old ugly orangutan, the kind with bald spots from constant scratching? Better yet, why not be married with twenty kids? Maybe a beer-barrel belly. And belching. Yes, belching would definitely turn her off. As it was, her hands touched a damaged Michelangelo, an expertly sculpted statue chiseled and smoothed to perfection.

Oh, how I want to squeeze any ole spot.

"I can strip naked if you want."

Heat flushed her cheeks and shot straight out her ears. She'd never blushed before, never. She had stared at more skin than most women saw in a lifetime. That was her job. She was a doctor who worked in an emergency room.

"You're beet red," he said, grinning.

"Hot flash. Too warm in here."

"I think the room's quite cool. Must be my near-naked state."

She glanced at him, and her breath caught at the look he flashed back. His gaze was intense, unwavering, causing the needle to shake in her hand. She coughed to clear the Sahara desert out of her throat.

How could she possibly be attracted to a man on sight? Hell, she'd worked on men fully naked without as much as a hiccup. But with this man, her hormones jumped around like cattle trying to get out of the corral.

She hadn't done the dance with a man in a long time. Her last serious liaison happened during med school. Even then, their romps bordered on ho-hum, enough to alleviate hormonal boredom. Sex, not love, like two animals in the weeds.

Concentrate, dear.

Yes, she was a professional. Professionals acted with a certain decorum. "You should be thankful the knife slashed instead of penetrated, Mr. Montero. The wound is right over your liver. We lose a significant amount of blood from that organ."

"You wore a ponytail earlier," he said with a faint dreamy air. "I like your hair either way."

Had someone already given him a sedative? She double-checked his chart. No sedative. The dreamy tone was a put-on, right? She should tell him her ponytail was a thing of the past, thanks to him.

"Are you married, Dr. MacDowell? I can find that out, too."

Dammit, she needed someone else in the room. A nurse. An orderly. Anyone with two feet. Why of all days was the ER so busy?

Because the ER was always busy. People should stay home and tend to their own injuries. They depended on doctors way too much.

Oh, hell. She was overreacting. His comments were the result of shock, and she needed an ice pack on her shoulder to calm the throb created by a thundering heart.

Relax. Get him out the door and send him on his way.

Famous last words. "No, I'm not married," she said as she tied a suture, "and I won't answer any more personal queries. Is that clear, Lieutenant?"

"Yes, ma'am." A grin stretched onto his lips. "How come I've never seen you before?"

She looked at him with a wide gaze. "How often do you come in?"

"I've had a few of my men get hurt. Your nice head of hair is hard to miss."

"Then you probably wandered in on my day off." *I dropped a stitch, dammit.* She compensated on the next one.

"I'd like to take you out to dinner."

He was making it extremely hard to concentrate. "I don't date my patients, Mr. Montero."

"Aw, that's not fair. We met before this."

"A collision is not what I call 'meeting' someone, and now, you're my patient." She grabbed a gauze pad to pat the forming blood drops.

"I'll change doctors."

The man was persistent. She laughed because she couldn't help herself. "You can do that."

"All right, consider yourself replaced. How about

dinner?"

"No, thanks."

"Why not?"

"Because I'm still stitching. You should replace me before or after, not in the middle."

She cut the last suture and covered the wound with sterile gauze. *Nice job if I do say so myself.* The Michelangelo was fixed. She grabbed the trash and hurried to the sink because again, a heat wave flushed her face.

Definitely a hot flash. Some women got them early. Her father had said so, and he should know.

She couldn't ignore the obvious. Her attraction toward Mitch Montero was an erotic dream come true. Visions of overwhelming passion and sex 'til all hours—

Friggin' dancing hormones. She might hump him right here on the stretcher. "Give your stitches a week, Mr. Montero, and no heavy lifting. Your family doctor can remove them. I'll write you a script for antibiotics. I suggest you take all of them. You have no idea where that knife has been. For the same reason, I'll have the nurse give you a shot of gamma globulin." She turned to the computer to complete his medical record and hit the Save button.

With a muffled groan, he swung his legs over the side of the stretcher and snatched his shirt from the bedrail. He extended a sleeve to study the damage. "I may as well toss this." He rolled the material and lobbed the ball into the wastebasket.

"Do you have a jacket?" She glanced around the area but spotted only an empty chair.

"Too warm for a jacket."

Warm? She wouldn't call the low fifties warm. "Well, you can't go out bare chested. Any of your buddies have a jacket?"

"I'm a little too messy for that, Doc."

"Then I'll get you a scrub top." Otherwise, every female from here to the entrance would slide into heat at the sight of his chest. She reached with her right hand for an extra large from the linen cabinet. Her shoulder locked in an upright position. *That wasn't a bright idea.* She turned her back to him and grabbed her rotator cuff to unlock the joint. The stars returned, floating around her head like a cartoon. She needed to get him out the door before her face changed to a permanent wince. With her left hand, she took the top and handed it to him.

"I don't need a shirt." He held the boxy garment in the air as his brows furrowed into a scowl.

"Yes, you do. It's October, not July, and no, I don't care if our weather is unseasonably warm. My boss will have my head if you leave half clothed."

A tiny smile curled one corner of his mouth. "And a very pretty head you have, Dr. Carisa MacDowell. Blonde like sunshine. Bright and beautiful."

Yep, too flirty. She narrowed her gaze. "I'll have the nurse come in with your shot and discharge papers." She turned to leave.

"Doc?"

Hearing the tentative note in his voice, she turned, one brow cocked with uncertainty.

"Are you really okay?"

She smiled at his concerned tone. "Yes, Lieutenant, I'm fine."

Outside the room, she leaned against the wall for

just a second. She had lied through her teeth. Her right shoulder was killing her.

Chapter Two

Lt. Mitch Montero stood at the inside entrance of the emergency room, watching the activity before him. The atmosphere was nothing like a TV show. People slouched in the waiting area, looking bored to death or staring at a receptionist who'd rather be somewhere else. No one ran around with an arm dangling. No blood squirting. The staff gave polite smiles as they hurried past, always with a professional air that never won an Emmy award.

He saw enough of the inside of emergency rooms to know what he was talking about. While on street patrol, he had dragged in busted-up criminals who pretended to be dying. Now, as a lieutenant, he dragged in some of the men under his command who pretended to be dying. Yesterday was the first time in a long while for himself. He looked around.

Several familiar faces glanced his way and waved. Carisa MacDowell wasn't one of them. She was hard to miss with that nice head of blonde hair with the soft waves and a golden glow that reflected the overhead lights. Not like he had a particular preference for hair color. If the woman was willing, he didn't care if she had purple spikes. He had even slept with a bald woman once. Actually, twice. Strangest liaison he'd ever had. No hair to run his fingers through, like rubbing a baby's bottom. She claimed he was using her,

18

which he was.

Maybe the doctor was in a back room. The ER had so many branches from constant expansion. The layout resembled a maze where people yelled for help, peeking behind doors and curtains for the door that would lead them to freedom. He only stopped by to thank her. His excuse, anyway. He had no idea why he bothered. Except for the ponytail. So cute. High on her head with a bounce that gave a guy erotic dreams of her ponytail brushing…well, never mind. When he saw her stroll in with her hair loose, he marveled at her windswept appearance, and his curiosity notched up a bit.

All right, a lot.

He craned his neck. She could be on break or in any of the countless rooms. He puffed up his chest, felt the stitches pull at his waist, and approached the main desk.

The same woman from yesterday flashed him a smile. She stood behind a counter where all check-ins took place. "Well, hi, Lieutenant. How are you feeling today?"

"Fine after I got myself cleaned up." Which was damn difficult. *Don't get the stitches wet*, the nurse had said. *Yeah, right.* Blood mixed with sweat had attracted every dust particle while chasing the perp, and then gravel and road tar stuck to the sweat after he tackled the SOB. He was in no mood for a sponge bath. "Is Dr. MacDowell working today?"

"No, she's off. Are you here for a follow-up visit? Any nurse will be happy to check your wound." She winked while a wry grin stretched onto her lips.

Under different circumstances, he'd flirt back, but he wasn't in the right frame of mind. He'd never had trouble attracting women. They eyed his six-foot-two, two-hundred-pound frame like he was the most virile man on the surface of the earth. Not that he tried to dissuade them, but getting them unattracted was the problem. They'd hang on him and coo in his ear while he silently prayed for his cell phone to ring as an excuse to scram.

Yet, here he stood in suit and tie with the hopes of impressing one particular woman. He had asked himself why several times on the way over, but something about Carisa MacDowell forced him to reevaluate his priorities concerning women.

Something about her...

She had blushed a deep scarlet. Carisa MacDowell was an experienced ER physician who handled a lot of male body parts. Her blush told him her mind had gone beyond the doctor/patient mentality, and that more than anything activated an insatiable curiosity. He liked the look and wanted to see it again. "When's Dr. MacDowell's next shift?"

"Not for a while, I'm afraid. She's out on medical leave."

Damn, I knew it.

When she had reached for the scrub top, she winced while the pain shot from those brown bedroom eyes. He had misinterpreted the grimace as too far of a stretch. *She lied to me.*

"Some guy plowed into her when she was jogging yesterday. Halfway through her shift, she could barely move her right arm. The entire shoulder is an ugly mess—oops, I shouldn't have told you any of this, you know, privacy issues." Her round cheeks turned red.

"But you are talking about an unreported accident,

especially if an insurance company is involved. Was anything broken?" Gad, he hoped not.

"She sustained a significant injury, but no breaks. I told her to file a report with the cops, but she said it was a minor collision. I think she's being too nice." She paused when an orderly handed her a piece of paper. "She stitched you yesterday. Didn't she say anything?"

"Not a word." His gut wrenched at the idea of hurting her. His weight exceeded hers by a good eighty to ninety pounds, and the impact was solid. Thank God, they had landed on grass. "Can you tell me where she lives?"

"No, sir. It's against the rules." She leaned forward onto the counter, her voice low. "You being a cop shouldn't have trouble finding her."

He smiled at that because she was right. He had resisted the urge to investigate Carisa on the computer when he returned to the office this morning. A casual thank you was his plan. But now, she was on medical leave because of him. *Damn*. Circumstances forced him to check her record.

He thanked the woman and turned to leave. Then, with a snap of his fingers, he leaned over the counter. "Does she have any particular favorite thing, like maybe flowers or candy?"

The woman laughed. "For anyone who knows Carisa MacDowell, they know the woman loves black cherry ice cream. Any brand will do. She eats them all. Oh, and Lieutenant—" Her eyes twinkled as she leaned toward him. "A half gallon, at least."

****

After spending the rest of the morning fighting with a computer that wouldn't cooperate, Mitch pulled to the curb in front of Carisa's town home and debated whether he should go through with this. It was mid-afternoon, naptime in his book of leisure activities. What if a man lived with her? He had asked if she was married. He'd gotten no further than that. *So what?* He'd simply say thank you, sorry for the inconvenience, and be done with whatever churned around in his gut. He wanted to find out how badly he hurt her, nothing more.

Then why bother with a stop at the supermarket only to wait in the five-items-or-less aisle with a woman in front who couldn't count? He stepped from his car.

The neighborhood was typical Philly style. Block after block of newly renovated row homes, all red brick. Builders gave them an outside facelift of fresh paint and new siding at the peak, changed the name to town homes, and bingo, higher price. Two stories, three bedrooms, one-and-a-half baths. Perfect for small families. Every unit had a fifty-by-thirty front lawn, a curved walkway stretching from the driveway to the front door, and a garage too small for a car. No deviation except for window color.

A step above his place. He lived in a condo in center city, a stone's throw from headquarters. The size and location suited his needs, which were minimal. What good was a house when he spent most of his time at the office?

He approached the front door and rang the bell. While waiting, he fidgeted like an inexperienced teenager, glancing around the street, hoping no one would see her slam the door in his face. No reason to feel so antsy except, deep down, he wanted to see her.

Why was the question.

Get it over with. Talk to her and move on.

The beauty from yesterday sans make-up opened the door. She wore jeans with a pale blue sweatshirt, no shoes or socks, her hair loose about the shoulders. Her right arm hung in a sling, which irked him to no end.

Her brown eyes grew wide. "What are you doing here?"

"Making a peace offering." He showed her the bag in his hand. "Black cherry ice cream, your favorite."

She scanned him from head to toe with a wary look passing onto her face. Not too many patients dropped in on their doctors, he guessed. He waved the bag in front of her face.

"You don't need a peace offering, Lieutenant."

"Sure, I do. I stopped at the hospital to thank you only to discover you were placed on medical leave. Don't you know it's against the law to lie to a police officer?"

A smile touched her mouth. "Yes, all right, I lied. And you don't have to thank me, even though the words are nice to hear once in a while."

"Your ice cream is melting." He jiggled the bag, creating a rustle of plastic that drew her gaze.

She clearly debated while biting a lip that looked soft and luscious. Her gaze shifted from him to the bag, a cycle she repeated without a change to her expression. He wasn't sure which factor won, but she ushered him inside.

To his surprise, her home had a just-moved-in look with boxes piled in the corner. The standard furnishings filled the living room. Nothing hung on the walls, no photos on the end tables. The kitchen had enough space for a large table and chairs, but a small yard sale fold-up with a radio stood in the spot. Three stools faced a counter for eating comfort with a laptop and coffee maker crowding one end.

"You're not looking at a doctor with a bankroll," she said.

Oops. "Sorry. Didn't mean to be obvious. How long have you lived here?"

"A little over a year." She headed for the kitchen. "I can't decide if I want to set roots in Philly or not. I studied at Jefferson, completed all my residency requirements in surrounding hospitals, but now I'm wondering if I should move on."

"Greener pastures?"

"Something like that."

"Why'd you buy a house then?"

"Short sale, a bargain-basement price. I also got a mortgage cheaper than my apartment rent."

Smart move. He'd love to bust his landlord for theft since he enjoyed raising the condo rent every year, but what the hey? "You want to eat now?" He held up the bag.

"Yes, I do. I need a bit of cheering." She grabbed two bowls from a cabinet. "You're having some, I hope."

"A little. I have to watch my figure."

She chuckled softly, and her entire face brightened in the process. He smiled in return because she had become the most beautiful woman in the world.

That was an odd declaration coming from the mind of a devil-may-care bachelor. Carisa was not the drop-dead gorgeous type where men drooled at her feet. She was, in fact, an ordinary-looking female with ordinary features. Nothing stood out—except her blonde hair. A wave caught every beam of light, whether from overhead or through a window. Yesterday, she'd worn a lab coat over a pair of dress slacks and blouse, a professional appearance so important to a doctor's image. Today, she wore casuals and ambled around in bare feet. She looked cute. Petite and cute.

She handed him a large scoop with a worn handle. "You have to serve me." She slipped onto a counter stool.

"With pleasure." He gave her a heaping spoonful, expecting a cry of protest, but heard her ask for more instead. He served himself a hefty amount, too.

"So, how bad are you hurt? Remember, I'm a cop. Don't lie to me." He leaned against the sink counter while eating.

Before answering, she shoved a spoonful in her mouth. "The glenohumeral—" She coughed. "The shoulder joint was jammed on impact. Our ortho specialist gave me a shot of corticosteroid to lessen the inflammation. No visible cracks. More like a bad bruise. The skin surface is a nice shade of green and purple. How's your side?"

"We're not changing the subject yet. Any other part of you damaged?"

"No. All your weight landed on my shoulder." She clicked the side of her bowl with the spoon. "This ice cream is pretty good."

"It's low fat. I didn't want you yelling at me. Here, have some more." He put another heaping spoonful in her bowl. Again, no protest. She simply dug in.

Her driver's license had listed her age at thirty, three years younger than himself, but she appeared older, perhaps more mature than a normal thirty-year-old. Her profession, no doubt. A constant barrage of trauma and death. No, not even that. Her face revealed an underlying sadness.

"I won't be back at work anytime soon." She dug around for a cherry.

"How long?"

"I asked for a few days, but my boss insisted I take accumulated vacation along with medical leave. I hardly ever take time off anymore."

"Same here. My captain complained about my accumulated days. He held the elevator door and practically kicked me in. I decided to take a ride to see my dad. I want you to come with me."

Her spoon stopped mid-mouth. "You're joking, right?"

"Not at all. I can use some company. Besides, you're on medical because of me. I'd like to make amends."

She stifled a laugh. "Meeting your father is not the way to a woman's heart. Any ice cream left?"

The woman had a knack for changing the subject. Maybe he should cut his losses and scram. He hadn't a clue what possessed him to ask in the first place. A sugar rush, perhaps. Too much ice cream. "Nope. We ate the whole thing." He shook the empty carton. "I'm sorry I didn't buy two."

"I'm glad you didn't."

He put the dishes in the sink then settled on a stool at the other end of the counter. Wariness returned to her face. Since the ice cream was gone, he had no reason to stick around. Like asking her to take a trip with him. He failed to understand his own motives. He had no time for a woman in his life. His chosen goal was to reach captain and after that, police commissioner. A woman would hamper his plans.

Yet, here he sat. For the first time ever, he didn't want to leave. "I think you'll like my dad." Maybe he lost too much blood yesterday. Not enough flowing to his brain to send signals to shut his mouth.

"Since we're hardly on a first name basis, why should I meet your dad?"

"You'll see some fall foliage, and I'll show you some sights along the way."

She eyed him through slits. "Where does your father live, Lieutenant?"

"Mitch. We're first names now…Carisa. He lives in Geneva, New York."

She stared wide-eyed, her mouth half open. "That's near the Finger Lakes, right?"

"Yes, a nice ride. Ever been there?"

"No, and it doesn't matter whether I've been there or not." She slipped off the stool and headed for the living room, shaking her head along the way. "I'd be crazy to go. We hardly know each other. You can't tell me the drive's a simple day trip." She faced him.

"No, a few days. A week, if you want. Two weeks, if you're game."

She again stared.

Perhaps he'd sprung the idea too quickly. He was never a man to beat around a bush. He said what he wanted to say and damn to the consequences. "I thought it might be fun." Those weren't the right words either.

She chewed on her lower lip, standing rigid in the middle of the living room.

Small wonder she didn't kick him out the door.

"Look, Carisa. I rarely visit my father. When I do, I get bored and leave after two nights. If I take you, I can show you around and extend my visit. My dad's getting up in years, and I should spend more time with him. You'll be a good excuse to stay a while."

An analytical gaze studied him. The rigidness had eased somewhat, but she wasn't jumping for joy at his trip suggestion.

"We both have time to use," he continued. "This is the perfect opportunity to get acquainted."

"You're on a guilt trip, Mitch. What happened was an accident. The last thing I want is to have you feel sorry for me."

She made a good point. Why else blurt out an invitation without thinking? Maybe a shrink should bore a hole in his brain to find out why he turned impulsive all of a sudden. Was it guilt?

No. He sensed an opportunity to correct an ever-growing problem. "I want you to come for another reason, Carisa. I have a meddlesome older sister who thinks she's in charge of my life. She's always fixing me up with one of her corporate friends. If my sister hears I'm coming with a woman, she'll leave her girlfriends home." He hoped anyway. His sister was overbearing to the point of rudeness. "I'll use you like a shield."

Carisa laughed. Her posture relaxed as she headed toward the sofa. Still chuckling, she curled up in the corner. Was she softening? *Say yes.*

"No," she said.

Rats. "You don't have to answer right away. You can mull it over. I'm not leaving until the weekend."

"I answered you, Mitch. You'll face your sister

28

alone."

Undaunted, he positioned a footstool by her feet and dropped onto a hard cushion. "My dad lives in a big house, Carisa. His housekeeper can ready a separate bedroom for you. Strictly platonic. I'll tell her you love black cherry ice cream, and she can stock the freezer." He leaned forward to touch her feet. An electric spark shot through him. He pulled back sharply.

An odd sensation. Totally foreign. Visions of cool sheets and a blonde head on his shoulder flashed through his mind faster than a blink. All from skin-to-skin contact?

Nah. Had to be the rug.

She watched him with half-veiled eyes.

Yesterday, her cheeks flushed while focusing on her work. They were reactions that had aroused his interest. Today, a stoic expression covered her face. She had a good grip on her emotions, a professional air even in the comfort of her home. Was he wrong about the attraction? Maybe he should head for the door, save himself from the embarrassment of making a complete fool of himself.

Oh, hell. He wasn't wrong. He wanted her to come for a very special reason, and the motive had nothing whatever to do with his father or sister. "I'm not asking you to be intimate. I'm asking you to protect me from my sister. She's the reason I leave early."

"You don't strike me as a man who has trouble attracting women, Mitch. Why don't you take someone you know?"

"Truthfully, because I don't know too many women. I'm a one-night-stand kind of guy. I don't have long-term affairs, and I'm not asking one from you.

Think of my offer as a free trip with a tour guide. Strictly on the up and up."

She smiled faintly without looking at him.

What other words of wisdom should come out of his mouth? Free room and board? Wonderful scenery? A great guy at your beck and call? *Yeah, right*. He pushed to his feet. "I'm leaving on Saturday. That gives you three days, but I need to forewarn Emily to get your room ready. I can drive the distance in five hours. She'll beat my butt if I waltz in with you unannounced. I'll call on Friday morning, okay?"

She cocked her head. "You have my address and phone number already. What else do you know about me, Mitch Montero?"

He leaned down to gaze into her face. They were too close. He had the unmistakable urge to kiss her lips, to taste her mouth and the ice cream on her tongue. Uncertainty stared back. "I'll tell you what I don't know, Carisa MacDowell. I don't know if you have a man in your life."

"You should have asked that before inviting me to New York."

"I'm waiting for an answer."

She shook her head. "No man."

All of a sudden, the world turned into a wonderful place. The bad guys, perps, and low-lifes disappeared from his mind. A first.

"I'm not finished. I don't know why such a beautiful woman has me captivated, and finally, I don't know if you'd rather bop me on the head or kick me in the rear to get me out of your hair."

She grinned on the last one. "Thanks for the ice cream."

He straightened. "You're welcome. For the record, this isn't a guilt trip. I want you to come. Will you reconsider?"

"I'll think about it."

She couldn't fool him. Her answer was still no. He needed to throw down the gauntlet.

Chapter Three

The man had lost all his marbles. How could he suggest such a trip? Two strangers on the road together. Finger Lakes, of all places. Smack-dab in the middle of New York State. What was it, maybe a hundred miles away? Hell, almost to Canada. And what possible interest would she have in meeting his father?

No, Mitch suffered from a guilt complex. He had made an offer to take her to New York because of an age-old culpability inbred by every parent in the world. He expected her to refuse, and he wasn't disappointed, but a smart man would have a contingency plan in case she accepted. *Oh, sorry, work calls. Maybe another time.*

Give me a break.

On Friday, she'd hear a big sigh of relief when she again refused. End of guilt complex.

But not the end of Mitch Montero.

Her mind couldn't shake him. She'd tossed and turned all night with his face drifting into her dreams. He had a way of looking at her with a warm, inviting gaze that excited her nerve endings, and his image persisted into the wee hours of the morning. Nothing calmed the excitement. She'd blamed the ice cream, too much sugar, too much fat, not enough cherries. Then her shoulder with its aching throb that refused to subside, and finally, her pajamas until she had no more excuses left. Even counting sheep jumping over a haystack had proved useless. The sheep fur resembled his brown curly hair.

Mitch refused to wait for Friday. The next day, he stood on her doorstep with a pizza box on his arm. No suit and tie this time. He wore an open collar shirt with a light sport coat perfectly fitted to emphasize his large chest. Handsome yesterday. Handsome today. The no-relationship man.

Go figure.

"Pepperoni," he declared with a wide smile. "I'm hoping you're hungry."

First, black cherry ice cream, her favorite. Today, pepperoni pizza, another favorite. She eyed him with caution. "This has to stop."

"No, it doesn't. I'm enjoying myself."

If she had half a brain in her head, she'd milk the man for every ounce of sympathy. He was the reason she wasn't earning those hard-earned bucks that she needed so badly. Instead, she found herself on an unwanted vacation, effectively pushing back her plans to make that one final payment. Like she had the gumption to go to some happy family reunion with an arm in a sling. She should slam the door in his face and tell him to get the hell out and never come back.

Take the pizza first!

The pie permeated the living room with the wonderful aroma of pepperoni, tomato sauce, and cheese. If the scent came in a spray can, she'd buy it in a second. She licked her lips like a wolf stalking a kill and ushered him in. "It was an accident, Mitch. Nothing more."

"I'm here to pamper you, not ease a guilt complex.

I happen to think our collision was the best mishap I've had in a long time." He placed the box on the kitchen counter. "Besides, I was hungry and hoped you'd like some. Did I buy another favorite?"

"You know damn well you did. I'd like to know who at the hospital is feeding you this info."

"My lips are sealed. Have a seat."

The man ordered her around in her own house. She should kick him out. She should do a lot of things, but none came to mind.

Aw, hell. A man hadn't pampered her in ages, and to have this handsome one catering like a slave confused her. He couldn't possibly lack female companionship. Yet, he stood in her kitchen being kind and thoughtful as if she was the only remaining female in the city of Philadelphia.

She slid her butt onto a stool. "I made a pot of coffee if you don't mind having a hot drink with the pizza."

"No beer?"

"Nay. I rarely drink the stuff. No soda either."

"Rats. I knew I should have bought some." He sighed with a slight pout forming on his lips. "Coffee's fine."

She pointed to the cabinet for the plates and coffee mugs.

He poured the coffee, placed slices of pizza on the plates, and then handed her the cream and sugar.

Her big job was to put out napkins. "If you keep this up, you'll spoil me." She took a bite of her pizza. *Yum.*

"I like spoiling women. It's a macho thing."

She'd already seen the macho on the gurney.

34

Macho men refused to show pain. He never once flinched while she stitched. "Are you gay?"

Eyes wide, he nearly choked on his pizza. "What made you ask that?"

"No relationships, remember? You don't have to be afraid to tell me." *I'll just die from disappointment.*

He grunted while shoving half the slice into his mouth. "No, I am not gay. I don't have time for an affair. My career comes first, and most women won't accept that."

"Fair enough except I'm getting mixed signals with your invitation to New York."

"I'm inviting you as a friend."

"Too bad. You look like the type who can satisfy a woman."

He stopped chewing. "You want to give me a try?"

She stifled a laugh. "I'm hardly in any condition for a romp in bed." Leaning forward, she took another slice of pizza.

He poured more coffee into their mugs while studying her. "You don't strike me as a woman who does casual sex."

"I'm not, but I do require maintenance every now and then." She had brass balls saying something so blatant to a stranger, but the man had a way of increasing her heart rate with a simple sweep of his gaze.

His brows shot upward. "Maintenance?"

"Feel-good maintenance." *Hell, why don't I just drag him to the bedroom?*

"Oh. I like that word. I'm sure I can help with your *maintenance* when you're ready."

She was ready now. She wouldn't mind taking on a

man like him, all muscle and meat and good-looking to boot. A feast waiting to be devoured. He was textbook male, and her response to him was textbook female. *Ah, the wonders of life and reproduction.* As a reminder that sex with one arm wouldn't be a whole lot of fun, she tugged on her sling.

"What about you?" he asked. "You should be in a relationship."

Chewing, she leaned back. "That's a sexist comment. Why?"

"You know, someone to take care of you. That sort of stuff. So guys like me won't plow into you and bust up your shoulder." He flopped onto a stool.

A wave of annoyance hit. Bad enough sexism existed in her medical profession, but to hear it in her home notched up her temper. She sipped her coffee so she wouldn't bite his head off. "That's the macho man talking, Mitch. I am perfectly capable of taking care of myself, have been for several years now. You can't keep women barefoot and pregnant anymore."

"I wouldn't think of it, but a man wants to be the protector. You know, protect and—"

"Conquer."

"No, not conquer. Satisfy." He shot her a quick glance. "Call me anytime."

A tempting offer. Her nerves tingled with excitement at the image of sex with this handsome man. She might shock the hell out of him and take him up on the offer. The perfect no-commitment liaison. "I don't suppose you brought over this pizza because you believed I was incapable of preparing food."

He stuffed the last of his pizza into his mouth before answering. "No, I'm trying to make you more comfortable, so you'll come to New York."

"Why, Mitch? Why is that so important?" She leaned toward him. "What aren't you telling me?"

He watched her with a steady gaze. Then with slow deliberation, he wiped his mouth with his napkin before turning toward her. "I've been a cop for a long time, Carisa. You get to hear a lot of stories, two-thirds of which don't make an ounce of sense. My dad's hiding something. He won't answer a direct question. If you came with me, you might get the words out of him."

"What do you think he's hiding?"

"My gut feeling is a terminal disease." The muscles in his jaw twitched. "My dad's a proud man who will never reveal a weakness. Headache, backache, head cold. He drives Emily crazy. I know he won't talk to me, but he might talk to you, a woman who happens to be a doctor, a woman experienced in getting answers."

And here she envisioned a more personal interest in dragging her to Geneva. He wanted a doctor to diagnose his father. This changed everything. *Aw, shucks.* "What about your sister? Was that true?"

"Oh, yes. Whenever she knows I'm coming, she's right behind with a girlfriend in tow. I have two good excuses to talk you into this."

Except for the one she wanted. Too many dancing hormones and misread cues. She needed a cork to stop the juices from seeping through her pants. *Just my luck.* The pizza lost its taste. She put her half-eaten slice back onto the plate. "I'm obligated by the doctor/patient confidentiality, Mitch. Even if he told me, I can't blab his story to the world."

"No, but you might convince him to talk to me or Emily." He stared down into his coffee while rotating the mug. "My dad was never a big talker. Over the years, I've learned to interpret the various fluctuations in his voice and figured out what he didn't say. My mother understood him a lot better, and I'm not sure my sister understands him at all. If I'm right, and he's suffering from a terminal disease, I hope he has his affairs in order. That's the least he can do if he wants to be so stubborn."

"Your mom is no longer alive?"

"She died a long time ago." He looked at her. "I realize I'm using you, Carisa, but I promise this will be a break for both of us. Will you come?"

"No." Cradling her arm, she slipped off the stool and headed for the living room. "For the record, I do feel comfortable with you, Mitch." No lie. A warm, fuzzy feeling had swept through her yesterday from the touch of his hands on her feet. The same warmth surfaced today when she answered the door. Too bad she couldn't figure out why.

He rotated on the stool. "Then why won't you come?"

"Because I don't want to be reminded of what I had and lost, that's why."

He jerked and folded his arms over his chest, his gaze like two slits. "Explain."

Ah, the cop persona. Interrogation time. She should explain. No one knew her story. No one cared enough to listen.

Mitch stood. "Maybe we should sit on the sofa." He took her hand and led her over. "Sit."

"No, you sit. I can't." She paced around the living room.

He took a seat in the corner of the sofa and, with a

relaxed air, stretched an arm across the back.

She wanted to put herself under that arm. She wanted to be comforted for a change, but she wasn't one to throw herself on any man.

"Tell me, Carisa."

She had told no one about her father, not even her best friends. The man had torn her heart into shreds and stomped on the pieces. But she started the subject. Mitch deserved some sort of explanation.

"My father has a busy OB-GYN practice in Dayton, Ohio, where I grew up. He was so proud when I told him I applied for medical school. He footed the entire bill, which was substantial. Once I completed my residency requirements, he invited me to join his practice, full partnership." She paused to stare out the front window.

The memory caused the pain to creep from the crevices of her soul where it had hidden for so long. What powerful spell had Mitch cast to allow the words to flow from her mouth?

"Go on."

She turned toward him. "I couldn't do it, Mitch. I had no interest in OB-GYN. I told him I wanted certification in emergency medicine. He went ballistic. He threw me out of the house. That was four years ago. I haven't been home since."

The memory of her father's angry face, his harsh words, still gouged her heart. Her own father, flesh and blood, mean and unyielding. What had compelled her to tell Mitch was a bigger mystery. No other man deserved to hear her troubles. *Oh, face it, dear.* Deep down, she wanted someone on her side, even if he was a man she had met only a few days ago.

She stood stationary, staring at the rug.

"What else, Carisa?"

The detective at work. He missed nothing. Or he was a mind reader. She settled on the other end of the sofa away from his outstretched arm, unable to meet his steady gaze. "He's demanded all the money back for my education. But he won't take payments. He wants one big check." She let out a sick laugh as she glanced his way. "He didn't give me a time frame so he'll wait for a while. I don't have that kind of money."

"Where was your mother during all this?"

"Right behind my father, cowering like always. She tried talking to him, but my father is a stubborn man. Once he makes a decision, that's it. The fact that I liked emergency medicine more than OB-GYN was incomprehensible to him. He told me to get out of his house. I packed and left that night. I talk to my mother, and occasionally, we meet in Pittsburgh, but she took his side, as usual. I haven't been home since." The pain gripped her heart like a vise. Their only daughter, tossed into the wind. She swallowed hard and fell silent.

"Keep talking, Carisa. It's good for your mental state."

She had always said that to herself. *Talk to someone. Spill your guts.* Four years of silence. As a physician, she understood the hazards of keeping anger bottled. "I lost a lot of respect for my mom that day." She toyed with a pillow. "She wasn't strong enough to stand up to her husband. Mom opted to let her daughter walk, and her lack of action devastated me. Consequently, we don't meet in Pittsburgh very often."

Not a pleasant topic of conversation. She'd rather

chew on nails.

Mitch leaned forward, his elbows on his knees. "I'm sorry. I never expected my invitation to cause pain." He glanced her way. "On the other hand, I'm glad it's out."

She gave him a crooked grin. "Now you understand why I won't go."

"Actually, I don't understand at all. You'll meet a lot of people with a good rapport with their father. Granted, I've drifted away from my dad over the years, but I have a great deal of respect for him. I know you'll like him. If you have a father stupid enough to disown his only daughter, then you should adopt another dad to take his place. You can start with mine." He touched her leg. "I want you to come."

Bruises covered his knuckles. With a gentle move, she touched them.

He raised his hand to turn the palm this way and that. "Kind of hard tackling a perp without doing a little damage. My knuckles, his face."

"How did you know I was an only child?"

"I'm a cop. I know a lot about Carisa MacDowell." He shrugged. "What I don't know are the personal aspects of your life, the facts that aren't part of a public record. Your favorite color, for example. Your favorite getaway spot. What you like to do in your spare time. Those facts will reveal themselves over time. I'm hoping while we're up in Geneva."

Words failed her. She had no argument nor a viable excuse for not going...except stubbornness. Her father's genetic trait. "Platonic?"

"Absolutely."

Now that she understood the real reason he asked,

she considered his offer. A trip out of state might not be such a bad idea after all. Better that than to sit around and feel sorry for herself. However..."I recently chastised my girlfriend for going off with a strange man, and here, I'm about to do the same."

"In that case, tell everyone you know that you're going with me." He shifted to the edge of the sofa and puffed his chest. "No secrets. Mitch Montero, Geneva, New York."

Excitement rose within her for a chance to explore new territory and a new man. She'd forgotten what fun was about. "All right. I'll go."

"Great!" He sprang to his feet. "I'll call Emily tonight. Pack for a week of cool weather. Nothing fancy. I want you to make this a week of relaxation. Emily's a treasure, too. You'll love her." He reached into his breast pocket and pulled out a business card. With quick strokes, he wrote on the back and extended it. "That's my cell number."

She stood to walk him to the door. He had a bounce to his step, as if he bubbled with the enthusiasm of a boy going on his first date. Maybe he was. *Or maybe I'm seeing things.* Either way, she enjoyed the look.

Mitch kissed her lightly on the cheek. A whiff of his aftershave drifted to her nose. A spicy blend, intoxicating. She almost stopped him to suck in a second whiff.

"Thanks, Carisa. I can't tell you how much this means to me." He headed out the door.

"Blue," she said, one hand gripping the doorknob.

He turned back, brow cocked.

"My favorite color is blue."

Chapter Four

On Saturday, Mitch proved to be a competent tour guide. He gave her maps of the region and pointed out landmarks along the way. He drove through Wellsboro, Pennsylvania, a cute little town with avenues of trees shading houses leftover from the coal-mining days. From there, he entered the interstate, the fastest route to Geneva, New York.

His constant chatter helped divert the uneasiness flooding her mind. She had agonized over the decision to accompany him. Twice, she picked up the phone to call and cancel. Both times, she'd hung up before the first ring. She wanted to go, and she didn't want to go—if that made any sense.

Her philosophy professor had said that everyone encountered several crossroads in life. Her father had created a major one. OB-GYN or emergency care. She'd made her choice and stuck to it. She stood at another crossroad now. Stay in her dull and mundane existence and work her butt off to pay back a father who didn't give a horse's ass about her, or see what this man in the driver's seat was all about. She wanted something different. Even though Mitch had expressed his desire for a platonic alliance, so what? He still offered a change from the dull and mundane. "I'm putting a lot of trust in you," she blurted.

He glanced sideways before zipping by a truck

convoy. "That doesn't come easily for you, does it?"

"Not really." She stared out the side window, wondering what would happen if a truck tire blew as they passed. "I've seen too much come through the ER doors. Domestics, date rape, anger, lots of anger from partners or spouses. I'm leery."

"Of men?"

"Of the human race in general. I don't understand what makes love turn into hate so quickly. One person confesses love to another, and then they turn around and rearrange their faces. I often wonder if people have a misconception of what love is." She adjusted her sling to relieve the way the strap pinched her neck. Probably made from pulverized glass. Annoying.

"Do you have a misconception, Carisa?"

With her free hand, she rubbed the back of her neck. "My father's love turned to hate pretty fast. My love for him shattered into a thousand pieces. I don't hate him, but I'll need super glue to put the pieces together. I'll never trust him again, and that, I think, is the essence of love."

"Trust is a big part of everyone's life. Cops trust their partners to watch their back. Without that trust, we stand alone."

She gave him a long look. "We're getting a bit philosophical, aren't we?"

"Yes, but before we change the subject, I want to tell you why you're sitting in this car with me." He glanced in his rearview mirror and changed lanes. "A lot of people cross my path, good and bad. Every once in a while, I meet someone who transcends above the others. I see purity, and that's what I see in you, Carisa." He took her hand and gave a light squeeze.

"You can trust me. You're here to rest and relax, not worry."

His touch shot warmth straight to her core. Like when he stroked her feet. The same fuzzy feeling surfaced, full of a strange awareness of comfort.

What the hell is happening? Blushing at the drop of a hat, tingling wherever his fingers brushed her skin. What was next, a flat-out melting?

Maybe she should monitor her blood pressure. "Purity? I'm hardly an angel."

He released her hand. "You and I see a lot of horror in our work. Several times, I swore I handcuffed the devil himself. When you walked toward me in the ER, a glow followed you."

She stifled a laugh. "That was my white lab coat. And if you think you envisioned a halo above my head, that was the lights reflecting off my hair. You were probably in shock from the knife wound."

After that, the conversation flowed light and airy, a get-acquainted time for two strangers heading into the unknown. For her, anyway. She relaxed in the presence of a man with a smile as bright as sunshine. Coupled with the smell of his aftershave floating around in the car and soft brown curls begging for her fingers, and— *oh, yeah*—a gorgeous dark blue shirt that looked fresh from a package. Hell, she hadn't wanted to hump a man so fast in a long time. Not that she could do anything with a damaged shoulder. Except dream.

After another hour of driving, he glided the car into a park where a game of midget football was in progress. A huge lake provided the backdrop. Spectators, some standing, some on lawn chairs, crowded both sides of the field. Other children, not interested in the activity on the field, chased each other in a game of tag.

"What's this?" She straightened for a better view.

"We're at the southern tip of Seneca Lake. We have only thirty miles to go, but a stop to stretch our legs might be nice. Besides, I want to talk to you."

They were talking easily enough in the car, but hey, whatever. She stepped out and headed for the football field.

"Where're you going?" He caught up to her.

"I love midget football. The kids look so cute in their oversized helmets and shoulder pads. Half of them can't see where they're running. Look!"

A little boy had tumbled face down onto the ground. He scrambled to his feet and immediately collided into a teammate, and down they both went. They jumped to their feet with faceguards clogged with grass.

While pointing at the duo, she laughed. "Aren't they cute?"

Mitch grunted in answer, took her hand, and guided her around the field toward the lake.

Concern showed on his face. She wondered why. Second thoughts?

"Something is on your mind," he said. "Talk to me."

The words surprised her. She thought she hid her emotions well enough. "Nothing's on my mind." Except the beauty of the park and its abundance of trees with the maple leaves of red and orange intermingled with the green of pine and yellow of oak. Fall colors brightened by a mid-afternoon sun, perfectly blended to create a fantastic work of art. Seneca Lake stretched as far as she could see with its surface reflecting the blue sky overhead like a mirror. A breathtaking sight coupled with the scent of freshly cut grass. She looked down to see blades of grass stuck to her sneakers.

Mitch tugged on her hand. "I'm a detective, Carisa, and a damn good one. I know when someone's lying. Tell me."

She attempted to break free of his hand, but he held fast. *Oh, damn him.* A groan escaped from her lips. "I'll never be able to lie to you. What gave you the clue?"

"I glimpsed annoyance on your face when you opened your front door. I expected nervousness, not that. Are you annoyed at me?"

She shook her head. This time, he released her hand, and she strolled closer to the lake. Several sailboats were on the water. A light breeze caught their sails and propelled them across the surface, cutting through the water without hardly a ripple. "Do you sail, Mitch?"

"Oh, sure." He stepped alongside. "I had a boat when I was a kid. Almost everyone does at some point here. And you're avoiding my question."

Indeed. She looked down at the water breaking on the shoreline. Small pebbles shifted lazily with each gentle wave. "Yes, I'm annoyed, and no, you aren't the cause. I got an email from my mother this morning. My father is requesting full payment by the end of the year. He said four years was long enough. My mother agrees, but she's under the assumption everything will go back to normal once payment is made." She faced him.

"I can never go home again, Mitch, not after this. I don't have the money either. He's forcing my hand. I either give up emergency medicine and go into private practice, or take out a loan." With a sigh, she turned

47

toward the lake. Falling in would be welcomed right about now, drown in a lake of sorrow, probably freeze to death, too. She touched the water with her finger. *Yep, like ice.* "Private practice generates more income than a salaried ER physician. My father is well aware of that."

"How much do you need?"

"The money's not the point. I can get a loan, but I won't because I want him to wait. I'll tell him one more year. If he refuses to accept the deal, he can put a lien on my house. He already disowned me. Anything else he does won't be half as bad as that." Her vision blurred as she stared at the water. "What he's doing hurts, Mitch. He put a knife in my back, and now, he's gouging my spinal cord. I don't understand why he's so cruel."

"He's vindictive, Carisa. He wants you out of the ER and back under his thumb. It's a human trait that has been around for eons." He placed a hand on her good shoulder and turned her to face him. "Forget about your old man. We're here to have a good time. Clear?"

That sounded wonderful. She'd love to forget everything forever, especially with Mitch as a distraction. "Clear." She gave him a left-handed salute and then started for the car.

"Wait a minute, woman. I haven't finished yet."

She turned to face him. "I'm not hiding anything else, Officer."

"But I am."

Her brows shot upward. "All right, shoot. What's on your mind?"

"Us. In particular, everyone's perception of us. Of all the years I've been away, I never once brought a

woman home. Everyone will perceive us as a couple."
He dropped his hand from her shoulder and stuffed both
into his jeans pockets. Change jiggled. "I don't know
how you feel about the charade."

"Wasn't that the whole idea, to fool your sister?"

"Infuriate is the word. I don't want you to feel
uncomfortable."

"I'm okay, Mitch, really. The situation doesn't
bother me. Although, they may question our sleeping
arrangement."

"I'm banking on your injury for that." He cleared
his throat. "There's one other important point." He
stepped closer and lifted her chin.

The maneuver startled her and she froze, staring
with wide eyes.

"We need to practice being a couple if we want to
pull this off. Couples kiss, and we haven't done that
yet."

His head lowered to her lips, a whisper kiss with
lips as soft as she imagined. When his head lifted, he
brushed his finger along her jaw line. "That was in case
they challenged us. Our first kiss is out of the way and
so is any awkwardness that comes with it."

She forgot her father. Hell, she forgot her arm was
in a sling! She peered at Mitch with a half-veiled gaze.
"I wouldn't call that a kiss, Mr. Montero. I think you
need more practice."

One brow cocked. He wrapped his arms around her
in a tender embrace and met her lips.

His tongue explored the recesses of her mouth, a
gentle unassuming kiss, forcing her to accept or rebuff.
She melted against him in acceptance. She shouldn't do
this. She was here on pretense to fool his sister and

diagnose his father. Everything else was secondary, including the excitement ebbing toward the surface of her skin. The man activated more than she wanted to feel including indescribable confusion. She wanted him to hold her closer, but her shoulder injury prevented that. She wanted to feel more than the hard muscles lining his back. Oh, hell, she wanted to see him naked. The no-relationship man. Too bad. He was a damn good kisser.

If she wasn't careful, she might blurt out a maintenance request before the sling came off. "You have me at a disadvantage with this arm."

Arms still encircling her back, he kissed her nose. "Not for long. You can't baby that kind of injury."

"Wait a minute! Who's the doctor?"

"Working out is a big part of survival for a police officer. We work with experienced trainers whether after an injury or trying to keep in shape. I think you need to put your doctor title aside and work with me on this one."

"Yes, sir." She conceded defeat but only because the man had a rock-hard body. Thinking of him in bed gave her shivers.

"Are you cold?"

Oh, God, she'd really shivered. "No, I'm fine. Just a breeze from the lake." *Liar, liar, pants on fire.*

A woman stormed toward them, her expression grim, her gaze fixed on Mitch. She blocked their forward motion, hands on her hips. "Well, well, I wondered if I'd ever see you again. I suppose the police notified a big city cop to come give them a hand."

Carissa eased away from Mitch and looked over the woman who stood before them like a stick wearing clothes. Pale skin, bones protruding from fingers and wrists, thin neck with a prominent tracheal line. Borderline anorexia for sure. A good wind should whisk her away.

"Is that what finally forced you to return home?"

"Hello to you, too, Cynthia. I doubt the police need my help. Is something going on?"

"Child murders, as if you care. But that's okay. I'm keeping a close eye on ours."

Ours? Carisa's gaze snapped toward Mitch, and she suppressed a gasp. His gaze remained on the anorexic.

"There is no 'ours', Cynthia."

"That's because you don't want to acknowledge your son, Mitchell. He's on the football field now. Number twenty-three."

Mitch scanned the field until he tracked one particular player. "He looks small. How old?"

"He's only eight. Of course, he's small. He doesn't have a father to nurture him." She stepped close and shook a finger in his face. "You choose to shirk your duties by living in another state. I'm about to take you to court for child support, you know, unless you want to save me the trouble and hand over some money." With a narrowed gaze, she turned to Carisa. "Watch him, honey. He'll screw you then leave you high and dry. Like me. And probably other women, as well." To Mitch, she flashed an expression of scorn. "You cops think you can get away with anything with all your fraternity shit. I'm raising our son without a father. How do you think that makes him feel?"

He waved her away. "I suggest you find who his real father is."

"Ha!" Both hands flew into the air as she stormed toward the crowd. "I'll see you in court, you bastard."

Wow. That was an eye opener. *All right, now, breathe. Let's not throw the heart into cardiac arrest.* When she saw that Cynthia was out of earshot, Carisa faced Mitch. "Something you want to tell me?"

Mitch stared at the crowd. "We dated while I was in college. She left me for a guy named Leo."

"And the child?"

"Not mine. We broke up twelve years ago, and I've had sporadic visits home. If the boy is eight, that means Cynthia had a four-year pregnancy. Math never was her strong point." With a shake of his head, he took Carisa's hand. "You'll understand why she made the claim when we get to my dad's place. Let's walk a little. I'll tell you the story about Leo."

They strolled along the shoreline.

"Leo and I attended high school together. He was captain of the football team and a star pitcher on the baseball team. Girls went crazy over him. For some reason, Leo's mission was to steal every girl I ever dated. I never understood why, except maybe a jealousy factor. Cynthia was another conquest. She dropped me faster than hot coal with all his promises of sex and good times."

"Why are you telling me this?"

"Because word will spread that I took a woman home. Leo will be at my door before the day is done." His jaw tightened. "He has this personal vendetta, and I doubt he's changed over the years."

She cocked her head. "And you think he'll whisk me away? Don't put yourself down, Mitch Montero. You have a lot to offer a woman."

His gaze sparkled. "Like what?"

"Good looks, great body. You're smart and have a noble career. I wouldn't be surprised if you told me Leo is a car salesman at the auto mall."

As he squeezed her hand, he snickered. "He is."

"Case closed."

Placing his hand at the small of her back, he turned her to head back. "That made me feel good, Carisa. Thanks." He stared at the boys on the field. "I wonder what the child murders are about?"

"Oh, no, you don't." She pulled on his arm. "No work. You're on medical leave."

Mitch stopped, his gaze straight ahead. "Well, I'll be damned."

A tall, dark-haired man advanced from the direction of the crowd by the field. He wore a business suit with a gold badge clipped to the lapel. In one hand, he carried a zippered leather folio and with the other hand, he waved to Mitch.

"Now, this is what I'd call a stroke of luck. Mitch Montero, how the hell are you?"

The two men shook hands. "Carisa, this is Bob LeBeau from the Geneva PD."

She shook Bob's hand and damn near melted at the close proximity of two very handsome men. Both towered over her like she was the stuffing between two pieces of bread. Both exhibited strength in their physiques, hair properly trimmed, no facial hair, and a commanding air. A military stature with legs spaced slightly apart as if they were airing out their scrotums. Bob was attractive, but Mitch caused her heart to skip a few beats.

"Homicide?" Mitch asked him.

"Detective Sergeant, Homicide Division. The boys tell me you're a lieutenant."

Carisa half-listened to their shop talk, which was okay. She felt tongue-tied anyway. Instead, she concentrated on the football game, but when Bob's voice lowered several decibels, his serious tone perked her ears up with curiosity.

"I'm not sure you've heard, Mitch, but we've had a series of child murders. Three this past year. I'd appreciate if you read the case file for some fresh insight."

"I came home to relax, Bob. This woman beside me is the reason." He squeezed her hand.

Bob gave Carisa a warm smile. His clear, dark gray eyes twinkled. "I'm not asking him to work. Just to read the file, that's all." To Mitch, he said, "I don't know why we can't catch the son-of-a-bitch."

"FBI's involved, right?"

"Full throttle. And we're getting nowhere."

Mitch looked at Carisa, eyebrow raised.

She merely shrugged. What could she say? If a person's arm dangled by a muscle thread, would she walk away?

"All right, Bob. I make no promises. Drop off the file at the house whenever you're in the area."

After a hearty handshake, the detective walked away.

Carisa watched him disappear into the crowd. "So much for leaving work behind."

Mitch grabbed her hand and kissed the fingertips. "I understand his frustration. Sometimes, a fresh pair of eyes will see what others miss, but I'm not a miracle worker. With the FBI on the case, I doubt I'll contribute much." He led her toward the car. "Are you ready to meet my family?"

"I'm ready, Lieutenant." A little voice told her to run. Too many doubts and insecurities had surfaced. About his family. About Mitch. Hell, about life in general.

Since when do I question yourself?

Well…like now. She was in a freefall straight into the arms of the man standing alongside.

Right or wrong, she didn't want the feeling to stop.

Chapter Five

The day was perfect. Cloudless skies overhead, the air clean and crisp but not too cool, the sun refusing to let go of summer. Carisa's heart felt light, a feeling she hadn't experienced in a long time. She made a mental promise to get away from the city more often.

Acres of vineyards stretched along both sides of the road as Mitch drove. Row after row of neat tied-up vines with yellow to brown leaves ready to drop off for the winter. Along the way, winery signs stood posted by an entrance inviting people in for taste testing.

"Will we do that?" she asked.

"Wine tasting? Of course. You can't come to the Finger Lakes without tasting some wine." He motioned toward the water. "We're driving parallel to Seneca Lake. My dad's house has a great view clear across to the other side. This area here—" He swept a wave with his hand. "All these vineyards once belonged to my dad. Over the years, he sold them off. Piece by piece, he sold his life."

"Good grief, a rather morbid statement. You must mean something else."

"No, I'm saying neither his son nor his daughter wanted anything to do with the wine business. My sister migrated into the corporate world, and I became a cop." He slowed for a turning vehicle ahead. "Dad hated my choice of career. As his only son, he expected me to take over the business and didn't acknowledge my profession for a long time. After I became a homicide detective, I received a little bit of acceptance. When he saw my lieutenant's badge for the first time, he finally showed some pride. I want to reach captain before age thirty-five. That will be my biggest accomplishment."

She cocked her brow. "For him or for you?"

"Both. I disappointed him over the years, but he's come around."

She wished she could say the same about her father. Just thinking about his unyielding ways made her stomach clench. "At least, he forgave you."

"Hey!"

Blinking, she started and turned to stare. "What?"

"Stop thinking about your father!"

Damn mind reader.

Mitch turned the car onto a narrow road that wound its way uphill. Several seconds passed before she recognized the curves as a driveway and straightened in her seat. "We're here?"

"That's the house coming into view."

The dwelling, poised at the top of the hill, slowly revealed its magnificence as they rounded the next curve. The architecture was Victorian, huge by her standards but not quite the size of a mansion with a roof boasting of so many angles and curves, an experienced roofer would break down and cry. The roof tiles were a rich burgundy color, the siding slate gray with gingerbread painted in black. A front porch wrapped around three sides, and windows galore glistened with sparkling glass. "Mitch, this place is beautiful!"

"It's my childhood home."

Her mouth fell open. "No!"

He stopped the car so that she faced the house and pointed. "Do you see the rounded balcony on the second floor? That's the master bedroom and my parents' favorite lounging spot. Their own private little heaven." He leaned onto the steering wheel as sadness clouded his face. "Dad hasn't used the balcony since my mom died. He's always on the front porch instead. The grounds, I think he's down to twenty acres, surround the house equally on all sides. Willie, Dad's full-time groundskeeper, takes care of it. Pretty, huh?"

"Pretty?" She choked on the word. "I've never seen anything so breathtaking."

"Wait 'til you see the rest of the place." He eased his foot onto the gas pedal to continue toward the house. "It has ten bedrooms, five-and-a-half baths, and a four-car garage, which you can't see from here. My mom and dad, sister, and I lived here along with Emily and her husband. My immediate family is small, but my dad had three brothers, and my mom two sisters. I have a lot of cousins. That's Dad waiting on the front porch."

Mitch maneuvered the car to a set of wide concrete steps built catty-corner to the house, exposing two sides of the open front porch. Well-trimmed evergreens accented the perimeter, and on one side away from the entrance, a flowerbed rested in peaceful tranquility for the winter.

An older man waited at the top of the steps, his gaze intense. He stood tall, although was slightly slumped at the shoulders. Two eyes like pieces of coal matched his hair, except for a hint of gray at the temples. She guessed his age in the late seventies, but even so, he was extraordinarily handsome with a straight nose and firm mouth. He wore simple clothes of white shirt and brown trousers with a gray work jacket that had never seen a day of hard labor. He strolled down the steps to greet them.

Mitch jumped from the car to meet his father halfway. They hugged and slapped each other's backs.

The men were preoccupied, so Carisa stepped from the car and stared in awe at the long winding driveway below them. Seneca Lake extended from left to right, boasting of acres of vineyards to color the countryside. Rooftops for houses she couldn't see dotted the shoreline, their shingles hiding behind trees with thinning foliage. The edges of boat docks were visible, some with the craft bobbing on the water, mostly sailboats with the masts rising above the trees. And quiet. Traffic drove on the road below, but the vines muffled the sound. She turned to comment to Mitch only to discover both men watching her.

"Carisa MacDowell, meet my dad, Jack Montero."

The two men looked nothing alike except in height. Mitch had the weight of muscles and youth while Jack had a slim build with clothes a little too loose-fitted. His skin, with the olive complexion of an authentic Italian, had a faint ashen color mixed in, creating a hue unavailable on a medical check list. His eyes, although clear, receded into his skull, leaving a tired look uncorrected by sleep.

Carisa circled the car with her left hand extended.

Jack slipped his hand under hers and brushed a gentle kiss across her skin. "This is the first time my son brought a woman home. I can't tell you how happy that makes me feel." He kissed her hand again before releasing. "MacDowell is Scottish, isn't it? Tight with a buck, are you?"

"Not me, but my dad sure is." She'd never considered such a description of her father, but moths always flew out of his wallet. That and George Washington had to wear sunglasses.

Jack took her arm and looped it in his. "Mitch got me wondering why he requested two rooms, but your sling gave me the answer. Are you a cop?"

"No, sir."

"Good." Smiling, he patted her hand. "One gunslinger in the family is enough. I can say for a fact I approve of his choice of women."

In that instant, she fell in love with the old man. He had a way of gushing his words as if he was an infatuated schoolboy. "Thank you, sir."

"Call me Jack. No formalities in this house." He led her up the porch steps. "Mitch, take care of the luggage while I escort this pretty lady inside."

So soon? Couldn't she enjoy the new environment for a little while longer?

Careful. I came to assess his father. A quick evaluation of the man on her arm showed unlabored breathing, facial skin dry but not flaky, moderate dehydration as evidenced by a subtle pinch of his hand, and hair lacking the shine of good health. He walked with a steady gait and had a good grip on his balance. A plus for his age.

"Well, what do you think?"

Oh, shit. Jack had been talking the entire time, and she hadn't heard a word. Even worse, she was inside the house and hadn't realized she'd walked through the door. As she absorbed her surroundings, she gasped. "I believe I stepped into a palace, Jack."

No exaggeration. A large foyer surrounded her

with a wide marble staircase and matching banister drawing her gaze to a second floor landing where her mouth fell open at its height. No Picassos or Rembrandts adorned the walls. Ordinary oil paintings of scenery hung instead. A huge chandelier of crystal and gold sparkled above her head, and porcelain figurines decorated small side tables along the walls.

The interior had a normalcy about it, neither gaudy nor plain, none of the extravagance of the Meet-The-Rich TV programs. The foyer floor was a beautiful unstained walnut, worn from wear but polished to reflect light. Mahogany trim surrounded each of the three archways leading to the foyer. Tiny nicks at the base showed evidence of a vacuum cleaner bumping one too many times. The place took her breath away by its size alone.

Mitch walked through the door with the luggage, and an elderly woman hurried from the left archway, arms outstretched. "Mitchell!"

He dropped the suitcases for the inevitable hug.

Her age was early seventies with the stock appearance of so many elderly women with short curly gray hair, slightly blue in color and permed to perfection. Her mature figure was full at hips and bust, covered in a flowered dress that was more for spring than fall. She wore a pair of wire-rimmed glasses, and behind those, were eyes a clear shade of summer blue. When she released Mitch, she turned those eyes on Carisa.

"Emily, meet Carisa."

Emily slapped Mitch on his arm, a playful slap where Mitch feigned pain.

"Why didn't you tell me she was hurt?" She took

Carisa's hand, her shrewd gaze giving her the once-over from head to toe. "How do you do, dear? Men never think to point out anything important like an injury. Is there something I can get for you?"

"No, ma'am. Please don't fuss. It's only a shoulder injury."

"Which I hope to strengthen in the exercise room," Mitch said. "She's been nursing the thing for a week." Bending, he grabbed the suitcases. "Are our rooms ready, Emily?"

"Yes, all ready. Help yourself to a snack if you're hungry. Dinner's at six."

Mitch led the way upstairs.

An overwhelming numbness enveloped her as she followed. She had never expected any of this. Mitch was a cop, a cop who had worked a beat. Big deal, the web had given a brief bio at various stages of his cop career, the awards and accolades received. Nothing out of the ordinary. Certainly nothing to indicate that he had grown up surrounded by vineyards.

"This way, Carisa." Mitch waited at the top of the stairs.

She had stopped midway, her attention focused on the marble steps. Each showed an indentation from years of footsteps. The banister, too, had a distinct wear pattern. "You slid down this, didn't you?"

"Every single day." He flashed a boyish grin. "So did Olivia until she decided she was too old. We had contests with my cousins to see who slid down fastest."

"And your mother allowed it?"

"To a point. Quite a few of us landed on our butts. But my mom wasn't the fussy sort. She always said a house was meant to be lived in, not put on display."

Carisa's mother was the opposite. Their living room resembled a window exhibit—never to be touched, only admired. When company arrived, they gathered in the dining room.

"Your room is at the top of the stairs," he said.

He could put her in the basement for all she cared. She was in awe of the house and especially Mitch. He'd never given her a heads-up about himself.

Mitch threw open her bedroom door with a flair and ushered her inside.

Stepping over the threshold, she entered a first-class hotel suite. She stopped, stunned at what she saw. "You never mentioned your family had money."

"I don't talk about it." He threw her suitcase on the bed. "Being a cop, people will assume I'm getting illegal payoffs. I live my life with no pretense or airs, like my dad. I prefer the anonymity of sorts. I hope you're not too surprised."

"Nah." Shocked into a stroke maybe. Like she'd complain because a guy had money. One surprise after another today. From the kiss in the park to Jack's mini-mansion and now Mitch's unexpected background. *What a roller-coaster*. What next?

"No wonder that woman wanted to extort money from you. She probably saw easy pickin's."

"My dad's the wealthy one. And Cynthia doesn't have a leg to stand on, because I'd demand a paternity test. I'm not even sure the kid's Leo's. He has a habit of stealing women from me and then moving on."

Carisa wandered over to the bed and fingered the array of fluffy pillows by the headboard. "Are we hiding the fact I'm a doctor?"

"No. I didn't want Dad's defenses to kick in. If he

asks what you do, fine. I'll tell him. Getting my father to talk will be a challenge either way. I think he already likes you, and that's a great start."

That was nice to hear. She looked at him. "How do you know?"

Mitch pointed to his eyes. "Observation. Dad's face got brighter than the sun when you stepped out of the car."

She had seen ash, a sign of poor oxygenation. Maybe Mitch was colorblind.

Mitch threw open a set of French doors that led to an outside balcony. "I hope you don't mind, Carisa, but I'm next door. We share the same bathroom and balcony. We can work out an arrangement for privacy." He stepped onto the balcony and waved her forward.

The rear view was as magnificent as the front. Nothing but acres of rolling hills filled with staked vines. A tranquil scene. Autumn colors of reds and browns. Better than any artistic rendition on canvas. "Wow!"

"My dad used to own all this, too. He built a successful winery over a forty-year time span, the first in the family to do so."

She peered over a thick concrete railing to a patio below. No swimming pool but several lawn chairs waited. With an upraised brow, she pointed to a plot of overturned dirt.

"Dad's vegetable garden. He still grows his own. He also owns enough vineyards to make his own wine. What he doesn't use, he sells. Keeps him busy."

His brown eyes glowed in the afternoon sun as he stared out into the distance. A faint trace of gold glittered close to the pupil while joy emanated from every muscle on his face. He was happy to be home. She faced him. "You don't resemble your father, Mitch. Maybe in height but nothing else."

"No, I take after my mother. She died when I was thirteen. It was a hard time for all of us." The glow faded into sadness. "Emily helped raise Olivia and me after Mom died. We became the kids she never had. Then her husband passed away. Dad always promised he would look after Emily, and he has."

"Yet, your father never remarried."

Mitch shook his head. "He loved my mother very much. He buried himself in the wine business and got a few prize-winning wines in the process. Now, he and Emily act like an old married couple. They know each other's habits, likes and dislikes. I can't say if they get intimate or not. I don't ask. Come with me to my room."

Leaving the balcony, he snatched his suitcase and headed for a side door. They entered a huge bathroom. He continued to an adjoining door, which opened to a large masculine bedroom.

"This was my childhood room." He tossed his suitcase onto a king-size bed. "Your room used to be Olivia's until I rebelled."

That surprised her. "Why?"

"You know, young man growing up. Overbearing sister. She had a knack for destroying my privacy. Dad finally fixed a room down the hall with the excuse that she was changing into a grown woman, which she was."

"Locking the doors was an option."

"Trust me, I wanted to, but Dad didn't like the idea. He said if a fire broke out, he'd have to break in.

He opted instead to move Olivia. She pouted at first, but the decorators created a great room for a growing young woman."

Carisa eyed the bed. Then she scanned Mitch. *Tempting.*

Too tempting. She adjusted her sling. "I'm glad you're close by, Mitch. I feel a comfort in that."

Something flickered in his eyes.

"Did I say the wrong words?"

"No, you said some very nice words. Then you don't object to sharing the bathroom? If you do, I can get Emily to prepare another room."

"No, this is a nice arrangement."

"Great!" He grabbed her hand and led her back into the bathroom. "As you see, we have two doors. You're to lock my door when you're in here, and I'll do the same with yours. Don't forget to unlock when you're done. Otherwise, you'll hear me pounding. The locks are independent by the way. I can't unlock your door on the bathroom side nor can you unlock mine." He entered her room and pointed to the French doors. "The balcony runs the full length of our two rooms. Make sure you lock your double doors at night so I won't sneak in."

Nice thought. "Sleepwalker?"

"I may start." Grinning, he headed for the hall door. "Do whatever you want. Rest, relax, take a nap. When you're ready, come downstairs. I'll be with Dad." He left but not without a glance over his shoulder and a wink.

Excitement surfaced. The house, the room, the man. All three triggered a dormant spirit that had died when she left Dayton. The spirit of adventure, of trying new things, like so long ago when life was more trouble-free. She had spent the last four years saving pennies with her house as her only extravagance. Even that had worked out better than she expected.

Now, with spirit revived, she let the excitement build. She had anticipated a typical family home in a typical neighborhood, not a place that resembled a resort. Her room had the dimensions of an efficiency apartment minus the kitchen. Soft colors of mauve and beige surrounded her. Pillows galore covered the queen bed. Cushy rugs. A flat-screen TV on the wall. A chaise lounge by the French doors to stare at the spectacular view. Even the balcony had lounge chairs waiting.

She wandered into Mitch's room. Darker, masculine colors decorated his room, the furniture a mixture of rich mahogany and cherry. A leather chair stood by the French doors with a backdrop of floor-to-ceiling bookshelves, the perfect spot for a man in a smoking jacket and a pipe in his mouth. Same cushy rugs and TV on the wall. Same view out the balcony doors. She liked his room, too, and could easily lose herself in his bed.

Hey, hey!

Yes, all right, she had to remind herself why he asked her to come. Father and sister. Two good reasons.

Except his kiss in the park had shattered those reasons. She'd felt more than a friendship kiss…or she was so friggin' confused she couldn't tell the difference.

Still exploring, she entered the bathroom.

The place sparkled when she threw on a light. A huge walk-in shower without doors looked big enough to wash a cow. An old-fashioned four-legged tub sat in the corner by dual sinks. She envisioned soaking in the tub for hours, sipping wine, with soft lights overhead, and then drowning in bubbles. Luxury plus. The bathroom topped anything she'd ever seen and would probably never see again. She wouldn't be a bit surprised to discover a heated toilet seat. *Now, that would be fun.*

She unpacked her suitcase, which didn't take long. Mitch had said nothing fancy so wrinkles became an afterthought. When she finished, she lowered her butt onto the edge of the bed and looked around. She could get used to a place like this.

Father and sister.

Well, he said something about an exercise room. And the foyer branched off into three directions.

Father and sister.

Oh, good grief. She knew why she was here, but she had a normal curiosity about the rest of the house. She'd keep her distance, somehow…maybe. Vacations meant fun, right? Then why not a romp in bed for a night of titillation and excitement? A simple maintenance request to top off a lovely trip to the wine country. No harm in that.

With her pulse kicking up, she ran into the bathroom to freshen up before joining Mitch downstairs.

Chapter Six

When she opened the door, Carisa stopped short.

An old dog huffed and puffed on the hall floor while staring up at her. A collie mix, judging from the amount of fur. He watched her with one good eye since the other revealed a clouded cataract large enough to block his vision. His tongue dangled over a gray muzzle, his body unmoving except for a thick tail thumping the hall rug.

"Well, hi, fella." She guessed he was male. Hard to tell with all the fur. "You must belong to Jack."

The tail thumped faster.

She never had a dog nor any kind of pet, when she thought about it. An animal in her mother's pristine house was a definite no-no. Too messy, too hairy. And God forbid, no table manners or bathroom etiquette. Carisa put her fist near his nose for him to sniff.

He licked her skin to show his acceptance.

Then she ruffled the mop on his head. "I'm about to go downstairs. Want to come?"

The dog forced himself onto stiff legs but stood wobbling.

Poor thing moved as if waiting for a brain signal to reach his muscles. Carisa ruffled the mop again, stepped further into the hall, and looked around.

Six doors flanked the hall. At the far end, another staircase led to a third floor and presumably more bedrooms. The hall had the breadth and length of another room, fully carpeted with a durable carpet meant for heavier traffic. Photos hung in frames on the walls. Mitch in various sport uniforms, a girl in dark hair painting on a canvas, Jack working in the winery. Ordinary snapshots arranged within circles and squares to show a history of sorts.

She strolled down the marble staircase with a hand sliding along the smooth banister. Marble had an elegant look. Earth's artistry at its finest. On a trip to Vermont many years ago, she had bought marble coasters. Her marble was gray with streaks of black. This marble was white with streaks of brown, a purer look than gray. Italian maybe? She'd read somewhere that Italian marble was the best in the world. This house deserved the best, polished to perfection by the butts of Mitch and his sister.

Hmmm.

Sliding down a banister sounded like fun. If she wasn't wearing the sling…

Another day perhaps.

The paintings decorating the wall of the staircase captured her attention. They were oil on canvas, different sizes and shapes with colors as vibrant as life itself. Scenery mostly. Flowers. Vineyards with mountains. The artist had talent. When she checked the signature, she jerked back with surprise. *Olivia Montero*!

Mitch entered from the front porch and waited at the bottom of the staircase.

Seeing him made her feel like Scarlett O'Hara strolling down to meet Rhett Butler. With a sling, of course.

He even leaned against the post with a smile.

Her heart fluttered. The man affected her. She wasn't sure why. Maybe if she hadn't tasted his lips, both soft and luscious that even now fueled a deep-seated desire for more. Maybe if he hadn't slipped his arms around her and pressed her breasts against his muscled chest.

Hell, she acted as if she starved for affection.

Well, maybe just a little.

Face it, I like the guy. That fact was becoming obvious.

"Rags! I wondered where you were." He clapped his hands to hurry the dog down the stairs.

Her chest fell. So much for Rhett Butler.

The dog gave a little woof and lumbered down as fast as his stiff legs moved.

Mitch squatted to give him a hug.

"Rags?" she asked as she reached the last step.

"Dad found him by the road wrapped in rags. He was only a month old. He's fifteen now."

At least, he clarified the gender.

Mitch straightened. "Looks like he accepted you already."

"I'm not hard to please." She pointed to the oil paintings. "Those are good."

"They're my sister's. She made a choice not to pursue an art career. I've no idea why." He held out his arm for her to hook into. "I'll give you a tour before dinner. We'll start with the living room."

The term "living room" was a definite misnomer. The room struck her as more like an oversized sitting area—formal in style with an assortment of Italian Provincial furniture, a portion of the house where one sat but by no means relaxed. The sofa with a stiff back and thin cushions was more fitting for a funeral parlor. Gray and pink flowers patterned the material. A sideboard, ivory with light brown trim, matched the sofa with armchairs completing the picture. Thankfully, no plastic slip covers.

The far wall had a beautiful fireplace chiseled from white and cream marble. Framed pictures decorated the mantel. If Jack pushed the furniture to the side, he'd transform the room into a great dance hall.

Not that she danced anymore. Never had time nor energy. "You know, Mitch, I never took you as Italian. You have an Italian name, but your skin and hair are fair. Is this your mom?" She pointed to the portrait over the mantel.

"That's her. She died too young."

"She's beautiful."

"Yes, she was." His face reflected the sadness in his voice as he stared at the portrait.

"She doesn't look Italian, either." She studied the features. "You have her hair and eyes."

The comment effectively dispersed the sadness. A faint smile arched his lips as his brows crunched together in a mock frown. "You call me pretty, and I'll put you over my knee."

"Promises, promises." She flashed him a smile and strolled to the opposite side of the room nearly tripping over Rags who plopped down in the middle of the floor.

A gold and white grand piano glistened from the sunlight shining through floor-to-ceiling windows. With an idle move, she fingered the ivory keys.

"Do you play?" he asked.

"I did a lifetime ago." Pain resurfaced with the

memory. She'd spent hours at the keyboard only to have the joy crushed when her parents redecorated and found no room for the piano. They shipped the instrument along with all her sheet music to Cousin Angela who had no interest in playing. Instead, she'd painted little flowers on the beautiful cherry wood. "Who plays?"

"My mother was the pianist. She played all types of music from classical to honky-tonk." He hit a few notes. "Dad keeps it in tune. I'm sure he wouldn't mind if you tinkered with the keys."

She doubted she had any skill left in her fingers. Junior year in college. That was how long ago she'd played a piano.

"Let's continue with our tour." He grabbed her hand and led her to a large dining room where a long mahogany table filled the entire length.

Visions of movie sets came to mind where kings and queens gathered to feast on a roasted pig. In one corner stood a huge china cabinet. In another corner, a tall glass case displayed hundreds of shot glasses. She pointed. "Who's the collector?"

"My mom. Every trip she took, she picked up a shot glass. Quite a few are from overseas, even though she never left the country. She got them from friends or relatives. Everyone knew she collected them. Funny part is she never drank hard liquor."

He again took her hand and led her straight out a set of double doors onto a patio, the same patio below their balcony.

"This house is amazing." She had always wanted a house with a lot of space. After growing up in Dayton and now living in Philadelphia, space was at a premium. *Someday, maybe*. She stared out into the vineyards and pointed. "I see a man moving about."

Mitch followed the line of her finger. "That's Willie Johnson, the groundskeeper. Nice guy. He lost his wife a few years ago. Dad wanted him to move into the house, but he said no. His house is down by the lake."

Willie hammered stakes into the ground with a slow, methodical rhythm.

The sound echoed through the vineyard as if he stood ten feet away. "How far does the property go, Mitch?"

"Do you see the high ridgeline? Dad owns to that. Pretty much the same distance right and left of the house."

"Wow! You gave up all this to become a cop. Why?"

"I have little tolerance for wine, Carisa. I'll drink the sweeter stuff once in a while, the stuff we call late harvest, but I prefer beer. It hardly made sense for me to continue the winery."

"A brewery then."

"A distinct possibility. I might try one in my old age. I'll have a lot of free time for taste testing." He squeezed her hand. "We're two of a kind, you know."

What would make him say that? She faced him. "How so?"

"I refused my father's business, and you refused your father's practice. Both of us succeeded on our own."

Well, when she looked at it that way…

"Both of us gave up the closeness of a family, too. You by choice. Mine by force."

She had debated staying in Dayton, accept a position as an ER physician in one of the area hospitals, but what was the point? Her father had made her an outcast. Family members wouldn't know what to do. Invite her? Leave her out? Whose side would they be on? A clean break was the only way.

"Come on. Your tour continues." He headed toward a large brick building with a faded Montero Winery sign stretching across the front. With a wave, he ushered her inside.

The smell of wine struck her first. She glanced around for the big oak barrels but only spotted four off to the side. Huge metal monstrosities filled the area instead.

He followed her gaze. "Most of the wineries up here use stainless steel to make the wine. The grapes are aged in the bottle, instead of an oak barrel. Wait here while I turn on a few lights." He opened a metal panel and threw a lever. The place lit up like a Christmas tree.

A crash snapped their heads in the direction of the far wall.

"Stay here!" Mitch ran between the stainless steel contraptions and disappeared. Seconds later came another crash. Then yelling. One voice sounded too young.

Carisa ran toward the commotion.

Mitch held a struggling teenager by the scruff of his neck. The boy had a decent set of shoulders despite his age, but his growth hormones hadn't kicked in yet to give him some height.

"Who are you?" Mitch demanded.

"Let me go!" The boy swung a fist and hit nothing

but air.

"No, I won't let you go. Who are you?"

"I said let me go!" He swung again and missed.

"You're a bit of a hothead for someone who's trespassing. Tell me your name, or I'll call the police."

The swinging stopped. "Tom Ewing."

Mitch jerked back his head. "Frank's boy? What are you doing here?"

"I don't know your name."

"Mitch Montero."

"Mitch? Wow, cool. I heard a lot about you."

Mitch released him. "Yeah, well, I don't know anything about you. Start talking."

Tom looked at Carisa and narrowed his gaze. "Who's she?"

"Dr. MacDowell. Now, tell me why you're here."

"A doctor, huh?" He adjusted his plaid flannel shirt. "I'm running away from home to become a man."

Mitch's brows shot halfway up his forehead. "You're hardly out of diapers."

Tom puffed his chest. "I'm eighteen!"

"Hardly," Carisa said, stepping forward. "More like fifteen."

Tom's chest deflated, and then he faced Mitch. "Don't tell Dad I'm here, please?"

"How long have you been hiding?"

"Since yesterday. Mr. Montero gave me summer jobs, so I know my way around pretty good. You're not calling my dad, are you?"

Mitch studied him. "Why'd you run away?"

"He won't let me have a girlfriend."

Carisa almost laughed. Nothing worse than teenage hormones.

"I'll get a job and support myself and my girl. I'll show my father I can make it on my own."

"Your old man is probably worried sick. He must have half the county looking for you."

"I don't care. I'm not going back, and you can't make me. If I can't stay here, I'll find someplace else."

"Oh, no doubt." Mitch peered at him while pursing his lips. He glanced at Carisa before speaking again. "You staying in the office?"

"Yes, sir. It's got a nice cot, and the bathroom still works."

"Okay then, let's go talk to my old man."

The young man stepped back, panic flashing from his gaze. "Why?"

"You want a job, don't you? I can't give you one, but maybe he can."

Mitch rolled his eyes at Carisa as he led the way to the front of the house.

Tom Ewing followed, looking more like a puppy on a leash.

What Mitch was doing for the boy surpassed anything anyone would do in Philadelphia or any big city for that matter. Most people would have hurried to get the kid out of their hair.

Jack rested on the porch in a worn wicker chair with ever-widening eyes as the three approached. He stood to his feet. "What's going on?"

Mitch explained. Then he stepped to the side and let the patriarch take control.

Jack gave the young man a concerned look. "Your father already called. He's worried sick, and he's got the police involved. You caused a lot of needless concern over a petty issue."

Tom clenched his jaw. "I'm not a baby anymore, sir. My father needs to understand I'm old enough to have a girlfriend."

"Fair enough." He bit his inner lip. "So, you want a job, huh? What about school?"

"I can do both."

"Oh, no doubt, no doubt." His gaze narrowed. "A summer job is a lot different than steady employment. Can you drive yet?"

"No, sir. Not for another year." He squared his shoulders. "But I'm a good worker, and I'll work hard."

Jack crinkled his brows together as he stared at the porch floor. After several seconds, he looked up. "I'll tell you what. You go out back and find Willie. I'll call and tell him you're coming. He'll put you to work. For now, stay in the office. What will you do to feed yourself?"

"I'm using the microwave in the office, sir, and there's a space heater to keep me warm. I'll be okay."

"All right, then. Go find Willie."

"Thank you, sir. I won't let you down." He jumped off the steps and ran around the house.

Jack frowned after him.

"Young man in love," Mitch said with a light chuckle.

Jack shook his head. "I'll take a ride to see his parents after I talk to Willie. Frank should be ripping out what little hair he's got left."

"Tread lightly, Pop. I got the impression Tom wasn't telling us everything."

The old man nodded. "I'll make sure Emily feeds him." After a last look, he entered the house.

Carisa touched Mitch's arm. "What do you think

Tom's hiding?"

"I don't know, but I guess it's better he's here than out on the streets of Geneva. We don't know what transpired between Tom and his father, but the dispute was enough to make him run away. Maybe Dad will uncover some details on his visit." He faced her. "I hope you don't mind, but I've no interest in talking about Tom right now. I want to show you a few more rooms before we sit down to dinner."

She wasn't sure why, but a bad feeling surfaced as she glanced in Tom's last known direction.

Chapter Seven

Mitch headed for a door under the marble staircase, which opened to a descending set of steps, uncarpeted.

Carisa followed into an exercise room full of an array of high-tech equipment. "Wow! This room is bigger than the perimeter of my house. You've got everything down here." Stationary bicycles, pulleys, weights, treadmills. Not to mention shelves full of trophies for football and hockey.

"I started weights as a teenager. Dad joined me when he saw how big I got." To prove his point, he flexed an arm muscle.

She couldn't resist and squeezed the rock bulging from his arm. "Very nice." All men wanted to show off their muscles. All women wanted to see and feel them, too. She was no exception.

He put a stern face close to hers. "I intend to strengthen that shoulder while we're here. I'll start you slow and work the muscles properly."

Yikes, panic time. She stepped back. "I've never done weights before, Mitch. I'll be a complete novice." And a woman so out of shape, she'd cry. "When should we start?" *Not like I'm in a hurry.*

"Tomorrow. Did you pack some workout clothes like I asked? I don't want any excuses. I'll be your trainer."

She'd like him to be more than that. But for now, a

trainer would suffice. "I thought you were taking me to the wine cellar."

"That's off the kitchen. Come on. I'll show you."

She followed him through the house and into the kitchen where the aroma of pot roast nearly melted her knees.

He passed Emily with a wave before heading down another flight of stairs. A heavy wooden door stopped them. He hit the latch and pushed.

A blast of cold air blew out. "Whoa!" She wrapped her arms around her chest. "This room is colder than outside."

"Temperature controlled." He pointed to the thermostat. "The wine keeps better."

Wine shelves covered three walls. In the center of the floor stood a heavy wooden table stained with bottle marks. The smell of fermented grapes permeated the air.

Mitch yanked a bottle from the shelf and wiped the dust. "Dad won first prize for this one. That's quite an accomplishment since he beat the big boys in California."

A Montero Winery label of gold and silver displayed a blue ribbon around the word Burgundy. "Impressive," she said. Not like she understood the finer details about wine. Red or white. Bitter as hell or sweet. She stayed away from the bitter as hell.

"Dad's back. I heard him come in."

Damn good ears. She only heard the fan blowing in the cellar.

"Dinner!" Emily called.

"Great, I'm starving. I still have a lot to show you, but we'll continue later. Let's go."

Everyone chattered at once while passing bowls of food. Pot roast, buttered peas, mashed potatoes with a wonderful garlicky aroma. When the creamy potatoes touched her tongue, she rolled her eyes from the out-of-this-world taste.

She listened with half an ear as Jack and Emily talked about local gossip with Mitch interjecting questions about people she had no clue who they were. Watching them triggered memories of a time long ago when she was part of a family. Four years had passed since she'd left, four lonely years with a void created by a father who once loved her. The MacDowells had never gossiped at the dinner table. Instead, her parents discussed the events of the day and included little Carisa as if she was the third adult.

The sling still pinched her neck. She reached to undo the snap.

"And what do you think you're doing?" Mitch demanded.

The tone surprised her. She met his disapproving gaze. "My shoulder is damaged, not broken. I think I can manage."

"Not yet." He redid the snap. "I'll be working you tomorrow. Don't be hasty." He picked up her knife and fork to cut her meat.

Jack and Emily watched with amused smiles.

"I'm not helpless."

"Humor me."

Wise guy. She handed him a roll. "Then butter this for me, too."

Jack chuckled as he poured wine into Carisa's and Emily's glasses. Mitch drank beer, Jack water.

"Now, Carisa," Jack began, "tell us about yourself.

Do you work?"

"I'm a doctor." She made a face at Mitch.

Jack jerked back, eyebrows high on his forehead. Then he burst out laughing. "And you let my son boss you around?" He laughed heartily.

Emily leaned forward, her face curious, eyes peering over the top of her glasses. "What kind of doctor?"

"Emergency medicine. I work in an ER in Philadelphia."

Emily sat back. "Is that how the two of you met?"

"You bet." Mitch stood and lifted his shirt. "She put these stitches in me."

Emily clucked her tongue. "Lower that shirt, Mitchell. No one wants to see your belly at the dinner table."

Except me. He could show her his nice flat belly any time...*aw, shit.* She'd grabbed her roll by the butter and got the stuff all over her hand. She licked it before anyone noticed.

Mitch pulled his chair closer to the table prior to sitting. "All right, Pop, I want to know what happened at Frank Ewing's house."

Jack shoved half a dinner roll into his mouth. "The boy's got a girlfriend who refuses to meet them. Frank's suspicious and demanded to know why. Tom stormed off in a huff. He figured Tom'd come home eventually. But he didn't, and Frank called the cops." He swallowed his food.

Thankfully, he didn't choke while talking. She wasn't in the mood to work. "Why doesn't the girl want to meet them?"

"Frank doesn't know. Tom's mother is beside

herself with worry. Since the beginning of the school year, Tom's grades have slipped. His whole life is this girl now. Nothing else matters." He sipped his water. "I'm glad you didn't do this to me, Mitch. Tom's trying to grow up too fast, and his parents are in a tizzy."

They debated the topic for several more minutes until Carisa changed the conversation to winemaking.

Jack obliged and talked about the various varieties of grapes, the aging process, bottling, even the synthetic corks.

Emily chimed in with which winery was doing what.

After clean up, they gathered in the family room, a room made cozy with soft lighting and comfortable furnishings. Jack and Emily lounged in recliners facing a large screen TV.

Though employer and employee, they were a cute pair. They bickered. They teased. They behaved like an old married couple familiar with each other in every way. When Rags wandered in, he settled between them and promptly farted before falling asleep. Carisa and Mitch sat on opposite ends of the pillowed sofa.

The local news was on, the same style of staccato and dread broadcast from every news station in the country. Murder, mayhem, robberies, beatings. Not one piece of good news. Even the weather report centered on the chill factor, instead of sunny skies.

One particular story about child abductions captured Mitch's interest. He leaned forward, riveted to the broadcast. "This is the case Bob's working." He explained to his father and Emily about meeting the detective in the park.

"It's awful," Jack said. "Three so far this year. All

local. All little girls. No suspects yet. The girls were kidnapped first. About a week later, their bodies turned up in a field. Horrible stuff. The community's in an uproar." He wagged a finger at Mitch. "Don't get yourself involved, son. You've got a pretty little lady with you. Work comes later." He winked at Carisa.

"Yeah, listen to your dad," she chimed.

Mitch gave a muttered growl, but his mouth lifted at the corners in a smile. He leaned back.

While Mitch, Jack, and Emily discussed the newscast including the trials and triumphs of the local football team, Carisa let her mind drift. The wine, of course. The excitement of a new adventure, meeting new people. The comfortable surroundings. She closed her eyes and nestled deeper into the couch.

She woke to the gentleness of a hand in her hair.

"Upstairs," Mitch whispered. "You've had a long day. I'll walk you to the staircase."

As they reached the foyer, the doorbell rang. Mitch swung open the door while she stifled a yawn.

A man entered, average looking in many ways except for the hooknose and gel-slicked hair. He wore blue jeans a trifle too tight.

The material cut into his scrotum, and she cringed with the inevitable infertility problems in his future.

He slapped Mitch on the shoulder while grabbing his hand since Mitch didn't bother to extend it. "Haven't seen you in years, old buddy. Heard you were in town and couldn't wait to stop by." He dropped Mitch's hand and approached Carisa, his eyes undressing her in one quick sweep. "You brought a beauty home, Mitch." He grabbed Carisa's hand. "I'm Leo, an old friend. We go way back."

85

Word spread super fast. The man had a death grip on her hand, as if afraid she'd run, which she was very tempted to do.

Mitch closed the front door. "What do you want?"

Without removing his gaze from her face, Leo answered, "To see this gorgeous creature, of course."

This man stole Mitch's girlfriends? Dear Lord, where was the eyeglass store in this town? She yanked her hand out of his.

Leo pulled up pants that weren't falling.

To cut more into his crotch, she guessed.

"Look, doll, we're having problems with child abductions. Before you know, our police will enlist Mitch's aid when they find out he's here. They'll call because I intend to tell them he's in town. Then, I'll come by and pick you up." He winked while a twisted grin stretched onto thin lips. "No sense sitting around while he's working. We've got some local hot spots that might get your juices going."

Yeah, vomit juices. "My name is Carisa, not doll."

He stepped back, hands raised in surrender. "No problem. I like assertive women. Gets all my masculine hormones jumping, if you know what I mean."

Oh, she knew what he meant all right. "Careful, Leo. I'm a woman who can cut off your penis and sew it on backwards so you'd screw yourself."

"Ooo, nice thought."

Good grief. Don't waste your breath.

Mitch stepped between them. "I'm not here to work, Leo. We're here for a visit."

"Then maybe we should let the little lady decide." He faced her and waggled his eyebrows. "What do you say, sweetheart? I can show you a real good time."

The man had brass balls. *Where the hell is a knife when I need one?* "I'm here with Mitch."

Leo pointed to the sling. "Can that come off?"

Mitch jabbed two fingers into Leo's chest and pushed him toward the door. "Out."

Leo shrugged. "Okay for now, but most of your women come my way." To Carisa, he said, "He can be pretty dull. I know Mitch like my own brother. I'll call when his buddies come around." He slapped Mitch on the back. "Yep, a real beauty. Sharp, too. I like that." He waved to Carisa. "Later, doll."

Mitch slammed the door in Leo's face without so much as a goodbye or *adios*. He glared at the closed door. "He'll work up a game plan now."

"He's a repulsive asshole. What's he think I am, a prize?" She shuddered. "How did such a jerk get all the girls?"

"Not *all* the girls. Just mine."

"I don't know about your other women, but he doesn't have a chance in hell with me. And for your FYI, you're not boring at all. Goodnight, handsome." She flashed him a smile before heading up the stairs, leaving wide eyes staring at her back.

Mitch was too nice a guy to let a sleaze like Leo destroy every relationship. Why did Mitch allow it? Leo was half his size and not even close in the good-looks department. Why would any woman in her right mind leave Mitch and go with Leo?

Obviously, Carisa had missed one too many psychology classes.

Father and sister.

Yes, all right already, but she liked Mitch. They had a friendship developing, and friends protected each other. So what if she'd come as a decoy? He merged her into a family again, and she wanted the feeling to continue. She hadn't grasped what she'd lost until dinner tonight with all the banter flowing across the table.

After a quick shower, she stepped onto the balcony for a cursory look at the nighttime scenery. Bright stars twinkled overhead, unobstructed by neither clouds nor lights. And quiet. Not a sound touched her ears. *Awesome.* She hopped onto the wide concrete rail to suck in the cool night air. At least until her hair dried.

"A chair will be more comfortable." Mitch stood outside his room fully dressed.

She sat perched on the rail in the far corner with her back against the wall. She wore only her silk pajamas, a little too underdressed for male company. And the weather. "I hadn't planned on staying out, but the area is so peaceful. You never know how much noise we live with until you come to a place like this. Am I allowed to sit here without my sling?" Not like she had any intention of slipping it on. *I'm the friggin' doctor.*

"I'll let you slide." He approached. "Bob stopped by with the case file. I told him I'd read it tonight and get back to him in the morning. I hope you don't mind."

What could she say? Men always did what they wanted anyway.

"Aren't you cold?"

She should be since she was fresh from a shower. "I rarely experience such a beautiful night. What's the time?"

"A little after ten."

His gaze seared into her. The heat generated

warmth that penetrated the silk and took away the chill. She should have thrown on a robe before stepping out. Slippers, too. Unfortunately, the night had captured her attention and blocked common sense. She'd probably end up with pneumonia and die.

"What's bothering you, Carisa? Are you having regrets about coming here?"

He stood with a confident posture, straight back, legs spaced apart, a man sure of himself, and more, so focused. "I envy you, Mitch."

His brows shot up. "Why?"

"You set a goal to reach captain by age thirty-five. I have no further goals. I became certified in emergency medicine, and my life stopped."

"Having a heavy financial debt over your head is a deterrent."

"Maybe." She stared out into the black vineyards. "I sometimes wonder if what I do is worth losing the closeness of a family. No one ever says thank you."

"Big city hospitals, Carisa. People take all that care for granted. Most want a reason to sue."

That didn't help. "Do people thank you?"

He leaned on the rail close to her feet. "When I worked patrol, I got a thank-you every now and then. As a lieutenant, I'm rarely on the street anymore. Our collision was fate because the detective with me couldn't run worth a damn. The perp definitely didn't thank me when I caught him."

She stared down at her toes. "I've often thought of trying a small community hospital somewhere in the sticks, maybe deal with farming accidents and horse bites. Patients might be a little more appreciative." The man's body heat tempted even her toes. She inched her feet under his butt.

"I envy you for another reason. I don't have a chance to enjoy a family atmosphere anymore. Sitting at the kitchen table and then in the family room hit me hard."

He crossed his arms over his chest. "You have to create your own family, Carisa. Your parents, at least your father, will miss out, but that's his problem. In fact, I'm surprised a man hasn't snapped you up by now." He stared at her feet. Then slowly, he let his gaze travel the length of her body before pausing at her chest. "You should have a robe on."

"Your gaze warmed me." *Again.* A flush of heat rose from her cool skin.

He smiled while toying with her silk pant leg. "I like these."

"They're too small for you." She slipped off the rail. "Thanks for talking me into this, Mitch. I love it here." She cocked her head. "Will you allow me to look at the case file with you?"

His brow arched. "You want to?"

"I've had my share of violent crime victims on a gurney. I could be another fresh insight."

"All right. My bedroom. Five minutes. A word of warning, Carisa. Bob dropped off three case files, but in police terminology, it's one case, all related."

After throwing on a robe, Carisa met him as arranged. He had turned on every light in the room as if destroying any inclination of seduction. Darn. *I shouldn't have slipped on a robe.* Ah, well, a woman could hope.

Grinning, he patted the bed. "Up here, woman. We'll go through the files together." He removed his shoes and socks.

Big feet, big…never mind.

Well, I'm on the bed sheets with this hunky man, barely an inch apart, propped against the headboard with pillows behind my back. And reading case files. How romantic. Her original notion shot to hell by reality. She chuckled to herself.

Mitch opened three files on the bedspread so they could read in unison. The abduction pattern repeated with each child. The little girls were three years old, brunettes, Caucasian, but from different family income levels. Cause of death for each was malnutrition, dehydration, and exposure. Sexual assault noted but no semen. All cleaned before disposal. Unexplained bruises surrounded their necks, possibly a choker collar. Each found wrapped in a gray blanket.

"No one witnessed the abductions," Mitch said. "No screams heard. A good possibility the child knew the kidnapper. Here're their photos."

Carisa gasped as she stared at the photos of three dead little girls. Contusions covered their faces, two bled from the ears, the third had a lip slit to her mandible. Who could be so cruel to torture such innocents? *An animal pretending to be human, of course.* She had seen it often enough. "The girls were wrapped in a gray blanket that looks fairly new. Why not a rag since the abductor is throwing away the child?"

Mitch flipped through the pages of Bob's personal notes. "Says here the blankets can be found at any dollar store."

"Gray signifies sadness or sorrow. Possibly remorse."

"I see cheap. What else hits you?"

"No diapers. The little girls were at the age to be potty trained."

Mitch read and pointed. "Correct. All three potty trained. The abductor's preference, perhaps."

Carisa read further. "They were taken in daylight while a mother or father was distracted. I've heard that story before. Tox screen negative. The kidnapper kept the child quiet some other way." She bit her lip. "How long were the girls missing?"

Mitch read from one case file to the other, flipping through pages. "All missing just short of four weeks."

"A child would cry from hunger pains. She was either isolated where no one could hear or had her mouth gagged."

Mitch pointed to the coroner's report. "Mouth taped. Residue found on face and hands."

What had possessed her to join him for an analysis of a crime that retracted every hair follicle on her body? Did she really believe she could offer fresh insight? She'd had her gut wrenched enough over the years whenever a child rolled through the ER doors. Then, she'd kept her emotions in check, performing her duty to save a young life and not always succeeding. Twice the tears came—the first when a child's skin dangled from a scorching bath, the second when the cops found a child stuffed in a trash can. The worst part was family members feigning grief. She wanted to strangle them with her bare hands.

Oh, hell. I know why I'm here.

Fresh insight aside, she had an insatiable curiosity about Mitch's job. The police added medical records to police files but never the other way around. Many of her cases had remained unanswered because she never knew what happened after the police had become involved.

Like the cases are the only reason I'm on the bed. As titillating as he was so close, within reach of her fingertips, the warmth of his shoulder touching hers, she wasn't ready to move beyond friendship.

She told herself that, anyway.

Mitch smiled.

"What?"

"I'm distracting you."

That he was. "All right, copper. Give me your opinion on the case."

"I have none, and neither does anyone else. The kidnapper took the little girls from the Seneca Lake region. He dumped them in Watkins Glen."

"A pattern."

"Yes. What do you make of the child being clean?"

"With no semen found, the abductor could be a woman."

"The FBI agrees." He beamed and gave her a sharp nod. "You're good."

She shrugged. "No fresh insight."

"I agree." He closed the files. "Any opinions about my dad?"

A subtle reminder of why he'd asked her to come. She wasn't surprised to hear the question, but a rush of disappointment surfaced. The no-relationship man wasn't interested in a fling either.

"His color is off," she said. "I can only guess at several conditions. I might discover more later." She slipped from the bed. "I'll go now. Good night."

"Sleep tight, beautiful. In the morning, I'll zip over

to Geneva PD to talk to Bob. I'm afraid we haven't anything new to add. After breakfast, I expect you down in the exercise room."

"Yes, sir." She saluted.

He remained on the bed watching her.

She glanced back before entering the bathroom to see an unreadable expression on his face. Would she have stayed if he asked?

Yes, dammit, without a second thought.

For some reason, she wanted to slam the bathroom door behind her.

Chapter Eight

Carisa had slept terribly. She tossed and turned on the unfamiliar bed, seeking a spot to help her drift off to sleep, but the bed was more comfortable than her own. So, she blamed the restlessness on the unfamiliar environment, the clean air and beautiful quiet, but that wasn't the answer either. Deep down, she understood what kept her awake: the man in the next room.

She couldn't shake him. Every time she closed her eyes, she'd see his face, like a ghost haunting her dreams. No plausible reason why. Because he was nice. Because he was good-looking, strong—hell, a friggin' list. Her purpose for accompanying him was clear enough. Just because her libido had created a sizable argument to hump him into submission, her conscience said no. So what if her insides jumped every time he touched her? A dog's cold nose did the same thing.

The man had filled her with too many doubts, dread even, and yes, regret. Regret for not opening her eyes a little wider, to enjoy life instead of working every second to repay her father, and regret for having no further ambitions beyond her current emergency medicine. When she'd made up her mind to let him be, she finally fell asleep. By then, morning brightened the room. She grumbled all the way to the bathroom.

Time for exercise.

Her psyche wasn't ready. The man had kept her

awake last night despite their distance. How could she tolerate his closeness in an exercise room? It would be akin to a torture chamber. He shouldn't have kissed her. That kiss had changed their friendship from one of pretense to one of...pretense. Nothing else had changed. Only her mind. She leaped so far ahead of herself she might as well head for a cliff.

Carisa entered the exercise room minus the sling to see Mitch busy with weights. He listened to a talk radio show as he pumped, oblivious to the audience of one standing in the doorway. Every arm muscle rippled around the bone into a gorgeous knot, straining against his T-shirt sleeve. She especially liked the tight gluteus maximus showing under the loose sweatpants. Her fingers itched to grab. Sheer torture, indeed. He created a stimulus by just being in the same room. She cleared her throat.

Mitch stopped and turned to face her. He wore a black T-shirt with gray sweatpants, both with the Philadelphia PD emblem. He switched off the radio.

"I hope you're not straining those stitches." She might as well take one last shot at playing doctor.

"I was working arm muscles. I was nowhere near my standard weight." He inspected her attire with a cursory scan.

"Is this okay?" She wore a T-shirt with sweatpants.

"Good enough. Let's get started. I can't work you too hard on your first day. After a few simple exercises, you can come down at your leisure."

"How'd it go with Bob this morning?" *May as well delay the inevitable for as long as possible.*

"He had nothing new for me, and I had nothing for him. The FBI is scouring Watkins Glen, going door to door to find someone who saw something. There's a lot of footwork to be done in cases like this." He pointed to a pulley apparatus against the wall. "We start with that."

Aw, shucks. What else could she do to delay? Maybe a slew of medical jargon to confuse him and assert her authority. *Yeah, right*. "How come you don't have mirrors on the wall like all the gyms?"

"Because I'm not a body builder. Mirrors are for the people who need to see their muscles rippling in the right direction." He narrowed his gaze. "You have a knack for changing the subject. Do I have to force you to do this?"

She stuck out her tongue at him, and they set to work.

She followed his instructions to determine arm flexibility. Then a lot of stretching followed by light weights. Painful, yes, but he didn't push. He acted like a professional trainer, all business. She, on the other hand, felt the pull of their close proximity. His spicy aftershave heightened her sense of smell while rippling muscles enticed her eyes. Any touch of his hand, whether to correct her grip or position her stance, drove her to distraction. By the time she reached the bench press, she had no concentration whatsoever. She held the bar in her hands, no weights, wishing this whole exercise shit was over and done with so she could get away and into a cold shower.

"Come on, Carisa. Just once. Then we're done."

Still business, damn him. Like any man, he concentrated on the task, and like any woman, she concentrated on him.

With a grunt and a groan, she forced her arms to

lift. *Ouch, ouch, ouch.* Her shoulder had had enough.

After he placed the bar on the rack, he leaned over with a big grin on his face. "You did very well."

"I'm paralyzed."

He straddled her and the bench. "One last order. Clasp your hands behind my neck and haul yourself up."

"You said we were done."

"I lied."

Submission wasn't part of her genetic makeup. She was a doctor who gave orders. Granted, Mitch knew more about weight-lifting, but really now…

She slipped her fingers into his hair to feel the soft curls. Like baby hair, and a sliver of pleasure shot up her spine. For a few seconds, his gaze flickered with surprise. Then a beautiful smile spread onto his lips.

He wrapped his arms under her body and lifted her to his lips.

She had wanted this kiss all morning, and her lips told him so. A big mistake for sure, but she'd worry about the consequences later. For now, she opted to taste and enjoy for as long as he allowed.

"Mitchell!"

Aw, damn. Not very long at all. Her fingers never had the chance to travel down to his tight butt.

"Emily says you're down there!" A singsong voice had preceded the heels clicking on the uncarpeted staircase.

Mitch groaned into Carisa's mouth, their moment of intimacy over. He lifted her to her feet before a tall, dark Italian sauntered through the door.

A female Jack Montero paused for effect, a breathtaking Jack Montero with long dark hair, olive skin, and coal black eyes. She surveyed the room in a split second, focused on Mitch, and headed for him, arms outstretched.

"I haven't seen you in ages!" She kissed him. When they finished their hugs, she turned to the other occupant in the room. The dark gaze analyzed and dissected then dismissed Carisa in a single sweep. "Dad said you had invited a friend."

"Carisa, meet my sister, Olivia."

The woman wore an expensive rust-colored dress that enhanced her dark Italian features. The material fitted to the curves of her body and showed a shape most men would die for. A head-turner, for sure. And tall. Carisa expected to see high heels on her feet, but they were only short pumps.

"Is my brother working you too hard, dear? He can be relentless, you know."

So, this was Mitch's sister. She had the air of a refined woman, a woman who associated with the upper crust of society, who spent time in a nail salon and soaked in a luxurious bubble bath on a whim. She definitely was a woman who commanded the attention of the room. Carisa couldn't take her eyes off her.

A sense of inadequacy sank in. Carisa MacDowell never had the body that turned a man's head. Her entire life, she had waited for her chest to grow. She even bought larger bra sizes hoping for the day to use them. Oh, sure, she had a shape but a small one. At least, she didn't resemble a beanpole. She'd given up all hopes of an eye-popping chest and donated the larger bras to the women's shelter.

"Let's go find Dad and have a little chit-chat," Olivia said. She headed up the stairs without waiting for an answer.

Mitch threw an annoyed glance at the doorway. "That's my sister. Authoritative and bossy. She's nearly at the top of the ladder in business, the fashion world to be precise."

Even though his face showed irritation, Mitch spoke with pride at his sister's accomplishments.

"Impressive. Judging from her oil paintings and now her dress, the woman has a great sense of color." Carisa grabbed his rock-hard arm and squeezed. "We're done here anyway, Mr. Trainer. You worked my shoulder enough for one day." She pushed him toward the staircase.

Mitch headed straight to the kitchen for water bottles and handed one to her.

She'd no sooner guzzled the fluid when Jack, Olivia, and Emily strolled in.

Jack was grinning from ear to ear while rubbing his hands. "It's settled. Now that you and your sister are here, the gang's coming."

Mitch groaned.

Carisa looked at him. "What's that mean?"

"We're having a party. The relatives are coming." His eyes flashed.

And how awkward for her? She barely knew Mitch, just met his immediate family, and now, the rest of the relatives were coming. She hadn't been to a family gathering in eons, but this wasn't the way to get back into the swing of things.

Shoot me, dammit! "Emily will need help. I'll run to my room for a shower. Then I'll come down for orders." That was one way to feel useful in a house full of strangers.

"That's sweet of you, dear," Olivia said. "The three of us can catch up while you help Emily."

"Well, don't rush down right away," Emily put in. "I'm not getting fancy on such short notice. You take a shower and relax a while, child. They won't be here until after four."

Carisa glanced at Mitch who stood with lips pressed together in a tight line. She gave his arm a light squeeze before heading for her room. "Thanks for the workout."

****

Mitch shifted his gaze from the doorway to Olivia then back. He struggled with every ounce of self-control not to run after Carisa and yank her into his arms. He had kissed those soft lips in the park and believed he'd never tasted flesh so wonderful. This morning, she'd initiated the kiss, and he liked how she pulled him in, despite her avoiding one last exercise. As usual, his sister had impeccable timing. And now, he had to share Carisa with the rest of the family.

His own fault. He had asked her to Geneva knowing the consequences. When did he ever come home and just visit his father? Olivia always made her grand entrance followed by someone in the family. Sometimes a party. A neighbor or two. Quiet moments with his father were rare. Rarer still would be a quiet moment with Carisa.

For the first time in his life, Mitch Montero wanted a woman to call his own. Not any woman. Carisa MacDowell, that beautiful doctor who stitched his side and melted his bones in the process. He desired all of her without hang-ups or resistance, to have, to hold, to love as a man should. Yet, he had no idea how to proceed.

She had displayed a curiosity when he arrived with the ice cream. Most women flaunted a nonchalance whenever he crossed their threshold, a pretense of sorts to make a man feel like he was wasting his time. Carisa's natural inquisitiveness shone like a bright light. She intrigued him, but on his second visit, he'd sensed a wall. Why? Because of her father? A man who had tossed out his daughter for the most asinine reason and never looked back? What fool was he to scar his only child because she chose a life of her own?

A selfish one, for sure.

When Carisa playfully slipped her fingers into his hair, she'd revealed her adventurous side. The wall had crumbled a little, maybe replaced by a lattice fence. Still a barrier but nonetheless encouraging.

Emily clapped her hands. "All right, everyone, out of my kitchen! I have a party to plan." She shooed them.

As Olivia led the way to the family room, she hooked her arm into Mitch's and pulled him to her side. "I want to hear all the details about your friend, little brother."

Why she persisted in calling him little was beyond comprehension. He was anything but little.

"Carisa's a doctor," his father volunteered. "Emergency room. She stitched up your brother's side."

Mitch unhooked her arm to lift up his shirt.

Olivia's dark brows shot halfway up her forehead. "At least you didn't pick her up in a bar."

"None of your business if I did, sister."

"Of course, it's my business. I've been looking after you since we were kids." She walked to the liquor table. "Anyone?"

His father refused.

Mitch nodded toward the bottle in her hand.

She poured whiskey into two glasses. "I still want you to meet Rosalie."

Uh-oh. That didn't sound right. Mitch eyed her through slits. "Who's Rosalie?" He took the offered glass.

"She's head of marketing at the company. I called her before I left Syracuse and arranged to meet in Geneva. Tomorrow, in fact. We'll have lunch together."

Mitch stepped back. *Are my ears playing tricks?* "You made a lunch date to match me up knowing I was coming with a woman?"

"Of course. I know Rosalie. I don't know this Carisa person." She gave a dismissive wave of her hand before settling on the sofa. "Rosalie seemed tolerant when I told her you were a police lieutenant. Really, Mitch, you must find another profession. A lot of women don't want a cop for a husband. I'm having a difficult time finding someone appropriate."

"I don't suppose you could leave the selection to me," he grumbled. He had never expected Olivia to be so brazen. He assumed with Carisa here, he'd force his sister to act a little more normal. *So much for assumptions.* "You're having lunch with Rosalie alone because I won't attend. I plan on taking Carisa sightseeing."

"Take her another day." She adjusted the pillow behind her back. "Rosalie's a good match for you. She's nice-looking, has money, a good education, and excellent family roots."

He frowned into his glass. "You sound like you're

talking about breeding stock."

"I'm keeping money with money, that's all. An emergency room physician can't possibly bring in the bucks like a cardiologist, for example. I believe ER doctors work for salary. And besides, should you get deeper involved, you need to keep your finances separate for malpractice reasons. Lawyers will have a field day with your bank account."

"What makes you think her family doesn't have money?"

Olivia snickered as she crossed her long legs. "Forgive me, dear, but she wouldn't hook up with a cop if she had money."

Mitch staggered and glanced at his father who merely shrugged his slumped shoulders and wandered toward the television. *Was Olivia serious*? She had always meddled in his life, but this was downright inappropriate. *Maybe I should get the hell out of here before I strangle her.* He stood by the sofa's end table and glowered at his sister. "I'm sorry you think so lowly of my profession, but I like what I do, and I'm considered one of the best."

"Oh, no doubt, little brother, but give Rosalie a chance. You might like her."

"And how do you suppose Carisa would feel if I left to have lunch with another woman? Are you out of your mind, Olivia?" He drank his whiskey in one gulp. He debated a second shot, but the fluid boiled in his gut. Anymore and he'd turn into a fire-breathing dragon. He placed the glass on a side table out of reach. Otherwise, he might hurl it at her.

Olivia studied her drink by holding it at eye level and rotating the glass from side to side. Then she followed suit and gulped the contents. "Look, Mitch, I know you're not sleeping together. Emily told me you requested my old bedroom."

"A necessary arrangement. She has a damaged shoulder."

"I didn't see any damage. She looked perfectly healthy to me." She placed her glass on the side table. "Are you sure she's telling the truth?"

His mouth fell open. *How could she suggest such a thing?* "I'm the one who damaged her shoulder!"

His sister had always created conflict. When he was younger, he'd faced a barrage of criticism about the girl on his arm. They were never good enough, smart or pretty enough. Hell, Olivia'd be unhappy with an automaton on his arm. As a consequence, he'd felt his temper flare faster with each visit.

"I hope she's not here because you felt sorry for her," his father said with raised brows.

Great. Two against one.

"Of course, that's why she's here," Olivia answered, "or he's trying to get on her good side so she won't throw this massive lawsuit his way. You weren't thinking clearly, hon. Now, she sees Dad has money. I hope you checked her out."

When he had accessed her driver's license to get an address, he found nothing—no warrants, no misdemeanors, not even a parking ticket. Olivia could pound sand with her accusation.

His father flopped into his recliner with a heavy sigh. "Your sister has a good head on her shoulders, son. You never know about people these days. Any lawyer will offer a get-rich-quick scheme."

Mitch stiffened. "You don't believe that about

Carisa, and you know it."

His father gave him a tired smile. "No, I don't. I like her. You'll like her, too, Olivia."

"You'll like Rosalie better."

Good grief, what had he gotten himself into? *Why won't she listen*? Had Olivia really expected him to leave Carisa home while he partied with another woman? Was she out of her mind? He never should have come home, never should have placed Carisa in this awkward family environment, but hearing his father's voice had compelled him to return. And he wasn't wrong. The man's color was way off. He looked exhausted with bags under his eyes and shoulders slumped. Even his gait shuffled. Hell, yeah, something was wrong. If Olivia took a good look around, she might see more than a little brother in the room.

"Olivia, you need to get married, instead of trying to match me up all the time." He snapped his fingers. "Here's an idea. How about I match *you* up?"

She stifled a laugh. "To your policeman friends? No, thanks. I'm satisfied with the direction of my life."

She would say that. Mitch Montero needed to be six feet in the ground before Olivia opened her eyes to the world around her, a world full of love and wonder, like her paintings.

Enough of this. "Time for my shower." He sprinted from the room.

Chapter Nine

A lot of banging penetrated through the walls of Mitch's bedroom. A drawer. A door. Then, the shower ran until a quick slam on the lever vibrated the pipes. Carisa listened to the noise as she flipped through a magazine. So much for a peaceful moment on the chaise lounge. Every slam indicated a man in a foul mood, and she had a good idea why. Her brief encounter with Olivia had revealed buckets of information about the relationship between the two siblings.

When Olivia had entered the exercise room, she dismissed Carisa as invisible, an object ignored, like a trash can sitting in a corner. Olivia's forced acknowledgment of her presence had occurred with their introduction, and the woman conceded, at best.

More slamming. Something crashed. Then quiet. Whatever he broke cooled the fire. She almost ran to him, afraid he'd hurt himself, but she waited. If the smoking dragon needed to talk, he knew where to find her.

After a time, a soft tap rapped on her side of the bathroom door. "Come in."

Mitch stepped through the door looking freshly scrubbed, his brown curls darkened from dampness. He also looked startled with both brows raised. "What's the matter?"

He pointed to the knob. "Your door was unlocked."

"Yeah, so? Do I need a lock?"

A wry smile curled one side of his mouth. "No, I keep my door unlocked, too." He strolled toward her and flopped in the chair opposite, his gaze blank and staring out the French doors.

The calm police lieutenant sat before her. No emotions. His face unreadable...a little too unreadable. "Trouble?"

His gaze softened as he focused on her. "How do you feel?"

He avoided her question. She wasn't surprised. The conversation downstairs was none of her business. "Stiff. I'll do without my sling."

"That's fine. If you're not too sore tomorrow, you can run down before breakfast and put in fifteen to twenty minutes. I'd like to take you out for the day."

What a pleasant surprise! She sat straighter on the lounge, excitement building. "That sounds like fun. Will we visit some wineries?"

"We can visit all of them if you want. I'll get you drunk and have my way with you."

A nice idea. She wouldn't put up a fuss at all. Too bad he said it as a joke.

His gaze shifted from her face to her bare feet.

She wiggled her toes to distract him.

He looked up with a slight twitch to his head. "I was only kidding."

"Yes, I know. I wouldn't be here if I didn't trust you, Mitch. The problem is you might have to reevaluate your trust in me. I plan on force-feeding wine into you then getting you in the back seat of the car." A damn difficult achievement even as a joke.

The comment put a sparkle into his eyes. A temporary sparkle. He again stared at her feet.

She didn't realize her feet were so fascinating. "What's bothering you, Mitch?"

He shook himself and sighed. "I shouldn't have come. I wanted to see my dad, but as usual, my sister drives me nuts. Even though Olivia knew you were coming, she still wants to play matchmaker."

Ouch, that hurt. Like having a rug pulled from under her feet. She forced a smile. "Oh, dear. Your little scheme didn't work. When's your date?"

He shot her an annoyed glare. "Can you honestly believe I will go on a blind date when I have the most beautiful woman in the world sleeping right next door?"

Her heart fluttered. Was he serious or were his words a casual comment spoken as one friend to another? "Do you realize what you said?"

He leaned forward and grabbed her feet. His hands were warm as they massaged. "My invitation wasn't for protection, Carisa. I used my father and sister as an opportunity to convince you." He met her wide-eyed gaze. "I brought you here to be with me, as simple as that."

She was right after all. Dammit, what now? She had already convinced herself not to get involved. She hadn't wanted another broken heart, and men had a habit of shattering the organ without an iota of finesse. "You said you weren't looking for a relationship."

"I wasn't until you fell into my life. I didn't want to pressure you."

Indeed. She hadn't felt pressure. A wave of indecision took its place. His kiss and his touch had told her so much yet she believed her response to be hormonal. A man and a woman together. A biological reaction. Nothing more than that, right?

"You lied to me." A defensive put-up-a-fuss comment, which had no sincerity whatsoever. So what if he lied? She hadn't heard such wonderful words in a long time. "What happened to the no-relationship man?"

He squeezed her feet. "That went out the window when we collided. As for lying, you wouldn't have come otherwise. I'm taking a chance to find out if you have room in your life for a cop."

The words jarred her insides. What could she say? How did she feel? Confused and bewildered?

No, totally befuddled. She'd concentrated on work for the past four years, never allowed time to deviate, and ignored flirtatious comments. Right or wrong, she wasn't interested in a relationship, placing the priority of paying back her father at the top of the list. Now, Mitch with an unexpected offer.

"I don't know what I want, Mitch. My heart has been empty for a long time." She stared out the French doors, unseeing. "I idolized my father. He was a little girl's hero. When my mother sided with him, she effectively collapsed my world. Both of them expected me to crawl back on my hands and knees, do my duty, and join my father's practice. They had no concern about my desire to live a life of my own. I vowed to tell both to shove the money up their asses."

Mitch stroked her insteps. "They hardened your heart, Carisa. That isn't healthy. You've got to release the anger even before you pay back the money. Learn to love again and accept the man willing to give you that love. You say you don't know what you want so when the time is right, I'm hoping you say me. All you have to do is come to me, Carisa, come to me and tell me I'm what you want."

Their gazes locked.

Oh, God, why is he doing this to me? She was more confused than ever. A fling, okay. Anything more and she wasn't prepared. Was he talking love? A relationship? *What, dammit?* Should she ask him to clarify or should she choose to ignore?

For now, the latter sufficed. She wasn't mentally ready for any of this.

With his warm hands, Mitch massaged her feet, restoring her sense of time and place. His calluses tickled her toes in the process. He watched her with a quizzical tilt to his head.

"And if I can't come to you?"

The grip on her toes loosened. "I'll admit defeat. For now, we'll keep everything above board. If you want casual sex, tell me. I expect to steal a kiss from you every now and then, and you can do the same with me. But if you want more in your life, and you decide to include me, you can be assured I'll always be there, no matter what."

She believed him. Even though she wanted to throw herself into his arms, she couldn't. Doubts flooded her mind. Yes, her father had hardened her heart. He filled the vessel with a deep-seated resentment that fermented over the years. That resentment had spilled over to include her mother, a weak woman who chose to lose her daughter rather than stand up to her husband. Never once was it a question about the money. They had come down on her hard for choosing emergency medicine. No one attempted to soften her heart until now.

"Mitchell!"

Mitch dropped his chin onto his chest while his hands tensed on her feet. "In here."

He shot an exasperated glance at Carisa as Olivia strolled through the bathroom door.

She had changed into slacks and silk blouse and looked as striking as earlier. Her dark eyes surveyed the room in one quick sweep as she approached.

"You and I are going to town. Emily gave me a shopping list." She spotted Mitch's hands on Carisa's feet and flashed a dark gaze at Carisa. "Don't tell me your feet hurt, too."

Her mouth fell open. "Too?"

"Shoulder, feet. What's next, back?"

"What in the world are you getting at?"

Mitch stood and faced his sister.

He gave the impression of a giant rising to full stature, but Olivia, with equal height, never flinched.

"That's enough."

She crossed her arms over her chest. "She's playing the sympathy card on you, little brother. Wise up."

"We were having a pleasant conversation. What you make of it is your business."

Undaunted, Olivia turned to Carisa. "Emily says when you're ready, go down. Do you think you can help her without injuring yourself?"

Well, well, well. So this was the topic of discussion during their brief family reunion. Olivia had formed an opinion about Carisa in what, ten minutes? Rather quick. "Why'd you stop painting?"

Olivia staggered. Her beautiful mouth fell open as

her dark eyes widened.

"I saw the paintings. They're good."

"That painter no longer exists." Olivia dismissed the comment with a wave and turned toward the door. "We're wasting time, Mitch. Let's head out." She left the room without him.

Mitch stared at the door. "What the hell happened?"

Carisa chuckled and rose from the lounge. "I changed the subject. I do that when my patients get confrontational. Works every time. Go on before your sister throws another fit." She shooed him out the door.

Since the exercises improved her shoulder's flexibility, Carisa lifted her hair into a ponytail. She slipped on her sneakers and ran down to Emily. The kitchen smelled of chocolate.

Emily was stirring the contents in a wide bowl. She looked up. "How's the shoulder?"

"Sore but the exercises helped. I don't think I'll throw a baseball anytime soon."

She chuckled as she placed cookie dough onto a sheet. "He's good with those weights. Started as a young man, if he hasn't told you already." She nodded toward the refrigerator. "You'll see three different blocks of cheese on ice. Cut them into bite-size pieces. Use the tray in the overhead cabinet to the right. We can't have wine without cheese."

Carisa agreed and set to work.

"I'm pleased as punch you came with Mitch." Emily licked a finger. "I can't tell you how happy that makes me. Time and again, we asked him to bring someone, but he never bothered."

"Probably because the outcome was always the

same."

Emily gave her a long, quiet look. "Olivia started already, I take it."

"Mitch warned me. I thought he'd exaggerated."

She shook her head, thumping the bowl like she was fighting the dough. "Olivia will get worse before your visit is done. I see the way Mitch looks at you, and Olivia isn't blind." She waved the spatula like a pointer. "We've got trouble ahead."

Carisa popped a piece of cheese into her mouth. "Mitch and I are only friends."

"Ha! He didn't request those two rooms for nothing, honey. They're the only rooms with an adjoining bathroom. He may resent Olivia barging in, but I've a strange feeling he'd welcome you."

Carisa laughed as she stacked the cheese. "You have a dirty mind." She had wondered about the room arrangements. With ten bedrooms in the house, he had a wide choice. Yet, he'd chosen the two with an adjoining bathroom, and, to her surprise, the only adjoining balcony. He had purposely created intimacy.

Oh, come off it. I'm delighted as hell. And flattered. No man had ever gone through the trouble.

Emily placed a tray of cookie dough into a secondary oven.

The clang of metal on metal snapped Carisa's attention back to the cheese. "Olivia's a beautiful woman. Is she going with anyone?"

Before answering, Emily took out a tray of cookies from the first oven. "I can't say for sure. She's all business. She makes a lot of money at her corporate job, but I tell her money isn't everything. Not like she's destitute. What she needs is to fall in love. She won't listen, of course. One day, she'll wake up and discover life passed her by." She sighed heavily while staring off into space.

"Ever since their mother died, Olivia used Mitchell to channel her sorrow. She was sixteen at the time, a young woman ready to blossom. She took her mother's death hard. She smothered Mitch 'til the poor boy screamed. I'm surprised they get along as well as they do even with her constant matchmaking. When he's had enough, he'll step to the plate. And honey, I can tell you it'll be soon."

"Why's that?"

Shrewd blue eyes focused on her over the eyeglasses. "You." Emily adjusted her glasses with her forearm. "Want a cookie?"

"Oh, God, I thought you'd never ask!" She grabbed one and bit into the confection. The cookie melted in her mouth. A wonderful combination of oats and chocolate. Heaven on Earth.

Emily arranged the cookies on a serving tray. The old woman had an amused glint shining from behind the glasses. "Milk's in the fridge."

What were cookies without milk? Carisa poured a glass. "Why doesn't Olivia paint anymore?"

Emily paused to stare at the cookie tray. "I don't rightly know. One day, she up and stopped. No explanation. She decided to pursue business."

"That's a shame. She uses a remarkable blend of colors." She took another cookie, whether allowed or not. Let Emily pry the goodie out of her hand. "How many people are you expecting?"

"Usually twenty-five to thirty. Depends on who's around on short notice. The living room adjoins the dining room so that's where they gather. When you get through with the cheese, you can start on some dips."

"Right." She shoved the last of the cookie into her mouth, gulped the milk, and set to work. Afterwards, she prepared dips with Emily's instructions. A little sour cream in one. Mayo in the other. Dill. Onions. She shouldn't lick her fingers so often, but hey, tasty stuff.

Occasionally, Emily threw furtive glances in her direction. She quickly averted her eyes when Carisa caught her, but the gaze slowly drifted back.

Concern replaced the amusement of earlier. "Do you want to ask me something, Emily?"

The old woman wiped her hands on her apron in a slow, methodical fashion while she chewed on the inside of her lip. "I want to talk to you about Jack." She shot a glance at the kitchen entrance.

Ever since last night's dinner, Carisa had sensed a hesitancy in Emily. The woman's mouth would open to speak and then clamp shut with a cursory glance toward Jack. They hadn't had a chance to be alone…until now. "All right. Go on."

She faced Carisa. "Normally, I'd never impose, but I know something is wrong with him. I've asked, begged even, but he won't talk. I'm worried. He doesn't look well and hardly eats anything. He says I'm imagining things when I tell him his clothes look too big. You're a doctor. You must see it."

Carisa tapped the spoon on the side of the dip bowl. "What do you expect me to do?"

"Talk to him. See if you can get him to understand that his silence is killing me." She glanced at the wall clock. "Now will be a good time. The kids are gone, and he's sitting on the front porch with Rags. Please,

Carisa?"

This was what Mitch had wanted. Now, Emily asked. The poor woman was so distraught, her blue eyes pleading for help, her voice quivering. The look was a common one in the ER with family members feeling helpless. "You're placing me in an awkward position. I'm not his physician."

"All I'm asking is for you to get him to talk, reason with him. If nothing's wrong, I'll add more fat to his food."

Carisa stirred the contents in the bowl. "I'll try. Let me finish the dips first."

"No, I'll do that." She grabbed the spoon from Carisa's hand. "I need you to talk to Jack before Olivia and Mitch return. He'll clam up for sure once the kids come home. Please?"

How could one refuse a kind little lady who made melt-in-your-mouth cookies? Carisa nodded and grabbed another cookie before turning to leave.

Then she paused in the doorway. "One question, Emily." Teenage insecurities sprang to the surface, which was ridiculous. She was a grown woman, for crying out loud, but she asked the question anyway. "How does Mitch look at me?"

Emily stared. Then a warm smile spread onto her lips. "Open your eyes, honey. The man is in love with you."

Why she asked Emily such a question was beyond reason. Maybe an affirmation of sorts, something she had felt all along but Mitch never verbalized. What to do with him was her problem. She had worshiped her father for his strength and commitment to his profession. The man had tossed her out like a used rag.

Mitch had said he would always be there for her. Her father had said the exact same words.

Carisa shook the comparison out of her thoughts and headed for the front porch.

Chapter Ten

Jack slumped in a worn wicker chair staring into space, his hands clasped together in his lap. He resembled a man shrinking in his clothes with a shirt collar drooping around his thin neck and jacket sleeves too long for his arms. Several possibilities had entered her mind as a cause. Tuberculosis was one. Sometimes the disease manifested with a cough, sometimes shortness of breath, but not always. Jack had exhibited neither symptom.

The most likely condition was intestinal cancer. That disease along with TB had a way of eating a patient from the inside out. Did Jack know he was sick? What if he hadn't sought medical help? She'd step into a hornet's nest with a diagnosis he'd want her to prove.

Carisa observed him from the shadows of the doorway, unsure how to proceed. Death was a part of her job. The hardest part was letting someone go when so much was available. But to what end? Half the time, infarcts destroyed the heart muscle beyond repair, or anoxia damaged the brain to leave the patient comatose for the remainder of life. Machines and pharmaceuticals were a modern marvel for mankind, but nothing brought back a lost organ. Medical science merely prolonged the agony for both patient and family.

Jack could be a man in denial. She'd seen the behavior hundreds of times and the anguish it caused family members who knew nothing. And here she was, a stranger, about to approach because Mitch and Emily wanted to know. The situation created a walking-on-eggshells moment.

Oh, hell. Now or never. She stepped out onto the porch. "I see why you like sitting here."

Rags responded first. He was sprawled by Jack's feet thumping his large tail on the wooden floor. The noise snapped Jack's attention to the world, and his tired eyes focused. He straightened in the seat.

"Can I keep you company?"

His face brightened, and he patted the chair next to him. "Aren't you helping Emily?"

"She forced me to take a break. I think I ate too many of her cookies." She took a seat and ruffled Rags' hair.

"She makes great cookies. If you taste her famous chocolate cake, you'll think you died and went to heaven." He turned slightly to face her, his head cocked toward her. "Mitch says he's the one who gave you that bad shoulder. Is it true?"

"It was only an accident. We literally ran into each other."

He straightened his head and rubbed the back of his neck. "Olivia was right. Mitch brought you here to pacify you."

"Pacify me?" She shot him a quick glance. "He said that?"

"No."

Of course. She should have known. "Olivia's words."

"She's always looking out for Mitch. You can't blame her for anticipating a lawsuit."

Lawsuit? Good grief, the notion hadn't entered her mind. What was next? A pay-off? A get-out-of-his-life check? "I like your son, Jack. I'd never do anything to hurt him."

Jack studied her with one eye half closed. After a time, a slow smile spread onto his dry lips. "I believe you."

The fallible ideas of the wealthy. They assumed everyone was after their money. Most of the time, they were right, but Carisa MacDowell wasn't one of them. Right now, she didn't give a horse's ass about Olivia's opinion. She had to keep Jack talking. "That's Seneca Lake, right?"

"Yep. Pretty, ain't it? That's Willie's house on the right by the water." He pointed to a rooftop between two very old oak trees. "Have you met him yet?"

"He was too far out in the vineyards yesterday."

"Well, he's been with me for years. Knows the vines like the back of his hands." He brushed dog hairs off his jacket sleeve. "Willie's wife died a while back. She always helped Emily when we had these parties. I'm glad you're giving her a hand. She's getting up in years."

"It's the least I can do for your hospitality. You have a beautiful house, by the way."

"Glad someone thinks so. The kids don't want it. Olivia's got this classy condo in Syracuse, and Mitch lives in Philadelphia with no intention of returning."

"How about Emily?"

"She don't want it either. When she retires, she wants a small apartment in Geneva, two rooms max."

"She won't retire, Jack. She'll leave when you do."

He frowned and fussed with his pant leg. "I

121

promised her husband I'd take care of her."

"How about when you're gone?"

He turned those coal-black eyes on her. They were sharper now, more focused.

"Did she send you out here?"

"She's worried, Jack. So is Mitch. They see the change and don't understand."

"There's nothing wrong with me." He stuffed his hands into his jacket pockets.

"Then you should tell Emily to fix up some fattening dishes. I see you've already bought a new belt to hold up your pants."

He peered at her through slitted eyes, his face a stone mask.

He'd either kick her off the porch or leave in a huff. She was forcing his hand and taking a chance with a slap. "You can't fool me, Jack. I recognize a man on borrowed time."

His lips pursed as he stared down at Rags. After a time, he looked up with a faint smile on his lips. "I guess you wouldn't be a very good doctor if you didn't diagnose right away." He slipped his hands out of his pockets and took her hand. "I've got Stage Four intestinal cancer. My doctor gave me three months, six months tops. That was a month and a half ago. I refused treatment." He patted her hand before releasing it. "Some fool surgeon wanted to take out my intestines and jump rope with them. He said I might get an extra six months. No guarantees. Big deal. Bad enough I can't drink wine anymore."

Life was cruel. Jack was a winemaker who couldn't taste his own wine. Like a musician who'd lost her hearing. Or a fashion designer who'd lost her sight.

In Jack's case, he faced a terminal prognosis. "Do you have pain?"

"Not much all things considered. I get a strong twinge every now and then. Nauseated once in a while. The doctor gave me pills for that." He wiped his brow, checked his fingers for sweat, but not a drop of moisture showed. "All my affairs are in order. Olivia will be my executor. She and Mitch can do what they want with the house."

"Your affairs might be in order, but you left out one important detail, Jack. Nobody knows how sick you are. Nobody knows your last wishes."

"They don't need to know, and you can't tell them."

A proud man and a foolish one, a patriarch unwilling to admit weakness. He faced a formidable opponent, a disease that could torture him to the end or allow him to go in peace. She hoped it was the latter. "I need you to understand something very important, Jack." She rotated to face him. "If you die in your sleep, and Emily comes in to wake you, nothing will stop her from calling 911 and activating the emergency response system. Then, the paramedics will stick tubes and needles in all parts of your body and pump on your chest to revive you, and all because they had no idea how sick you were. This will continue all the way to the hospital, and the code team will stick more needles and tubes in you."

Hoping to impart the topic's importance, she touched his arm and inwardly cringed. Jack's arm was a bone with no muscle. "People come into the ER every day, Jack. We revive them then they burst into tears because they wanted to die in peace. Instead, they find themselves hooked to every apparatus known to modern medicine. You have to tell your children, Jack, or at least Emily—especially Emily. She's the one who will find you first. Someone needs to know your wishes."

He studied her with a narrowed gaze. "They can bring me back?"

Holy shit, he doesn't know? "Yes, Jack, we can bring you back. What treatments you refused will be aggressively administered because family members will want everything done."

"My doctor knows my wishes. I got one of those living wills."

That's a start. "Do you carry a copy in your wallet?"

"Yep."

"All right, let me tell you what happens in the real world. The family who has no clue finds you. They call EMS. Your family or EMS starts CPR. No one thinks to look in your wallet. The tubes and needles are put in place." She shifted to the edge of her seat and leaned toward him. "Don't you see, Jack? If your family knows your wishes, nothing starts. However, if by chance one member of the family doesn't know or has doubts about the validity of the living will, that member can request the continuation of life support. The physician must legally wait until all family members agree to terminate. That's why it's so important for you to tell everyone." She sat back in the chair with a sigh. "You can thank our legal system for that."

His dark eyes misted as his face changed to a shroud of indecision.

Why hadn't his doctor talked to him? Death wasn't

a cut-and-dried situation these days. Advance directives. Living wills. Do not resuscitate orders. All used different terminology and generated loopholes big enough to pass a planet through. She touched his arm to force his gaze toward her. "You need to tell your family now, Jack. Don't rely on someone searching through your wallet."

"What about my doctor? He knows."

"He will be contacted after the establishment of life support, never before. The ER team has just minutes to save a brain. No one will waste time on a phone call."

He sighed heavily and patted her knee. Then, he eased his frail body to his feet and shuffled across the porch. Rags lumbered after him. Both descended the steps and disappeared around the side of the house.

Carisa slumped in the chair, feeling totally inadequate. She had wanted Jack to head into the house and straight to Emily. She felt her heart sink to her toes to see him walk down the steps. Jack breathed on borrowed time, and someone needed to know. She prayed he told Mitch because she sure as hell couldn't. *And please tell him soon.*

She'd never understood why some patients were so secretive. They placed their doctors between a rock and quicksand all because of the doctor/patient confidentiality. Angry family members screamed malpractice. Hospital administration screamed unnecessary costs, and the doctors found themselves sitting in front of a review board. A catch twenty-two for the books. Like now. If Jack kept his silence, then she could do nothing except follow suit.

Aw, well. Enough brooding. Work waited. She reentered the house.

The sound of crying stopped her. Carisa crept to the kitchen entrance to peek around the opening to see Jack holding a weeping Emily.

Thank you, Lord.

With no desire to interrupt, she headed through the dining room and out onto the patio to bright sunshine. *Time for a jog.* A vineyard jog, something different besides her boring run around the streets of her neighborhood. She jumped off the patio and ran a few hundred feet before turning for a view of the back of the house.

As magnificent as the front. Wine barrels decorated the perimeter of the patio and the garage entrance. Some had plastic flowers popping from the top, white and yellow, never to fade or wilt. Other barrels glowed with murals of vibrant colors, and still others had children's handprints pasted all over. *Cute.* Judging from the color blend on the murals, this was Olivia's work again. Carisa turned and headed toward the ridgeline.

A dirt road ran parallel to the vines. An access road at one time, overgrown but nonetheless discernible. She followed the ruts, hopping on and off the median to give her hamstrings a bit of a stretch. A quick jaunt to the ridge and back should allow Jack and Emily sufficient time for privacy.

A beautiful day. Clean air. Quiet. She heard every crunch of dried weeds beneath her sneakers, every snap of a twig, and even the pump of her heart. Cities were never quiet. Too much traffic, too many people.

She ran beyond the ridge. Not intentionally. When she glanced over her shoulder, she spotted the ridge behind her. She stopped to take in the acres of vineyards before noticing a wooden shed about a hundred feet ahead. The door was ajar with a heavy lock dangling from the latch.

A man stepped out, still conversing with someone behind him. When he spotted Carisa, he held out his hand to stop the person from following. "What are you doing here?"

The voice made her jump. The sound was more masculine than the man and more powerful than the body. He had a ferret face, a penguin shape, small feet, small hands, and no neck, a man who looked forty-five going on sixty. His complexion had a washed-out look except for the red flush that covered his cheekbones. Like rouge on a pale face. Definitely not the flush of an outdoorsman by any stretch of the word. A desk jockey more likely with his starched white shirt and black trousers, spit-polished black shoes and an ass flat as a seat. Not a speck of dirt on him. She searched for some sort of vehicle and caught sight of an electric cart tucked between two rows of vines. "Sorry. I'm obviously trespassing."

"Yes, you are. Where did you come from?"

"The Montero house. I'm really sorry."

He glanced briefly inside the shed with a quick nod.

The shed door closed by an unseen hand.

He stepped toward her with a strained smile on fat lips. "All right, I'll let you slide. Mr. Montero used to own all this land before he sold it to my father. I went to school with his son."

Not forty-five then. Wrong on that one unless he was held back twelve…no, impossible.

"I suggest you not walk around these parts without

an invitation. Wine growers are possessive of their vines."

And not very friendly either. "Thank you. I'll remember that." She turned to leave. "I'll head back now."

"Please do. I don't want to see you out here again. Do I make myself clear?"

"Yes, sir."

Rags hobbled to the ridge, growling and doing his best to look threatening on wobbly legs.

He succeeded. Ferret-face lost the red flush and stepped back, wide-eyed and frightened.

"Keep him away from me!"

She doubted Rags had the strength to hold onto a leg without yawning, but she grabbed his collar anyway.

"Both of you, get out!"

"Okay, we're going." She started back, taking Rags with her.

"And if you're out here working the vines, please wear a hat."

She opened her mouth to speak but words wouldn't come. Why would she need a hat? "Come on, Rags. The guy's a loon." Or overprotective of his vines. Then again, the wine industry was a world onto itself. His behavior could be perfectly normal. His reaction to Rags was another matter. What a wimp.

She looked down at Rags. "I agree with your assessment of him. He's not a likeable man."

The dog gave a weak woof in answer.

Maybe Rags bit him once. That would make a person wary. Still, something wasn't right about the entire scene. Ferret-face wore clothes that looked a little too prim and proper for stepping out of a tool shed. Unless the person in the shed was a woman. Or another man. Carisa swallowed the last explanation easier since no woman in her right mind had the guts to kiss a ferret.

For every trash can, there's a lid, her grandmother used to say. Carisa shuddered. She glanced back to see him watching her from the ridgeline. "I guess he wants to make sure we disappear." Rags wasn't alongside. She rotated to find him sprawled out under a tree, wheezing. She walked over to check him. The poor dog had his tongue hanging halfway to the ground.

"A bronchodilator might help you tremendously." She patted his rump. A white something or other dangled from his lower lip. She removed it and placed it in her palm. A tooth! "Good grief, Rags. What'd you do?"

"He loses teeth all the time," a voice said.

Chapter Eleven

Carisa rotated to see a black man standing nearby with a red-handled shovel over his shoulder. His height exceeded any of the Monteros' by at least four inches, and she heard her neck vertebra crackle as she strained to see his face. *Must be something in the water to make people grow.*

His wrinkled face broke into a smile. "You must be the doctor. I'm Willie, Mr. Jack's groundskeeper."

He was a wiry sort of man, boney with strong arms and callused hands, a man used to hard outdoor work. His dark skin had a leather appearance from too much time in the sun with deep crow's feet around both eyes. He was not as old as Jack, perhaps ten years younger with a cut through his short hair that made a permanent part. "Carisa." She stood and extended her hand.

He backed off. "Oh, no, ma'am. I've been playing with dirt all day." To prove his point, he swung the shovel off his shoulder and clapped his hands together. Dust blew. "I saw Harvey staring after you from the ridge. Did he bother you?"

"I trespassed. He never introduced himself. Just told me to get out." She pointed to the dog. "Rags doesn't like him. He growled the entire time."

"That's new for him. He usually barks until Harvey shakes in those shiny shoes of his." He leaned on his shovel. "Strange toad, that Harvey Fergus. I don't like him either. Can't say what he does with his time all day 'cept count his daddy's money." He nodded toward the ridge. "The boy's mighty possessive of that shed of his. I was too close to the property line one day, and he barreled out like a steam engine. He accused me of trespassing. I politely told him I still stood on the Montero grounds. He got rather indignant. My guess is when his papa dies, he'll put up a six-foot fence with razor wire around the perimeter of the estate."

"Which is substantial, I assume." *Must be nice to have money, which is something I'll never see.*

"Oh, it's substantial all right. The father's a nice man, but the boy will cause trouble. He don't know nothin' about wine. Don't think he wants to learn either." He scratched his head, leaving smudges of dirt on the surface. "Selling the ground just about broke Mr. Jack's heart, but nothin' else he could do. His kids aren't interested."

Like her father would sell his practice because his daughter wasn't interested. She and Mitch were indeed two of a kind. "Is it customary to wear a hat in the vineyard?"

Willie stared. "Where'd you hear that?"

"Ferret-face."

"Who?"

"Sorry. Harvey. He wasn't wearing a hat. Neither are you."

Willie rolled his eyes. "Like I say, he's a strange toad. Don't pay him no mind. Besides, you shouldn't cover that nice golden hair of yours." He chuckled as he kicked his boot against the shovel blade. "Ferret-face. That's rich."

She liked Willie. He was easy to talk to. However,

duty called. "I should get back to the kitchen. Emily probably thinks I got lost."

Willie's dark eyes brightened. "Yeah, Mr. Jack tells me the family's coming. Quite a crowd as you'll see."

She made a face. "I'm not used to big parties."

"Can't avoid it especially if you hang around young Mitch. I'll be there."

"Good. That makes me feel better." She glanced down at Rags. The poor dog huffed and puffed like a steam engine. "Will Rags be all right?"

"Oh, sure. He'll lie here 'til he catches his breath. When he's ready, he'll look for Jack. You might find a few more of his teeth along the way. The vet says something genetic is going on, and we can't do nothin'. If he loses any more, we'll need to liquefy his food. And don't you worry about the crowd, miss. You look like you're gonna fit in fine." He threw the shovel over his shoulder and headed into the vines, whistling.

She ran the rest of the way to the house. Once she hopped onto the patio, she stopped as Tom Ewing stepped from behind a wine barrel. He fidgeted, shifting from one foot to the other as if the stones beneath his boots were too hot. His face had a contorted appearance, as if he was chewing the inside of his cheek. "Hi, Tom. Something wrong?"

If he had a hat, he'd be toying with the rim. Instead, he tugged on his jacket. "My girlfriend's puking her guts, Dr. MacDowell."

"Oh?" She walked toward him. "Stomach flu or something she ate?"

"Don't know, ma'am. She can't keep anything down. She won't go to the doctor."

"Where is she?"

"In the winery office. She's been staying with me. Please don't tell anyone." He glanced toward the patio doors.

"She's been with you all along?"

"Yes, ma'am. That's why when Mitch turned on the winery lights, I made noise to draw him away from the office. You can't tell anyone she's here."

What do I look like, someone who can harbor secrets? She gave him a stern look. "Jack needs to know, Tom. You're on his property."

"You gotta promise not to say anything...please."

Great. First Jack's secret, now this. "Do her parents know where she is? There are laws about getting parental consent when working on a minor."

"Her parents don't care. She comes and goes as she pleases. Talk to her, Doc. Maybe I can grab something from the drug store."

Carisa relented. *Better to see with my own eyes than have a teenager give a haphazard history.* "Lead the way."

Her mind listed the common teenage scenarios as a cause for vomiting. Drugs, alcohol, junk food. Kids had a way of experimenting with the strangest substances. The biggest cause shot to the top of the list. Tom, being fifteen, was a little young to handle the responsibility, so hopefully, she was wrong. She entered the office.

The starkness of the room struck first. White cinder block walls, old linoleum floor, minimal furnishings. A worn desk stood in the center with an open backpack spilling contents of clothes. Above that, two large fluorescent lights illuminated the office, emphasizing a coldness akin to the inside of a refrigerator. A microwave and coffee maker stood on a small stand by one wall, on the other wall was a cot where a girl hugged a blanket. She was a petite redhead with a chalky face and sunken green eyes. A bucket stood on the floor by her head for easy access. Within seconds, Carisa summed up her diagnosis.

The girl's green eyes shot an angry glare at Tom. "I told you not to get her!"

Carisa grabbed a chair and placed it alongside the cot. "Tom's worried about you. What's your name?"

"I don't have to tell you nothing."

"Her name's Rachel," Tom said. "You can't call her parents."

"I have no intention of calling her parents because I don't have to, right, Rachel?"

"I've got the stomach flu. No biggie."

"Well, if you don't mind, I'm the doctor. How about I make the diagnosis?"

"I don't want a doctor."

"Yes, you do." Tom stepped close. "You need to eat. Listen to me. I'm the man here. I'm supposed to take care of you."

Carisa turned to Tom, surprised to see his eyes blazing. *What the hell is he so mad about*? "Why don't you step out while I conduct an examination?"

"No. I need to watch over her. She's my girl."

"And I'm the doctor. We need a little privacy, if you don't mind."

"Rachel won't want me to leave." He puffed out his chest.

Unusual possessiveness for such a young man. Then again, this was a clandestine coupling. Carisa looked at Rachel. "Does he watch you go to the bathroom, too?"

Rachel waved toward the door. "It's all right, Tom. You're supposed to be cleaning out the garage anyway. Come back in a little bit."

"No!"

Carisa stood to face him. "You go, or I go. Your choice."

Tom's face turned beet red. He glared at Rachel. With a low growl, he slammed the door on his way out.

The boy had a temper. *No wonder he ran away from home.* Carisa took her seat.

Rachel hugged the blanket closer to her body. "I don't have to let you touch me."

"True, but I want some answers without Tom butting in. How old are you?"

"I don't have to answer your questions either."

"No, you don't have to do anything, Rachel, except stay here and vomit all day, become dehydrated and weak, and worry Tom to death. Now, since I already know what is wrong with you, I can discuss some options, or I can go to the house and get my cell phone."

Rachel eased herself to a sitting position and put her back against the wall. She threw up her chin in defiance. "I think you should leave."

"You know I can't."

Her chin lowered. "This is Tom's fault. He got you involved."

"That's because he doesn't understand the seriousness of the situation." She leaned closer to lock onto Rachel's averted gaze and spoke in a soothing tone. "How old are you?"

"Seventeen."

And I have as much money as Harvey Fergus. Carisa cocked her head. "I also expect to hear the truth. You have to be fair to the baby."

Rachel shot her gaze around the room, darting from the window to the door. She looked like a trapped lab rat searching for an escape route. "Twenty-eight. How'd you know?"

"Your voice told me your age. As for the pregnancy, you have increased pigmentation near your hairline. That's the beginning of what is called the mask of pregnancy. Not all women get it, but your fair skin gave you away." Hanging around her father's OB-GYN office had served a purpose after all. "How long has the vomiting been going on?"

"Three weeks." She tucked the blanket around her legs.

"You took a home pregnancy test?"

"Twice. Tommy doesn't know."

"I assume he's the father?"

"Yes. We fell in love."

Carisa leaned forward on her elbows. "What you're doing is against the law. He's only fifteen."

"We fell in love," she repeated with a shrug.

Like that was the answer to everything. Why couldn't her job be simpler? *I should have gone to veterinary school.*

"You have to be quiet about this," Rachel said. "I know my rights."

Carisa ignored that. "Where do you live?"

"With my parents."

"Do they know about Tom?" *Of course, they don't.* "How about a job? Do you work?"

"I drive a school bus."

Tom's school bus more likely. *Shit, what a dilemma.*

"You can't tell anyone."

Carisa sighed as she leaned against the chair's backrest. "Honey, you're only two years younger than me. Tom is a minor. What you're doing is legally wrong. The boy can't even drive."

"You going to report me?"

"At the moment, I don't know what I'll do. You, however, need to get yourself to an OB-GYN specialist. You have a life inside you, and that is an immense responsibility. Whether you tell Tom or your parents is for you to decide." She stood and brushed off the seat of her pants. "Try to get some fluids in yourself. Have crackers or whatever stays down. This is normal in the early stages of pregnancy."

"Can't you prescribe something?"

"I have no jurisdiction in New York, but more importantly, I can't prescribe without a proper examination. That's where the baby doctor will help. I don't recommend you stay here either. You need the comfort of your own bed and maybe the help and support of your parents." She put her hand on the doorknob and looked back. "You dug yourself into a pretty deep hole, Rachel. Think carefully about your choices."

Carisa left the office. She didn't expect to hear a thank you and didn't get one. Without question, she needed to talk to Mitch.

Chapter Twelve

Mitch and Olivia returned a short time later with arms full of grocery bags. Then, Mr. Muscle Man carried in several cases of beer and soda while Olivia cradled an armload of flowers.

Carisa helped Emily unpack the bags.

Emily handed her the carrots. "Cut them for the dips, dear. I'll do the celery."

Olivia grabbed a piece of cheese. "I'm going to take a quick shower before everyone comes. Leave the flowers. I'll make an arrangement when I come down. Where's Dad?"

"Taking a nap," Emily answered then she sniffed.

Olivia stopped short, brows arched. "Emily, have you been crying?"

"Strong onions, dear. Make sure Rags is in your father's room. You know how the dog gets with Sal."

Olivia left the kitchen.

Mitch shifted his gaze from Emily to Carisa and back. "What did you make with onions? We bought the potato and macaroni salads."

"Never you mind." She waved a celery stalk toward the cellar staircase. "Get some wine from the cellar. Did you buy the ice?"

"It's still in the car. I'll pack the cooler as usual." He turned toward the back door but not without a glance at Carisa and a puzzled lift to his brow.

Carisa waited until the door snapped shut. "Why didn't you tell him?"

Emily clanged a spoon and huffed. "Because Jack made me promise. He said he will tell his kids in his own time. So, you and I are holding his secret." She jammed the spoon into the potato salad. "I don't like the idea either."

Wonderful. Secrets in a new relationship. Just what she needed. "Keep at him, Emily. Jack doesn't have a whole lot of time."

Their gazes met and held. Emily's blue eyes filled with tears before she turned away.

The family would have the convenience of hospice if Jack opened his mouth and told everyone. With any luck, Emily would slip the news to Mitch. He, in turn, could tell Olivia. End of secrets. "What's the problem with Rags and Sal?"

Emily emptied the macaroni salad into a large bowl. "Sal doesn't know when to stop teasing. We can't keep them in the same room because Rags acts like he'll tear Sal's leg off. The younger children get scared."

Mitch returned with a huge cooler, which he clunked onto a bench by the door.

He jammed soda and beer into the ice with arms rippling as if the ice put up a fight. Man against nature. No more dull and mundane existence for Carisa MacDowell. The man dragged her into the throes of a family again, and a certain bit of pleasure rose in her heart. Plus, he stimulated her libido like hell because a flush of heat touched her cheeks just by watching him.

Not again. Maybe no one would notice if she stuck her head in the freezer. Heat-fueled desire. *Can't beat it. I'm gonna ask that man for a maintenance request before he knows what hit him.* "Do you need help with the cooler?" *Yeah, right, get real.*

"If you mean carrying while full—" He grabbed the handles and turned toward her. His arm muscles bulged. "No." He winked before leaving with the cooler.

What was it she said about no heavy lifting? His strength was intoxicating. The vision of him as a lover with all those muscles and power created a flood of moisture between her legs that she swore was an open faucet. Even worse, she was peeling a carrot that had a shape of an enlarged penis.

Dear Lord, help me.

Why couldn't Emily give her the celery to cut? The stalks with their ribs and fibrous strings never conjured images of passionate sex. *Well, neither should the carrots.* She had better clear her mind of the obscene before chopping.

"Don't forget the wine," Emily said when Mitch returned.

"Right." He pounded down the stairs to the wine cellar.

"Oh, darn. I forgot to tell him Aunt Jean is coming. Would you mind, dear?"

She still stared at the wine cellar stairs. Emily's voice had broken the spell. Carisa shook herself. "Aunt Jean?"

"He'll know. Pass the word before he comes back."

Carisa hurried to the cellar.

Mitch already had several wine bottles on the table. He looked up from one of them.

"Aunt Jean's coming." *Brrr!* She hugged her arms.

"Good. Stay here and help me carry this stuff." He turned, plucked a bottle off the shelf, and wiped off dust with a rag. "She loves Dad's port. Let me see here." He counted the bottles. "Two more for good measure." He searched the racks.

She approached the table. "You should have some kind of carrier for all these bottles."

"I do." He pointed to an eight-bottle carrier in the corner.

"Then what do you need me for?"

In answer, he grabbed her by the waist and lifted her onto the table. Without missing a heartbeat, he captured her mouth, clamping his hand behind her head to hold her in place, forcing her lips apart to allow his tongue to probe. A cool hand slipped under her sweatshirt to stroke her back, shattering all thoughts—except the one involving a bed and two naked bodies, a man with muscles and soft curls in her face. And something else surfaced. An unfamiliar emotion, one she rejected as impossible. An overwhelming surge of heat mixed with…happiness?

Well, I'll be damned.

He bit her upper lip as he lifted his head. "That's why."

Smiling, she slipped her fingers into his curls and pulled him back. This time, her tongue explored. She returned the heat with equal fever. The man tasted so damn good.

"Mitchell, hurry up with the wine! The gang's coming."

Olivia again. The woman had radar. Carisa looked around at the ceiling.

"What?" he asked.

"I'm looking for surveillance cameras. I think they activate whenever we touch." She pushed on his chest. "I hear car doors."

He lifted her off the table and slid her down his body.

The feel of his hard erection sent her hormones into a rage. She rested her forehead on his chest, not in the least willing to leave his arms.

"I can't go upstairs yet," he whispered.

She met a gaze dark with desire. "Anything I can do?" Well, that was a stupid question. All the blood had pooled in her pelvic region and not a drop reached her brain.

He bit her nose. "I need you to turn into an ugly gargoyle so that I cringe when I see you." He released her, dragging his finger along the length of her arms. "Here, take several bottles with you. If anyone asks, tell them I'm cleaning the bottles."

"Mitch, by the way—" In as few words as possible, she told him about Tom and Rachel. "Back home, I'd call child services, and they'd notify the police. I don't know what to do here." Pedophilia was a punishable crime, no matter what the perpetrators claimed. And here, Rachel was pregnant. Her situation made everything worse.

Mitch touched her chin. "When I get a chance, I'll slip away and have a talk with them. This kind of stuff is never easy to handle."

She kissed him lightly and hurried up the stairs.

Carisa had no time to dwell on the heat of his kiss or the feelings that surfaced. The guests poured in by the time she reached the top step. Olivia's singsong voice echoed clear through to the kitchen with every ring of the doorbell. Carisa and Emily rushed back and forth to put food trays on the dining room table while Mitch carried in the wine.

The atmosphere was jovial and loud with a lot of hugging and kissing. Jack had thrown open the adjoining doors between the living and dining rooms giving the place the look of one big hall. They needed a hall. Thirty plus people from the very young to the very old gathered. Everyone came to see Mitch and Olivia, two long-lost relatives returning to the tribe.

"My word, we're rushing around so much, I hadn't time to introduce you," Emily said while scanning the kitchen for any forgotten food. "You should join them."

"You are more a part of this family than I am. I'll finish cutting the rolls."

The old woman bit her lip.

"Go!"

Emily threw off her apron and grabbed a bowl full of chips before leaving.

****

Mitch excused himself from the party while everyone was busy hugging and kissing. He wanted to get this business about Tom and Rachel over with. Hell, he hadn't come to Geneva to solve any abduction crime, and he sure as hell hadn't time for a teenager's problems. He headed for the winery only to see Willie emerge while shaking his head.

"That boy's got a hard head," Willie complained.

"What happened?"

"I took him a plateful of food and interrupted him and his girlfriend snuggling on the cot. I might be wrong, Mitch, but the girl looks too old for him."

"She's twice his age, Willie. That's why I'm here.

Carisa made the discovery."

Willie again shook his head. "The stupid shit blames me for causing her to pack up and leave."

"She left?"

"Yeah. She said too many people found out. She blames Tom. Tom blames me." He kicked a stone toward a bush. "She got in her car and drove off."

Mitch cocked a brow. "I didn't see any strange cars around here."

Willie gestured with his thumb. "She used the secondary access road and parked behind the winery. I didn't know it was there until she squealed away. Tom's in the office banging everything in sight. He wanted to go with her, but she refused. Said she was going back to her parents because she needed a nice bed. That got Tom real hot. She promised to come back tomorrow, all that crap." He rubbed his chin. "Maybe I better check to see if any of the cars out front have their keys in the ignition. The boy doesn't have a driver's license yet, but he's dumb enough to chase after her with someone's car."

"Good idea." Mitch stared at the dark winery. "Dad promised Tom's father to keep an eye on him. Now that we know the real reason he ran away, we should try to keep him here. I'll talk to him."

Willie slapped Mitch on the shoulder. "The boy's hotter than coal. Watch your back."

Mitch entered the winery. He reached the office as the door swung open with a bang.

Tom stepped out hauling a backpack over one shoulder.

Mitch stopped him with an upraised hand. "You plan on hitchhiking to your girlfriend's?"

"It's all Willie's fault. He scared her away."

"She's too old for you, Tom. She's breaking the law, and if you leave, you'll lead the police right to her. Is that what you want?"

He squared his shoulders. "We're in love. We belong together."

Yeah, right. 'Til death do us part. "Don't you think you should finish school first before you get serious with a girl?"

Tom attempted to circumvent Mitch. One sidestep blocked his path. "You sound like my old man. I'm going to find her."

Mitch put a light hand on the boy's chest. "Willie heard her say she'll be back tomorrow. Why not wait?"

"I don't want to. Let me go."

"I'm not holding you back." He wasn't giving him any room to get around either. "Do you know where she lives?"

He looked up with a blank stare. "No, I don't."

Yeah, funny that. "You should wait for daylight. I don't think she'll stay away long. Dr. MacDowell said she was sick. Maybe she got embarrassed throwing up in front of you."

"Maybe." He stuffed his hands into his trouser pockets. "We love each other and belong together."

"Pedophiles get thrown in jail, Tom."

He flushed a deep scarlet. "She's my girl, dammit! I don't care what anyone says!"

A touchy situation. Young man in love with an older woman. Hormones out of control. The media loved stories like this, and the outcome was never a happy one. "Look, Tom, wait for tomorrow. Give her a chance to come back. If she loves you, she won't be away long."

"Willie's gonna pay for this." He ground his teeth.

"What makes you think Willie's to blame? Rachel knows she's breaking the law."

"We're in love, dammit!"

The answer to everything. "If you don't calm down, I'll call your dad and tell him you're here. Is that what you want?"

"I don't care if you call him. I'm going after Rachel."

Hell, what a dilemma. The boy belonged in a locked cell to cool off. One last try. "Daylight's a smarter option. If you don't know where she lives, then you can't find her in the dark. If you're so intent on chasing after her, at least go when the sun's up so a car won't take your legs off. But a real man would wait for her to come back on her own." *Yeah, words of wisdom.* Hormones ruled.

After several moments passed, Tom stepped away. "You're right. I'll wait for her."

The tactic worked? Since when?

No matter. He had a woman of his own to contend with, and the boy was wasting his time. Tom would be on the road by morning searching for the love of his life, and no one, not even Mitch Montero, could stop him.

Chapter Thirteen

Carisa took her time cutting the rolls, moving the knife like the blade was duller than dirt. She wasn't used to large crowds, and a congregation of strangers made her want to scrub the kitchen floor.

Her family was small, a few cousins here and there, two uncles, one aunt. None got along, and they avoided gatherings like the plague. Her mother had hosted the bridge club or a ladies' social but never a big party, and never anything for children. Her father had often worked late to avoid the crowd, and on those nights, he'd taken his daughter for an ice cream or a walk in the park. The memories seemed ironic now. She had loved spending time with her father. Obviously, he hadn't felt the same.

A man walked into the kitchen. His jet-black hair brushed the top of the doorframe as a deep-set black-eyed gaze swept over her like she was pole-dancing on a stage. He wore an excessive amount of gold jewelry on a wide-open neckline that showed a little too much of his curly-haired chest. His clothes were expensive, the shirt a white silk, his trousers black and pressed to perfection. *Definitely a man who checks himself in the mirror.*

A grin stretched across his face. "I wondered who you were. Don't tell me Uncle Jack finally got Emily some help?" He walked across the room. "I'm after the mustard." He reached into the fridge, grabbed what he needed, strolled back, and extended his hand. "I'm Salvatore Montero."

Ah, Sal and Rags. She accepted his hand. "Carisa."

He held firm. "Nice name. Married?"

"No." She yanked her hand out of his. "You want to take these rolls with you?" She shoved the tray against his chest, whether he wanted it or not.

"Sure." He swept a gaze over her from head to toe. "You're pretty. The ponytail gives you a nice sporty look."

Not like she had time to take down her hair. Nor change her clothes. Sweatshirt and jeans. *Tough toenails.* "Thanks. Here, take more napkins, too." She threw the napkins on the rolls.

"I like sporty women. They have great stamina in bed."

The next thing I'll hear is the length of his penis. She peered at him. "The rolls, Sal?"

He glanced down at the tray in his hands. "Right." He hurried out.

Carisa grabbed Emily's apron and began cleanup. As the sink filled with bubbles, she let her thoughts drift to Mitch.

She'd never had a steady man in her life. They had come and gone after a few dates. A mutual agreement. Never anything serious. Fun times. Sex. Physical connections. With Mitch, she couldn't deny the strong emotional connection. The man made her happy. She couldn't understand why. They were still strangers, two people who literally ran into each other. Yet, his kiss warmed every cell in her body, forcing hormones to vibrate into action. Especially down yonder. And quicker than she ever believed possible.

Was she in love with him? No, that wasn't the right question. She liked Mitch. They were two people enjoying each other without the L word. A much-safer option. Love had a way of causing needless pain. She had learned that hard lesson from her father.

Salvatore returned. He carried two full wine glasses and handed her one.

She promptly dumped the contents into the sudsy water and washed the glass.

He cringed. "You threw away good wine."

"Oh...sorry. This was for me?"

He sipped his wine. "I see no reason why you can't enjoy yourself while working." He pressed his body to her back and pushed her against the sink, forcing his hard erection against her butt.

She gasped and jumped to the side. "Have you lost your mind? I'm not a sex-starved kitten waiting for the lion to pounce. Get out of here!" She glanced at the entrance.

"I can be in and out before you know what hit you, babe. Try me."

Body roiling with irritation, she backed away while wiping her hands on the apron. *Bad enough I put up with this shit at the hospital.* "No, I won't try you, but if you leave now, you can forget we met."

"What agency are you from?" He slowly matched her backward steps.

"I...huh—agency?" *What the hell is he talking about?*

"I'd like to hire you for a little private party...if you get my drift."

She got the drift all right and clamped her jaw.

Somebody, please interrupt us! "I'm with Mitch."

"Yeah, right. That's why you're in here, and he's out there. Look, you can't be making much for this job. I've got a hundred bucks in my pocket if you'll come down to the wine cellar. You've got a nice firm butt that I want to enjoy." He leaned close. "I also want to see if you're a natural blonde."

Was he kidding? She couldn't keep her mouth from falling open. He wore a wedding band, for crying out loud. Jamming her hands on her hips, she slapped her mouth shut. "I think you better leave the kitchen before Mitch comes in."

He moaned. "Mitch again. You naïve, beautiful blonde." He placed his wine glass on the table. "If you knew Mitch, you'd know that he is the most career-oriented man in the family. He's a confirmed bachelor and doesn't have time for a woman. Frustrates the hell out of his sister. If you were with Mitch, you'd be alongside him, and Olivia'd be jumping for joy."

Yeah, right, and doing cartwheels, too.

"I happen to know that Olivia's got a date arranged for Mitch tomorrow." He shook a finger in her face. "You should find out a little more about your employer before you make any claims, sweetheart. Will you stop backing away!"

"What the hell else am I supposed to do? You want to back me into a corner, and I won't let it happen." She side-stepped toward the kitchen entrance.

He flashed a crooked grin. "Relax, I won't hurt you. I do regret that Olivia can't tell me a thing about you, just that you're helping Emily. Are you just for the party, or will you be a permanent fixture around here? If the latter, I might stop by to see Uncle Jack more often."

Carisa staggered. *Helping Emily*? "Olivia knows perfectly well why I'm here."

Sal waved aside the comment. "Oh, come now. It isn't to match you up with Mitch, which she's always trying to do." He reached into his trouser pocket and extracted money then wagged it in her face. "Now, about the cellar. An easy hundred bucks, Carisa. For what, five minutes?"

A little boy ran in. "Daddy, Mommy wants to know what's taking you so long?"

"You tell Mommy I'm going to the bathroom. Go on, tell her."

The little boy ran out.

Again, Carisa couldn't stop her mouth from falling open. "Your wife and kid are here?"

"Kids. I have three."

"Are you crazy, Sal?" She darted for the entrance.

Sal caught her right arm and jerked her toward the cellar steps.

The move knocked her off balance and caused a twinge through her scapula. She fell against him. "I'll scream, Sal. People will come running."

"And I'll tell them you solicited me. They'll believe family over the hired help. Think about it, Carisa." He narrowed his gaze, his grip tightening on her arm. "You'll never work in this town again. Let's go." He yanked hard.

Her right shoulder snapped, and pain shot straight down to her fingertips. She cried out and swung wildly with her left fist, hitting only his chest. Fear seized her throat. Her mind raced. *Fight or flight?* What should she do? And how the hell could a kitchen stay empty so long with a house full of people?

Stay calm. Beat the crap out of him. Hit him where it hurts. Her father's words echoed in her brain.

She swung a knee toward Sal's crotch and hit his kneecap. *Friggin' tall men*.

Sal gave a cruel laugh and yanked again. They were within inches of the cellar steps.

Now what? Scream her head off? Instead, she swung her fist into his erection. *Take that, damn you!*

"Ommph!" Sal released his hold to protect his sensitive parts and then quickly grabbed her before she got away. "Oh, no, you don't."

She stomped on his foot, which was a ridiculous maneuver. Her sneaker against his heavy shoe was like hammering a nail with a marshmallow. Tensing, she readied another swing at his crotch when he released his hold.

With a muffled expletive, he inched away, eyes wide while staring at the back door.

Mitch stood on the threshold, his face red, his eyes like glistening daggers, jaw tight, lips pressed into a thin line. He resembled a man struggling to contain an explosion.

The bottom fell from her gut. Her legs wobbled, and she caught herself on the kitchen table. Her vision changed from clear to a strange sparkling, as if she peered through a hole and everything else was distorted. *Dilation of the pupil. Oh, God.* A whirling of the room was next. *I will not faint*.

She'd never fainted a day in her life, and she wasn't about to start. She clamped her eyes shut and sucked in several large breaths to get herself under control, wishing Sal would disappear in the process.

Feeling steadier, she opened her eyes.

Neither man noticed. Their gazes were locked in mortal combat.

Sal backed away first with one hand up in surrender, the other hand holding his private parts. A nervous smile stretched onto his face. "Just having fun with the hired help."

Mitch approached, his steps slow and deliberate. "Hired help, Sal?"

"Look, she flirted, okay? Then, she attacked me. How am I supposed to explain this to my wife?" He rubbed his crotch.

"You had a grip on her arm, Sal. I'd say the lady was defending herself."

"All right, yeah, so I grabbed her. She should learn to control her urges with her employer's guests. Never know when one might take her on."

"Like you?" Mitch gripped Sal by the scruff of his neck and dragged him toward the back door. Sal had more height, but he was no match in muscle. He gave little resistance to Mitch's hold on his neck.

"Mitch…really, man, I'm playing her. You know me, how I love to flirt and tease. I wouldn't hurt her. It's just a game, man."

"Is that right? Since when does a game drain the blood from a woman's face?"

Mitch's practiced calm compared to Sal's panic was almost comical. If she wasn't feeling so woozy, she'd laugh.

"Look, she solicited me. You know my wife and kids are with me."

"So you decided to force her down to the cellar? I wouldn't call that fending her off, Sal. Maybe we need a statement from the lady. Carisa?" Mitch searched her face, his burning gaze softening. "Did he hurt you?"

"Yes." The word slipped out as a croaked whisper. "He offered me a hundred dollars for five minutes. I told him I was with you."

His chest heaved with heavy breaths.

Sal struggled against the grip. "She's lying!"

"My woman has no reason to lie."

"Mitch, come on, man—"

Mitch dragged him out the back door.

Carisa tossed off the apron and ran for the staircase with tears streaming down her cheeks. She didn't care who saw her. She wanted the security of her room to cry, to scream, to be alone. *Oh, God, help me.*

The pain was unbearable. Inside the room, she collapsed on the floor by her bed, clutching her arm. Several minutes later, a knock rapped on the bathroom door. Carisa jumped since every nerve in her body fired.

"Carisa, it's me."

She had locked all the doors. She hadn't meant to lock out Mitch, but she didn't want someone following her either. Like Sal. She let in Mitch and showed no embarrassment for the tears streaming down her cheeks.

He embraced her and held tight while easing her head onto his chest. "I'm sorry," he whispered. "Please don't cry."

"A whole week of nursing this shoulder shot to hell because of that bastard."

"He was an ass as a kid, too." He kissed her hair.

The sensation of his warm lips shot a stream of comfort straight to her shoulder. Which wasn't possible. Only in her mind. "I never tasted fear until tonight, Mitch. I was about to scream bloody murder when you showed up. How could he be so stupid with the family in the other room?"

"He's not a rocket scientist, Carisa."

"Olivia—"

"Shhh." He put his hand behind her neck and massaged. "He told me what Olivia said. I'll settle with her later." He placed a finger under her chin and lifted her head. "I'll run down and get an ice pack."

She didn't want him to leave, but the sooner she put ice on her shoulder, the better. "Yes, thank you, and Mitch, please, something to drink. My mouth has gone dry."

He cursed audibly and hurried from the room.

Ten minutes later, he rushed back, carrying an ice bag and large glass of colored liquid. With a commanding finger, he pointed to the head of the bed as he placed the glass on the night table and wrapped the ice in a towel.

Carisa rummaged through her purse for a painkiller. Anything would do. *I'm a friggin' doctor. I should have something in this damn purse!* She found a buffered aspirin in a packet, ripped it open with her teeth, and gulped down the pill with the liquid. She jerked sharply and stared at the glass. "Whoa, what is this?"

"Water with a shot of whiskey." He wrapped the ice pack on her shoulder.

"You've done this before," she said, marveling at his skill.

"You have a common football injury. I wore quite a few ice packs in my day." He sat on the bed facing her, staring.

155

His gaze was like burning embers. She stroked his cheek.

With a wink, he grabbed her hand and pressed his lips against the palm.

Words eluded her. She had always taken care of people, never the other way around, and to have this man come to her defense and then handle her shoulder like a delicate flower generated an intoxicating sense of security. She wasn't sure whether to cry or shout with joy. "Thank you for coming to my rescue. When I saw you standing in the doorway, I'd never experienced anything more wonderful in my life. You didn't beat him to a pulp, did you?"

"I wanted to, but I knew once I started, I wouldn't stop. I told him to get out and never come back. If he wants to see his Uncle Jack, he'll need to visit when I'm not here." He again kissed her hand before releasing it and turned away.

The expression on his face surprised her. Not anger. *Pain*? She searched for evidence of a bruise. "Did he hurt you?"

"No, Olivia hurt me. I don't understand her at all."

She seized the long-awaited opening and touched his arm. "As a doctor, I'm telling you what she's doing is not healthy. She's overly possessive, Mitch, and has eyes only for you when she enters a room. All others are invisible. It's a classic blindness. In her eyes, no one is more important." She slipped her hand down to his thigh. It was a powerful leg that belonged to a powerful man. "I'm flattered, by the way. You surprised everyone."

"I surprised myself."

His smile was slight, but she caught the faint lift at

the corner.

"Olivia drove me nuts in high school."

"Yes, when dating was a big part of adolescence. She not only hindered you as a young man entering adulthood, but she hindered herself as well. Her focus centered on you and still does."

Carisa again touched his leg, caressing perfectly hardened muscles beneath the trousers. She couldn't resist. "You're the one who can correct the problem, Mitch. Olivia will never accept the women you choose because they will never be as good as the one she picks—the one she can control." Carisa patted the thigh. "You should get downstairs. I'm sure everyone is wondering where you are."

He placed a hand on her cheek. "I don't give a crap about the party, Carisa. My concern is you, always has been."

The words sounded nice. The man made her feel important, protected, and so…unsure. Was he in love as Emily suggested? More like an old woman's yearning for a touch of romance. *But really now, Carisa, isn't it obvious*? What were words when his gaze, his touch, his kiss told her so much? "You called me your woman." She'd said it with hesitation, half-expecting a retraction.

Their gazes locked. Doubt flooded his. "Are you?"

She stopped breathing. This was a different form of possessiveness, a more normal connection between a man and a woman. "Yes, I am."

He leaned over and kissed her.

She wanted this one to last, to keep him by her side and forget about the people downstairs. His mouth tasted wonderful, soft and luscious with a hint of ham and cheese with mayo.

He lifted his head.

A disappointment, yes, but how far could one go with an ice pack on her shoulder? "Were you coming back from the winery?"

He fingered the golden strands that fell from her ponytail. "The girl was gone." He released her hair and explained about meeting Willie. "I had a serious discussion with Tom, but like any young man in love, he was unreasonable. He doesn't care what the law says. All he cares about is the happily-ever-after without any idea how he'll achieve it." He took her hand and squeezed. "She'll go to jail if caught."

And become a media uproar in the process. "What should we do?"

"I have no jurisdiction here." He readjusted the icepack on her shoulder. "If she ran away to have the baby, fine. If she demands support from Tom, then the court will throw the book at her. I'm hoping she disappears."

"What if Tom disappears with her?"

"Then I'll tell the police everything I know." He rubbed the back of his neck, his expression grave. "They will want a description of Rachel from you and Willie and that will help them hunt down a school bus driver named Rachel. If she was Tom's bus driver, she'll be on record at the school."

Carisa grabbed his shirt collar and pulled his lips to hers. She wanted to forget about Tom, Olivia, and Sal, to enjoy her time with Mitch, and to explore the possibility of love and the wonderful feelings that went with it. *His woman. Her man.* Who would have thought…

"Mitchell, where are you?"

Cameras in the bedroom, too?

"I'll kill her," Mitch whispered into her mouth. He bit her lower lip before pulling away.

Olivia marched through the open bathroom door, riveting her gaze onto Mitch, nothing else. "What are you doing here? Everyone thinks you fell down a drainpipe."

Carisa wondered if Olivia noticed how close and personal Mitch placed himself by her side. If they were lying naked intertwined, would Olivia see that? *Classic textbook*.

"Well, let's go!" Olivia demanded.

Mitch's jaw muscles twitched. He rose to his feet like a monolith breaking through the ground ready to cast a giant shadow onto an unsuspecting crowd. He faced his sister. "You told Sal that Carisa was here to help Emily."

His threatening posture hadn't fazed Olivia in the least. She merely folded her arms across her chest. "Yeah, so?"

"Sal hit on her."

"Don't be ridiculous. Sal's married. She obviously flirted." She tugged on her blouse sleeve.

Mitch's face turned scarlet. "And have you noticed Sal is no longer at the party?" His voice quivered.

"Well, sure. He and his family said their goodbyes. He was called into work." She had spoken the last sentence with some hesitation as she shifted her gaze from Mitch to Carisa.

Mitch threw Olivia an annoyed glare. "He's a mail carrier, Olivia. Since when do they call him to work on a Sunday evening? He doesn't work in a distribution hub."

"His wife says he does lots of overtime on Sunday evenings. He makes extra money." She bit her lower lip.

Mitch ran both hands through his hair, yanking the ends.

Carisa winced. *Please don't ruin your curls.*

"I interrupted Sal about to force Carisa down to the wine cellar!"

Olivia started. Her arms fell to her side as she looked at Carisa for the first time. "Are you hurt?"

"I'm wearing an ice pack on my shoulder. What do you think?"

Denial flew across Olivia's beautiful face. "What did you say to him?"

The accusation tensed her muscles, creating a twinge under the icepack. "Nothing to suggest he stick his hard erection into my butt." *Oops!* She shouldn't have said that with Mitch standing nearby. She expected steam to shoot out his ears.

Mitch clenched his fists. "I want to know why you passed off Carisa as Emily's helper."

Olivia jumped at his sharp tone. "He asked me who she was. No big deal." She flipped the hair off her shoulder. "You have to admit I don't know anything about her."

"You never thought to say she was with me?"

"Oh, stop playing cop. You'll blow a gasket." She turned toward the bathroom. "Are you coming or not?" She paused in the open doorway with her head cocked. "Well?"

Carisa watched the interaction between brother and sister with a physician's analytical eye. Olivia's body language expressed dominance, and she dismissed their conversation with a wave. Her mind was downstairs with the rest of the family. Mitch wasn't by her side, and she needed to correct the problem. What Sal attempted was of no consequence.

No, this was not the explosive argument to break Olivia's hold. A more powerful one was yet to come. Carisa grasped his hand and motioned for him to lean over. "Kiss me."

The anger fell from his face as his brows shot halfway up his forehead. Carisa clutched onto his collar to lower his lips. She kissed him with the depth of earlier, mindful of Olivia's audible gasp. After she suckled his lips one last time, she lifted her head and winked.

Without turning to face Olivia, Mitch said, "I'll be down when I'm ready."

"Well, don't take long. The family's here to see you, too." She walked off with a huff.

Mitch smiled. "That worked."

"For now. Go downstairs and visit your family. I'll join you in a little while." She wanted to say before Olivia spread rumors they couldn't retract, but she bit back the words.

Smiling, he kissed her nose and left.

She debated locking the door, but the debate lasted too long.

Olivia returned, her face like stone.

"Mitch went downstairs."

"Yes, I know. I waited for him to leave." She approached the bed. "I wanted to give you this." With a narrowed gaze, she tossed a piece of paper onto Carisa's lap.

A ten thousand dollar check! Carisa stared, mute, her breath hitched in her throat.

"I want you to cancel your outing with Mitch tomorrow. I've arranged an important lunch date, which he refuses to attend. Because of you, dear." She folded her arms across her chest.

Well, well. I received a get-out-of-his-life check after all. "Even if I cancel, I can't guarantee he'll go, Olivia."

"Then you need to convince him. It's in his best interest to go whether he understands or not. Rosalie's a much better match."

Wow. Talk about a swift kick in the pants. The medical profession had fallen to the bottom of the social ladder. Funny that. "Mitch is old enough to handle his own life, Olivia."

"Doesn't matter. Just do as I say. If everything works out with Rosalie, I'll give you a bonus." She turned to leave but paused in the doorway. "You might want to use some of that money to make your way back to Philadelphia. A cab can take you to the airport." Lifting her chin, she left without another word.

Carisa stared at the check in her hand. Ten thousand. A sizable amount. She could pay off her father by the end of next year if her overtime schedule continued. Was this a lucky break? A too-good-to-pass-up moment?

Without a doubt, this check required some serious consideration.

Chapter Fourteen

God help me.

Mitch struggled with the overwhelming desire to be with Carisa every second of the day and the uncontrollable urge to strangle anyone who interfered. That someone was usually Olivia. She had turned into a royal pain-in-the-ass.

Carisa was right. He had never seen Olivia's behavior as anything more than a loving sister, a buttinsky at times, critical of the girls he dated, but she had stopped after a time. No, he corrected. She ceased because he'd kept his girlfriends away, a safer tactic for the most frustrating time of his young life.

Now, after all these years, he'd invited a woman home for the world to meet. Olivia's obsessive conduct had jumped to the forefront, as if his choice of mate would be the ruination of all mankind. Well, that was too damn bad. He was a grown man and could chose whomever he pleased. As it happened, Mitch Montero was too far gone this time. He had fallen in love with the blonde-haired beauty. When they collided in fact, Carisa had looked up with a pair of bewildered brown eyes, and he was lost.

He had waited on the gurney with her face flooding his mind, oblivious to the noise of a busy ER or the pain of his wound. Then, she strolled in. What a shock. A happy shock. He'd talked her into this trip to give her a chance to fall in love. With him. With the house that he loved so much. With the area. He didn't need his sister to create a roadblock.

He glanced toward the foyer, over the crowd of heads, hoping to see Carisa step off the staircase. He wanted to introduce her to the family, brag that he had snared the most beautiful woman in the world. Each glance proved fruitless. Was she brave enough to confront the rest of the family after her encounter with Sal? *Please try, Carisa.*

"So, what do you think?"

He jerked. Aunt Jean had been talking a mile a minute in her usual staccato voice. What the hell had she asked him? "Sorry, I was distracted."

"No matter. You don't drink wine anyway."

She rattled on about Sal's rapid departure, speculating on the why and what for until he steered the conversation toward other topics. He'd put his self-restraint to the test when his hand gripped Sal's neck. He'd come so close to rearranging that smug expression on his cousin's face, to make him permanently resemble a raccoon, and he didn't need his aunt's chattering to remind him how close he came.

When he'd stepped through the back door and saw Sal yank on Carisa's arm, he felt every hair on his scalp bristle. Her pain shot straight out of her eyes and into his heart. Even now, the vision caused his nails to dig into his palms. *His woman.* He had never said those words before. Even better, she had agreed.

"Are you with us?" Olivia whispered.

He jerked again. "Oh, sure." He pretended to participate in the constant banter between family members with a nod of his head. Like a bobble-head on a dashboard. Nod, nod, nod. A reaction to movement.

Olivia hardly noticed. She behaved as usual, hooking her arm in his as if they were a couple.

Over the years, this hadn't bothered him, but now, he could barely control his annoyance. Olivia had gasped, of all things, when he and Carisa kissed. How silly was that? Like he was a schoolboy sneaking a smooch in the playground. Hell, Olivia needed a man of her own, not her brother.

No man could deny his sister's stunning beauty. She had a fiery air, a hotheaded Italian look that wasn't a bit true. She was, in fact, docile around men. He had uncovered this hidden part of her character early when several football buddies followed him home. The guys had gone gaga over her. To this day, men melted when she passed, but she chose not to notice. Instead, she doted on her brother like a martyr. He loved his sister, but he wanted Carisa on his arm, not Olivia.

From a few feet away, Emily approached. "Where's Carisa?"

He opened his mouth to speak when the piano echoed from the direction of the living room.

Emily gasped. "Someone's playing your mother's song!"

Indeed. Chopin. The player had the skill of a concert pianist. The entire dining room emptied and headed for the living room.

Carisa pounded on the ivory keys. She had changed into a blouse and slacks, her hair loose with the waves shaking in synch with each accented note.

His father sat next to her on the piano bench, tears streaming down his cheeks. He turned the sheet music as he had so often for his wife, reading along with

Carisa because he knew the music by heart.

The memory jarred everyone in the room. Several of the older relatives dabbed tissues to their eyes.

"That song hasn't been played in this house since your mother died," Emily said through the tears rolling on her cheeks. "Look at Jack! He's so happy."

No one recognized Carisa and whispers abounded. Several of his cousins turned to Olivia who merely stared, dumbfounded. No one asked Mitch Montero, the career man who never bothered with a woman.

Carisa's performance was flawless. Afterward, the crowd applauded. His father hugged her, followed quickly by Emily.

Mitch stood alongside the piano and faced the crowd. "Ladies and gentlemen, meet the woman in my life, Carisa MacDowell." His chest swelled with a pride he'd never experienced as everyone lined up to say hello.

Carisa looked around, wide-eyed with all the accolades. She met his gaze on several occasions with a face full of surprise, shyness, and awkwardness, each one fighting for dominance.

Mitch stood back and observed with a smile.

His dad talked her into another composition, an Irving Berlin song that got the crowd singing. Life had changed so much after his mother died. His father stopped socializing. Olivia stopped painting. Mitch had joined every school sport to work out his sorrow. After a time, his father rejoined the world, thanks to Emily's persistence. Olivia never picked up another paintbrush. None of them had expected to hear the piano again.

The hour was late when he returned to his room. His father couldn't stop talking about Carisa's concert.

The old man had fallen in love all over again, and his joy bubbled out his pores. As much as Mitch wanted to be upstairs with Carisa, he let his father ramble. The man was, after all, bragging about the girl Mitch took home.

After a slow shower, he slipped on a pair of pajama bottoms and a robe before stepping onto the balcony. Her side of the balcony was dark, and a wave of disappointment flooded him. Not like he had expected her to wait. She'd left after clean up while he reminisced with his father in the family room.

He loved this time of year—late October, the sky clear and twinkling with stars, the air crisp with no threat of an early winter. He missed the place with its lazy days after the fall harvest. Most of all, he missed the silence. Philadelphia had too much noise, too many cars and people.

He stared at the quarter moon rising. Perry Como's swing-on-a-star song came to mind, another of his mother's sing-along favorites. He had spent many nights on the balcony as a kid, always with a pair of binoculars. *Keeping an eye on the vineyards*, he'd told his mother. Of course, the countryside turned into a black void at night with visibility barely fifty feet from the house, but his self-appointed task made him feel important. That had stopped after his mother died.

"Hi."

Carisa's voice had resonated from somewhere within the darkness. He stepped closer to her end of the balcony and spotted her outline on the rail. This time, she wore a robe. Its color was dark, purple maybe, or perhaps deep blue. She looked like a chameleon blending into the shadows on the wall. "I didn't think you'd be up this late." He approached. Actually, he was thrilled to see her. He had hated the idea of not saying a proper good night. "How's the shoulder?"

"Better since the ice pack. All the hugs and handshaking nearly did me in, though."

The family had said hello in the traditional Italian fashion—a hug and a kiss. Her face had shown the awe of a custom both new and different. They had hugged and kissed Mitch, too, as if he'd announced their engagement. "I said this last night. A chair will be more comfortable."

"But I can't see over the rail if I sit in a chair. This way, I have an unobstructed view."

She had a point. The rail was concrete with thick spindles, an obstruction no matter what angle. "You made my dad very happy tonight. I want to thank you."

She chuckled softly. "I'm surprised I remembered how to play. I thought your dad would bawl out loud when I picked the Chopin piece."

"You played beautifully."

"Thank you. It's a shame Olivia never learned. Was your mother disappointed?"

"Probably, but she never pushed. Mom had big dreams about Olivia's artwork on display at the Met. She was very proud of her talent."

"But Olivia gave up. You should ask her why."

"Yeah, well, I never understood why she studied business. She's a natural for the arts." He hardly understood his sister. She loved painting, yet she stopped. She hated business, yet she studied for an MBA. No confusion with his life. He wanted to be a cop. Period.

Carisa put her head back against the wall and

stared out into the blackness. Contentment covered her face.

The look pleased him. Everything about her pleased him.

"It's lovely here, Mitch. You have acres of vineyards surrounding the house, Seneca Lake in the front, and no neighbors on either side. A picture-perfect setting." She looked at him with a heavy sigh. "What made you move to Philly?"

He rubbed the back of his neck. "I never wanted to leave, but I had to start my own life."

"Away from Olivia, you mean."

"Yes." The words hurt even after so many years. "I was young at the time and couldn't control my sister. I had no choice. I applied to several police academies, every one out of state. Philadelphia intrigued me the most."

"Weren't you afraid she'd follow you?"

"In the beginning, yes. Then, she got that job in Syracuse, and her career took off."

He leaned on the rail near her bare feet. Last night, she had wiggled her toes under his butt, not in the least shy. This time, he intentionally lifted his hip. The woman didn't need a neon sign. She inched her toes under.

"Why are you sitting in the dark? You don't even have a light on in your room. I thought you were asleep."

She took a deep breath and then let it out through pursed lips. "I'm clearing my lungs before we head back to Philly." She wiggled her toes.

Whenever that would be. He had always kept his trips short and sweet, shorter still if Olivia visited.

Right now, he hadn't a single reason to leave and all because of the woman with her toes under his butt.

"I ran to the ridge today and met Harvey."

"Harvey Fergus?" He shuddered. "The guy gives me the creeps. What was he doing on the ridge?"

"He has a shed in a clearing. He stepped from that when I inadvertently trespassed onto his property. Someone was with him, but that person stayed in the shed. Rags doesn't like him. He followed me and growled the whole time. Harvey's nothing but a big priss."

That wasn't how Mitch described Harvey Fergus. The man fought like a girl, cried like a baby, but had the brain to go on and do big things. He'd chosen to skip college and handle his father's books. A boring existence.

"On the way back, I met Willie. Nice guy." She wiggled her toes again.

An animalistic urge rose inside him. He wanted to nibble on those toes tickling his butt. He wanted to nibble on the rest of her even more.

"Mitch—"

Her voice was hesitant, cautious. Shadows hid any clues from her eyes. "Something on your mind?"

She chewed on her lower lip while watching him.

Something was indeed on her mind. "What is it, Carisa?"

She shook herself and forced a smile. "Are you still taking me out tomorrow?"

"I'll take you on one condition. If you remove my stitches. They pinch like hell."

"Poor baby, but it might not be time."

"Then I'm not taking you anywhere." To make his

point, he crossed his arms over his chest.

Her mouth fell open. "Blackmail! From a cop." She laughed, a deep nervous sound that belied the humor of her words.

He studied her. "Besides Sal, has anything happened tonight that I should know about?" Dear Lord, had someone else hit on her?

"Nothing worth mentioning." She fingered his sleeve, smoothing her finger over the robe's material then dropped her hand. "Tell you what. I'll take a good look at your stitches in the morning. If I'm satisfied and you find me the supplies I need, I'll remove them. I make no promises. The last thing you want is to split the incision wide open."

"You've got yourself a deal, woman."

He preferred to sit here all night, but the hour was late. Under no circumstances would he waste half the day sleeping when he finally had a chance to be alone with this woman. He had ample opportunities to uncover what troubled her. Another time and place. For now, the night must pass before tomorrow began. He stood and leaned inches from her face. "I'm getting you up at six."

"No way! I'm on vacation."

He kissed her. Sweet heaven! Every time he tasted her lips, he reeled from the softness. He desired more of her, here, in his bed, and he wanted her soon. Would she come to him like he asked? Had her father hardened her heart to the point of no return?

No, her lips told him too much. He had to make her realize what she refused to feel. He would thaw that heart, but these damn stitches had to come out first!

Chapter Fifteen

In the morning, Carisa inspected his wound and gave the okay.

As much as Mitch tried to contain his joy, he hooted anyway and ran from his room with her supply list in hand, waving it in the air like a man on a mission. Her supplies covered the essentials of stitch removal—small scissors, latex gloves, tweezers, gauze pads, and surgical tape or the equivalent of which only the gauze he knew to be in the house. He enlisted Emily's help for the rest.

Emily, in turn, had followed him back to his bedroom to watch the doctor in action.

Olivia waltzed through the door, dark brows raised. "What's going on?"

"Stitches," Emily answered. "Carisa's taking them out." She cleaned her glasses on her apron.

"Oh, good. That never entered my mind. Smart."

Rags lumbered in. He stared at everyone expectantly before he flopped onto the rug and spit out a tooth.

Mitch frowned at him. "I should have sold tickets." He picked up the tooth and tossed it in the bin and then removed his shirt.

Olivia shivered. "Maybe I better not watch. She might hurt my little brother. I'm leaving." She turned toward the door. "Don't forget our lunch date, Mitch.

Twelve-thirty downstairs. Wear a suit jacket. We're not doing casual." She left without waiting for a reply.

Emily replaced the glasses to her nose and faced him. "I thought you were spending the day with Carisa."

"I am. Olivia insists on playing matchmaker."

Carisa walked in while wiping her hands on a towel. "Olivia thinks Rosalie's a better match for you, Mitch."

His head snapped around, and he narrowed his gaze. "She told you?"

"She doesn't trust your judgment."

So, this was what had bothered Carisa last night. Olivia had caught her alone and what? Threatened? Coerced? "She asked you to cancel?"

"Pretty much. I told her you were old enough to make your own choices."

Emily clucked her tongue. "That's a bit brazen for Olivia. You need to talk to her, Mitchell. She's getting out of hand."

Olivia was already out of hand. Only now, the hands choked him. "I'm spending the day with Carisa, Emily. Case closed." *Come hell or high water, nothing will keep us apart today.*

"She'll be pissed, not to mention the other woman."

"Too bad." Like he gave a shit how Olivia or Rosalie felt. He cared only about Carisa's feelings. *A first in my book.* Because Carisa was the first woman he truly cared about.

Emily turned toward Carisa. "I'm sorry we don't have any gloves, dear. They're not something we use every day."

"That's okay, Emily. A good hand-washing will do the job."

Mitch flew onto the bed, propped his head with one hand, and waited.

Carisa frowned at the display, but her eyes sparkled. She sat next to him and spread out a towel as a work area.

Emily stood, looking over her shoulder. "Those are nice stitches. Do you also make your own clothes?"

Carisa laughed as she dropped a cut stitch onto the towel. "I hardly have time for that, Emily."

The old woman shuddered. "All right, that's enough. I never had the tolerance for medical dramas either. Come on, Rags. You don't need to be here either." She clapped her hands to hurry the dog along.

Alone…finally…unless his dear old dad popped in.

"I don't want to come between you and your sister, Mitch."

He fingered her shirt sleeve, a brushed cotton, soft like a woman should be. "Olivia and I are already separated by a wedge, Carisa. She pounds the thing deeper with each visit." He dropped his hand. "What other wonderful words came out of her mouth?"

"She wants you to meet this Rosalie person." She patted his skin with gauze. "Maybe you should go."

"And cancel with you? Are you crazy?" Doubt filled him. He studied her. "Do you want me to cancel?"

A sly smile spread onto her lips. "Hell, no. I'm afraid of the consequences when we return."

"You let me worry about that."

She opened her mouth to speak, but no words came. She also avoided eye contact.

Something still troubled her. *What is she hiding? And why won't she tell me?* He touched her chin. "I need to cheer you up."

"I'm fine."

"Then smile."

"I'm a doctor. This is serious work."

"And the most beautiful doctor I've ever had the pleasure to meet." *That* put a nice twinkle in her eyes.

She flicked her head to toss her hair back onto her shoulder then shot him a one-eyed glare. "You're staring."

"I have no interest in the stitches. Do I make you nervous?"

"No, of course not."

"Good because I have no intention of looking elsewhere—ouch!" Frowning, he pulled back. "You did that on purpose."

"Oops. I guess you make me nervous after all."

"Liar." *Gad, she is cute.* "You assaulted a police officer, I'll have you know."

She dabbed the wound with the gauze. "No witnesses, copper. Come on. I only have a few more."

"Hmmpf. I'll get you for this."

"Careful. I might send a hefty bill. A house call even. Big bucks." Finished with the stitches, she leaned back to look over her work. "You heal well. I'm covering it to prevent any serous fluid from staining your shirt. The gauze can be removed in an hour or two."

He jiggled his chest muscles and watched the flush rise on her cheeks. "Gotcha!"

She cleared her throat. "You assume I was admiring your chest."

"I'm a cop. I never assume. You turned red in the emergency room, too."

"All right, I was admiring your chest. I never used to blush, you know." She taped the gauze over his wound and then swept the trash into a small waste bag, and tied a knot.

He sat up and grimaced. "I think you forgot one."

Her brows shot halfway into her hairline. "That's not possible. Let me see."

Gotcha, again. He grabbed her waist and rolled her onto the bed.

She shrieked. "You tricked me!"

"Entrapment, my dear. Simple entrapment." He lunged at her mouth, but she turned him onto his back like a wrestling champ. He stared at her with wide eyes. "Hey, I'm injured. Have some sympathy."

"Yeah, so? Do you think I could roll you otherwise?"

She kissed him. Oh, God in heaven, how he'd wanted this, how he dreamt of her naked beside him, to feel her softness pressing against his chest, to kiss and taste every square inch of her skin and experience all the magnificent sensations a woman created. He gripped her butt cheeks to hold her hips against his erection.

What am I doing? Not yet. She needed to heart-soul-mind-body desire him, open her heart, and initiate lovemaking from deep within, not just a playful romp with no meaning. He rolled her onto her back and gazed into a pair of warm brown eyes. A playful romp could be just the thing…

She stretched upward and kissed his nose. "Your door is open."

For the world to see. "Don't care." He suckled her neck.

In response, she slipped her fingers into his hair and mussed the curls.

Then, her lips shattered his thoughts as they toyed with his ear.

To hell with his sister or anyone else walking through the door. This woman caused every cell in his body to come alive. He captured her mouth. She had to know how he felt about her. Hell, his need was so damn obvious.

She broke away, breathless. "Wow! You put a lot of feeling into that kiss."

"If I'm not mistaken, I felt an equal response." The pressure of her soft breasts against his chest created visions of pure ecstasy. He seriously considered retracting his outing for the day.

"This is not what I call getting an early start," she teased.

He lifted his head. "We'll spend the whole day together. I'll show you around the Finger Lakes, we'll do a little tasting on a few wine tours, and then find a nice place to eat. Actually, I know several good restaurants."

"But you don't like wine."

"Doesn't matter. I won't deprive you." He kissed her nose and sprang to his feet, marveling at how well he accomplished the feat with a full erection in place. "Meet me downstairs in twenty minutes."

"What about Olivia?"

"I'll handle Olivia. We will have a good time. Got it?"

****

Carisa followed Mitch to the car feeling light and giddy. She hadn't done any sightseeing in a long time, and the prospect of exploring a new area emptied her heart of Olivia, her father, and everything in between. She would enjoy this day with Mitch, a day of wine and scenery filled with perfect fall weather, the air as cool as oxygen through a cannula without the city stench of car exhaust and open garbage cans. Her personal tour guide had rolled down the windows so that a sense of freedom blew in with the breeze, causing havoc to her hair. Absolute heaven.

Mitch drove into Geneva and pointed out his high school. He passed the airport, the town hall...the police station. His hand gestures were often swift and frequent, like so many Italians. The mannerism hadn't manifested in Philadelphia, but he bubbled with enthusiasm at his endless reminiscing.

Her history lesson for the day included the area not only around Seneca Lake but Cayuga Lake, the body of water adjacent to Seneca. Eleven lakes in all existed, the four largest representing the fingers on a hand. At every winery, someone always hailed Mitch and ran over. Hugs and kisses abounded from male and female alike. After one such stop, her curiosity reached overflow. "Everyone knows you, Mitch. Wasn't it hard to leave?"

"Sheer torture." He maneuvered around a car. "I left my family and friends and transferred to a city where I knew no one. I had made a hard choice to succeed on my own, even though Geneva PD offered me a position. I don't regret the decision." He turned at a crossroad. "I couldn't live in my father's shadow anymore. He made some good wine in his career of which I was expected to follow suit."

"Except you don't touch the stuff."

He glanced in the rearview mirror. "Ironic, isn't it? What good was a winemaker if he can't sample his own product? Now, if I had a choice, I'd consider a brewery."

He had talked incessantly. About his high school football career. Weekend hockey games. His status as captain of the debate team. None of those surprised her. The trophies in the exercise room had substantiated his diversification. What surprised her was his original career choice. "You wanted to be a librarian?" If she wasn't already sitting, she'd be on the floor, passed out from shock.

He flashed a grin. "Yeah, I love books. You haven't seen my dad's library yet. Floor-to-ceiling shelves full of all kinds of books. I think a library would be a great job to go to every day."

"Yet, you decided to be a cop. Why?"

After flashing her a wink, he glanced both ways before crossing an intersection. "Oh, you know, television, macho. A knack for following clues. Instincts. All that. I worked patrol for two years then switched to vice. After that, homicide. I had good mentors." He turned the car into a parking lot. "Here's another winery to try."

Unfortunately, after completing the tour, she realized she had walked into one winery too many. A glaze covered her eyes when she returned to the car.

"It's time for something to eat," he said.

"I'm full of crackers and wine. I don't have room for anything else."

"You need substantial food, and I know the perfect

place."

He drove the car onto a long winding road before pulling into a crowded parking lot. A neon sign over an old nineteenth century mini-mansion flashed Mama's House. "Obviously a popular place," she said, looking around.

"This restaurant has great Italian food, Carisa. Wait 'til you taste it."

She yawned and lifted a hand to cover her mouth. "I need a nap first."

"Nonsense. The food will wake you up."

He ushered her through the doors where the smell of garlic and tomatoes walloped her senses. A crowd waited, some fidgeted, a few danced in place to the overhead music.

I'll never last. She stifled another yawn.

"Mitchell!"

A round, short elderly woman broke through the crowd and hurried toward him, arms wide. They hugged and kissed.

"It'sa beena too long, Mitchell. How'sa your father?"

Since she had listened to the same questions from one stop to the next, Carisa let her gaze wander around the restaurant. Yes, a popular place. People of all ages filled the polished wooden tables and booths. A long circular bar hadn't a single empty stool. Servers in black uniforms carrying trays full of food hustled to get orders to the tables. The wonderful aromas woke her along with the noise. Everyone talked at once.

"Mama, meet Carisa."

Mama roamed a critical eye over her then nodded her approval. "Come. I givea you the best seat ina house." She ushered them toward a secluded corner booth where the decibel level was noticeably lower. Servers whisked beer and rolls onto the table.

She stared at Mitch, mouth ajar. "Beer?"

Mitch grabbed a roll. "You've had enough wine for one day. Besides, Mama makes her own beer. Great stuff. Take a sip."

"I think you're trying to destroy my liver." She could count on one hand the number of times beer had passed through her lips. But she sipped the amber-colored liquid.

He watched with anticipation. "Smooth, right?"

Smooth? It tastes like an oak keg. She shrugged. "I guess."

He leaned back, mouth open. "You guess? Mama's is the best beer around!"

"If you say so." Beer was beer. No big deal. She picked up the menu and read. "Gnocchi! I love gnocchi." One of her favorite foods from childhood. Her mother, a non-Italian, had made the best ever.

While he waited for their orders to arrive, Mitch continued his tour guide role, recounting the history of Mama's, the surrounding vineyards, and even the roadway out front.

She hardly heard a word. Only one detail occupied her mind.

He scrunched his face in a mock frown. "What are you smiling about? I'm talking about the winter that destroyed all the vineyards."

"Sorry. I wasn't listening. I can't picture you as a librarian." She leaned forward, her voice low. "You're a bit too hunky for the part."

"Hunky?" He suppressed a smile. "If I'm boring

you, say so. Don't let me ramble like an idiot."

"If you were our local librarian, you'd attract every female in the neighborhood, myself included. I'd find a reason to stop by every day." *Maybe twice a day.*

"Eat some bread. Your eyes are glazed over again."

Happy to comply, she slathered the bread with butter. "I like you, Mitch."

"I like you, too, but you're a little drunk right now. Eat the bread."

She dunked it in the beer and took a bite.

Grinning, he rolled his eyes. "Was the medical profession your first career choice?"

Before answering, she chewed a few times. "I wanted to be a concert pianist."

He sipped his beer. "I'm not surprised. You played beautifully last night. Yet, you became a doctor. Why?"

She stuffed the rest of her soggy bread into her mouth. *The three B's: bread, butter, and beer. Not bad.* "Blackmail." She glanced at him. "My father was willing to pay for my medical education. He didn't give a horse's ass about music."

Mitch frowned into his beer. "I don't think I want to meet your father. It sounds like it's his way or the highway."

"You're right. I chose the highway. I gave up a concert career for him. I will not let him take my ER career. So, no, you don't have to worry about meeting him." She gulped the last of her beer.

Before the next breath, two beers appeared.

Eyebrow cocked, she eyed Mitch with rising suspicion. "Is this your doing?"

He curled his lips into a wry grin. "Mama knows I love her beer. You might be better off with coffee." He gestured for the server and pointed to Carisa. "Coffee, please."

The server nodded and hurried off.

He reached across the table to touch her hand. "I'm not the type of man who drugs a woman to force her into sex. I think you know that."

His hand was warm on hers, his gaze tender. A comfort flowed through her body, and she fought the urge to shift over to his side of the table and rest her sleepy head on his shoulder. Why did this man make her feel so damn good?

It's obvious, dear.

What, a sexual urge? Hell, why not? A romp in bed would make their trip extra special, a nice rousing day and night of great sexual intercourse. Uninterrupted, of course. Impossible with Olivia nearby. Probably why he'd held back this morning. They were both aroused. Would he be different if they were back in Philly?

No, she had missed something. Maybe the excuse wasn't Olivia. Maybe it was his father, or the house…or her. *I'm the one holding back, idiot.* Like now. What was she fighting? Closeness? Afraid to fall in love? Why? Somehow over the years, she had turned into an automaton. *Safer that way. Safer to never fall in love.*

Oh, shut up.

Mitch released her hand when the server returned with the coffee and two salad dishes. "Any dreams, Carisa MacDowell? What do you plan to accomplish in life besides save lives?" He dug into the salad.

Before she answered, she stared at her plate of gnocchi and cheese. The server had delivered their meal orders in the space of a blink. "I haven't had these in a long time."

"That's your fault. Philly is loaded with good Italian restaurants."

She leaned forward on the table, her voice low. "Aren't they supposed to wait for us to finish the salad?"

Mitch cut his fork into his serving of lasagna. "Mama's from Italy. They eat the salad with the meal. She says if people don't like it, they can eat somewhere else."

She tasted the gnocchi. The little dumpling melted in her mouth. "These are so good."

"You haven't answered my question."

"I've given up on dreams." She watched as he forked one of her gnocchi. "Hey!" She forked some of his lasagna and bit into the cheesy pasta. "Wow, this is good, too."

He chuckled softly. "You have dreams, Carisa. Tell me."

Yeah, shattered dreams. Must he be so persistent? She sprinkled Parmesan cheese on the gnocchi. "My dreams are smothered by reality, Mitch. They're never happy ones. In fact, my happiest moment was graduation from med school. Now, the experience triggers a sense of irony. I gave up a music career to satisfy my father. I've lost both. So, no, I don't have dreams anymore." She tasted a bite of the salad. Creamy Italian dressing—another favorite. Could be she liked too many foods. One of these days, she could blow up like a balloon. "I sometimes wonder what I'll do once I present my father with that one big check." She dipped her bread into the tomato sauce and took a bite. "Move maybe. Look for a small community hospital where people say thank you." She toyed with the gnocchi before continuing.

"I used to love my father very much. He was my hero, a little girl's prince. I went into medicine to please him and look what happened. I'm isolated and alone." She stuffed a few gnocchi into her mouth to hide the tears forming in her eyes.

She'd cried enough, dammit. Buckets in fact. Night after night of tears for months on end. Why now? The liquor effect? Too much wine. An oh-woe-is-me depression. She glanced at Mitch. "Sorry."

Mitch lifted her chin with his finger. "You can love again, Carisa. Don't let your father rob you of that joy. Allow another man a chance to be your prince, but you have to want love enough to go after him. Chase the man down. Tell him you love him. Tell him the words he's waiting to hear before taking the relationship to the next level. But don't lie. You must speak from the heart, and that heart must be open for him."

She wanted love, but love had a way of biting her in the ass. She wiped her mouth with her napkin. "You make it sound easy."

He shook his head. "Love is never easy, but I will tell you this." He gripped her hand. "For you to love again, you need to turn around and look at the man standing behind you. You won't see your father." With a slow caress, he released her hand.

So, this was what held him back this morning. He wanted her to make the first move, both in action and words. *Come to me and tell me I'm what you want.* Those were his words echoing from a prior conversation. Was he asking the impossible?

Oh, God, I don't know what I want.

She wanted simple answers. She'd like to get lost in love, have a man to call her own, and share the intimate hours together. A man she could depend on who would always be there no matter what. *Now, who was asking the impossible?*

After placing his napkin on the table, he stood and leaned close. "I'll be right back. Think about what I said."

Think? She was on an emotional roller-coaster with brain waves short-circuiting within her skull, bouncing around like a rubber ball. Indecision collided with uncertainty. She wanted to run, hide, jump off a cliff. Nothing made sense.

"Hey, beautiful!"

Chapter Sixteen

Leo stood alongside the table.

Tonight, his blue jeans cut a little less severe into his scrotum, but the legs hugged a pair of spiny limbs. She'd seen better extremities on a chicken.

He pushed his way onto Carisa's side, forcing her to slide down the bench. "I waited for this opportunity ever since I came through the door. I knew Mitch would have to use the men's room sooner or later after all the beer. How about it, doll? Ready to move on?"

If the man licks his chops, he'll have a fat lip before Mitch returns. She glared. "Go away, Leo."

He leaned back with a gasp, hand over his heart. "The man has you brainwashed. He's career oriented, doll. You don't want to stick with a guy like that."

"Will you stop calling me doll!" Carisa slid to the wall and turned to face him. "Mitch already told me about you. I'm not interested."

He gave her a lecherous grin. "Is that any way to treat a man coming to your rescue? Mitch isn't the only one with money, you know."

"I'm not interested in anyone's money."

"Like I believe that. All his women tried me despite his money. I'm over and above anything he can offer."

Blind as bats, every one of them. She looked at him, at the slick-backed hair and pointed chin. "Are you jealous of Mitch?"

He waved aside the comment. "Of course not. His women flocked to me because his work came first. You'll never be able to compete. I, on the other hand, know what a woman wants."

Yeah, a puke bucket.

"Leave with me now, doll. We'll have a glorious night together."

Maybe two puke buckets.

Mitch approached. He stood calmly alongside the table, watching Leo with a half-grin on his lips. "I wondered when you would make your move, Leo. I saw you fidgeting at the bar."

Leo threw a light punch at Mitch's arm. "She's a beaut, Mitch. You know how to pick 'em." He turned to Carisa, eyebrows lifted. "Now that the little lady has had time with you alone, let's see if she changed her mind. Boring cop or dynamic lover? Your choice, doll."

Oh, good grief. "I need an appointment with an ophthalmologist because I don't know what other women see in you."

Mitch leaned close to Leo. "I think the lady said it very well."

Leo pulled back, mouth agape. "You're taking a stand on this one? Why now all of a sudden? What makes her so special?"

"Because up until now, I didn't care about any of the others. You took a lot of problems off my hands, Leo. I should thank you for that, but this woman is worth every ounce of fight I possess." Mitch grabbed onto Leo's jacket and tugged. "Now, you'll get up quietly and leave. We don't want to cause a scene. Mama will disapprove."

Leo squirmed to loosen Mitch's hold on his jacket. "You never fought back, Mitch. What's come over you?"

"I want this woman to stick around for a long time, something you'll never understand. Let's go."

Carisa stared after him, not certain she heard right. Or maybe she heard but took the statement the wrong way.

A minute later, Mitch returned and slid into his seat.

She checked his knuckles. "You didn't hit him?"

"Nay, he isn't worth the trouble. I saw him come in. I figured he'd follow the same old pattern and wait for my girl to be alone before he put on his Romeo act. I've had enough of his games, Carisa."

She leaned forward on the table, her gaze intent on his face. "Did you mean that about me? I'm worth a fight?"

Smiling, he took her hand. "I meant every word. I finally met a woman who makes my heart flutter. I won't let a sleaze like Leo come between us."

Their gazes locked. She wasn't sure whether the confusion flooding her mind came from her heart or the booze. *And why am I?* She wasn't a naïve schoolgirl, ignorant of mating rituals or sexual liaisons.

Nah, it was the booze.

Mama broke the hold when she placed two cordial glasses before them. "Anisette. For luck." She left with a smile on her lips.

Carisa glanced from the glass to Mitch, her gaze narrowing. "This will truly rot my liver."

"It's impolite to refuse." He lifted his glass toward her and waited.

Not wanting to embarrass him, she made a face but followed suit.

"To love," he said and clicked her glass.

"To love." She downed the drink with a sputter and a gasp.

****

Carisa had fallen asleep in the car. She looked so peaceful. All the doubts, the worries had disappeared from her face. She slept now without the weight of reality on her mind. The anisette was the crowning touch. She should be out for the rest of the evening and well into the night. Mitch started up the long, winding driveway to his father's house.

Something had bothered her. He tried to get her to talk, to open up and tell him, but she'd always changed the subject. The doubts in her gaze would lift then return, as if she struggled with an internal debate. The wine hadn't loosened her tongue. Nor the beer. And now, she was out like a light.

He lifted her from the car, like a child fast asleep in his arms. The image gave him such a feeling of contentment. This was love, he knew, a sense of belonging, a desire to cherish the woman in his arms forever. *If she lets me.*

As usual, his father and Emily sat on the porch bundled in blankets and heavy coats, winter attire for a beautiful fall night.

Mitch carried Carisa up the steps and met their amused gazes.

"Now, that's a sight we don't see every day," his father said with a chuckle. "Too much wine?"

Mitch nodded with a grin. He kissed Carisa on her forehead.

"She's a gem, Mitch."

A precious gem. He winked in agreement and carried Carisa to her room.

He'd love to put himself on the bed with her, to hold her while she slept, but she wasn't ready. She might never be ready. What if her father had destroyed her will to love? *No, I won't believe it.*

Her lips had revealed the hunger buried deep within her soul. She wanted to love, but she resisted. A trust issue perhaps. She was afraid to give her heart to a man who might shatter it again. *Not me, honey.* He would never break her heart…never. He covered her with the quilt, kissed her soft lips and left the room.

Before he stepped from the staircase, he heard Olivia call from the direction of the kitchen.

She charged out, her dark eyes blazing. "You have your nerve. I had that lunch date set up, and you left with that woman."

"I told you I planned the day with Carisa. What didn't you understand?" He headed for the kitchen. "Did you have a nice time?"

"No. I was embarrassed as hell. You had no right to do that to me." She followed, stomping as she walked.

"Do what to you, Olivia? You arranged the date without consulting me. I'm a little old for that, you know." He glanced over his shoulder and forced a smile. "Carisa and I had a wonderful time." He grabbed a bottle of water from the refrigerator and took a hefty swig before continuing. "I don't need you to manage my love life. I do fairly well on my own."

"But Rosalie was perfect. Smart and pretty, good career, no excess baggage."

He flashed her a glare. "What do you think I've got upstairs, Attila the Hun? Open your eyes, sister. I've got a beautiful woman who happens to be a doctor. You should be happy for me."

She grunted as she slammed a kitchen chair under the table. "I might have known. My check was a pittance compared to what she can get from you."

Check? He snapped his head. "What are you talking about?"

"I took it back. She ripped the thing in two, and I won't give her a chance to change her mind. She reneged on our arrangement."

Is she kidding? Mitch stared. "You bribed her? To what end?"

"To cancel your friggin' outing. I wanted you to meet Rosalie." She threw her hair off her shoulder. "Did she try to dissuade you?"

Well, well. So, this was what Carisa had on her mind all day. She had said she didn't want to come between them, but a bribe? This was new for Olivia. He scrutinized his sister. "Were checks to my girlfriends a habit in the past?"

"Of course not. I'm surprised you suggested such a thing."

"In other words, the first woman I introduced to the family made you grasp that I was serious?"

She blinked. "Well, aren't you?"

"Oh, yeah." He smiled and drank another swig of water. "How much was the check?"

"Ten grand."

He stared, the bottle poised mid-mouth. "She turned down ten grand to be with me?" Carisa needed money to pay off her father, and she chose him over the check. *Well, I'll be a son of a bitch.*

"You're worth a lot more than ten grand, brother dear. She knows that."

But Carisa hadn't known when she agreed to come nor had she a clue when they kissed in the park. Her lips had told him so much even then. She was in love with him. All he needed was to get her to admit the fact.

This was great news. He should be boiling mad at Olivia, but her refused check confirmed what he'd already suspected. He floated out of the kitchen and headed for the front porch, feeling like a teenager after his first kiss.

Olivia followed.

"You might want to get on Carisa's good side," he said with a quick glance back. "She's going to be your sister-in-law."

Olivia's mouth fell open. She grabbed his arm and stopped him by the staircase. "You can't be serious!"

"Of course, I'm serious. She doesn't know yet, and I don't want you to tell her. Am I clear?"

In a matter of seconds, Olivia's face changed from wide eyes to flushed skin. She didn't like the idea of Carisa coming into the family. She'd rather he spent his life under her controlling thumb. *Well, no more. Time for everything to stop.* "If you weren't so fixated on me, Olivia, you might actually take the time to get your own life in order."

Her back stiffened. "What's that supposed to mean?"

He guzzled the last of the water and crushed the container. Recyclables were back in the kitchen so he put the bottle on a side table. He faced his sister. "You took over after Mom died. I guess you believed I was your responsibility and put your own life on hold."

Her posture stiffened even more. "That's not true."

"Isn't it? Then why are you always trying to fix me up when I haven't seen a man on your arm in years?"

She crossed her arms over her chest. "I don't have time to date. My career keeps me busy."

He pointed to the staircase wall. "You don't have time to paint either. Look at those colors. A buyer would snap up every single one of the paintings in seconds. You were only sixteen at the time. Why don't you paint anymore?"

Something emanated from her face as she stared at the wall with a gaze shifting from one painting to the next. Sorrow perhaps? Regret?

Her back loosened. "My love for painting died with Mom."

His gut twisted with the words. After all these years, he hadn't bothered to sit and talk with his sister. "Explain."

She looked at him with a vacant stare and shrugged. "Mom was my encouragement. After her death, I couldn't paint anymore. I tried several times to pick up a brush, but I had no inspiration."

A wave of sadness surfaced with memories of a time when nothing felt right. His mother had left him, and he pumped iron with a fierceness that strained young muscles. Not once had he thought of Olivia or her painting. He placed a hand on her shoulder. "You channeled your sorrow on me, Olivia. It smothered me. I had no choice but to revolt." He rubbed her strong shoulder, feeling the strength that came with the Montero genes. "Mom's death hit me hard, too, yet I found myself fighting you more."

She stared at nothing in particular, probably the buttons on his shirt.

"I thought if I made you happy, then that was all that mattered. I didn't want to lose you, too, Mitch."

He had dealt with his mother's death in the weight room. His father buried himself in the winery. Olivia, uninspired with painting, focused on her brother. Emily—bless her—had done her best with all three of them. *If only I talked to my sister sooner.*

"You ignored your own needs," he said. "The family jokes about me not bringing a woman home, but you haven't brought anyone home either."

Turning away, she gave a harsh laugh. "I'm an old maid now."

He dropped his hand to his side. "Don't be ridiculous. Men melt when you pass. Unfortunately, you don't give them a second look."

She cocked her head, her gaze searching his face. "I'm beautiful?"

His insides flipped. *My God, she doesn't know!* Who would have told her but a mother? He took her by both shoulders. "Yes, Olivia. I'm not saying it because I'm your brother. You turn heads everywhere you go."

She broke away. "My height turns heads. People gawk because I look like a giant."

"I've got news for you, sister. When you and I were shopping yesterday, I felt like your bodyguard. More than one man ogled you and not because of your height."

She threw back her head and faced him. Tears welled in her eyes. "Men want women Carisa's size, Mitch, not a woman six foot and towering over them. I've had some men ask if I played basketball. Do you know how that made me feel?" She choked on a sob. "So yeah, I don't date. I refuse to be the object of ridicule." Tears rolled in a silent stream down her cheeks.

Pain gripped his heart to see them. All these years, his sister had stayed single not because of him but because of her own insecurities. *I'm a detective, dammit. I should have picked up the clues.*

Mitch wrapped his arms around her in a tender embrace, a gesture he hadn't done…well, ever. "You'll be surprised to discover what a man wants in a woman. A secure man will accept you as you are. The insecure ones—the immature ones—will always find a flaw. They haven't learned to appreciate a real woman." He loosened his hold and touched her chin. "You have so much to give, Olivia. All you have to do is open your eyes and ears. Those two senses will tell you a lot." He squeezed her before pulling away then took her hand. "Come on. Sit on the porch with us."

His father and Emily turned their heads to look at them. They overheard, of course. Both needed to be stone deaf not to hear.

"Those words had to come from you," Emily told him. "She didn't believe us."

Olivia flopped into a chair and slumped with folded hands dangling between her legs. "I was so afraid of losing Mitch, I smothered him." She sniffed at her brother. "Am I the reason you left for Philadelphia?"

"I'm sorry, Olivia. I had to live my life, not yours. Don't think my heart wasn't broken to leave this house, to leave my family and friends."

She dropped her chin to her chest. "Me, too. I

didn't want to work in Syracuse, but the decision turned out to be the best move of my career." She shuffled her feet on the porch floor. "I lost you anyway despite everything I tried."

"Does this mean one of you will take the house?" his father asked.

Mitch smiled at his father's animated tone. "Olivia deserves the entire estate, Dad. She should fill every bedroom with kids as beautiful as her."

"No way!" Her face brightened, and she straightened in the chair. "This house is yours, too. *You* fill the rooms with kids." She covered her face with her hands and groaned. "Carisa's going to hate me. I treated her like dirt."

Mitch took her hands and lowered them. "Carisa knew what you were doing long before I had a clue. She's a doctor, Olivia, and a damn good diagnostician. She picked up your body language and tone of voice from the moment you were introduced. I don't think she'll hold a grudge."

His father turned to Emily with a shrug of his stooped shoulders. "We're back where we started. Neither one of them wants the house." He nudged Emily's arm. "Are you sure you don't want it?"

Chapter Seventeen

Carisa pried open her eyes and blinked away the sleep with temples throbbing from a drummer who took up residence, playing a Latin beat that vibrated her eyeballs. Liquor had that effect. The wine, beer, and, oh yes, the last drink, the one that had burned her esophagus and turned her tongue into overcooked shoe leather. After that, she couldn't remember walking to the car.

Shadows filled her bedroom, created by faint moonlight seeping through the open draperies. She was still fully clothed except for jacket and shoes. The clock on the night table showed nine forty-five. She kicked off the quilt covering her, swung her legs over the side of the bed, and yawned.

She was alone. Why she expected differently was beyond reason. Mitch had said he would return her safe and sound. He hadn't meant to his bed. She was, after all, a little drunk...all right, very drunk, but not drunk enough to miss the feel of being lifted in his arms. The movement had awakened her. She'd instantly fallen back to sleep with the scent of his aftershave filling her nose.

More than any man before him, Mitch had awakened the woman within. His touch had activated a yearning. For him. For love. For the very essence of human existence with children and pets, but not necessarily the white picket fence. Yet, she silently argued about the suddenness of such feelings. People couldn't fall in love in a week's time. And should she? Why take a chance to have her heart broken again? She adored a man once. Her father was a smart and handsome man, and despite his busy practice, he'd always made time for his little girl. Like bouncing her on his knee. Or taking her to the bank to teach her the value of money. Her time at home was carefree and happy—until his unreasonable demands.

Everything stopped. The love, the yearning. She had become isolated with no one on her side. Carisa MacDowell had fought the adversary alone, and all because she hadn't wanted to stare at only vaginas for the rest of her career.

And then Mitch came along.

She had sucked in everything he offered: the protection of his arms, the awareness of unbridled security, the tenderness of his touch. Wonderful feelings. He wanted her. Every fiber in her body received the message. Why hadn't she wanted him back?

Because unfamiliar sensations had churned around in her gut. His closeness created a thundering heart. His touch froze her breath. His smile caused blood to surge straight to her pelvis. Was that love or just a simple hormonal reaction to stimulus? How the hell would she know?

Maybe all she needed was a little potassium.

Doubts. Always doubts. She sighed heavily, slipped off the bed, and glanced toward the window.

A lone light lit up the darkness somewhere out yonder. At a guess, beyond the ridge. The shed more likely. The priss working late. She approached the French doors to get a better look and spotted a second light. This last one moved about like a flashlight. Both snapped off within seconds as the light in Mitch's room lit the balcony. She closed the drapes and flipped on a light.

She knew this would happen. She had developed feelings toward Mitch, even while she convinced herself otherwise. Why was she fighting the emotion? Because she doubted herself? Or did she doubt him? Nothing was certain. Even more important, could she trust Mitch enough not to break her heart all over again? *How did I get myself into this mess?*

She wasn't emotionally ready. She had too much pent-up anger toward her father. Mitch deserved more than a woman confused by her own feelings. She undressed for a shower.

Maybe she should do like that song from *South Pacific*. The one where Mitzi Gaynor washed the man out of her hair. *I'll wash away the doubts and confusion, scrub away the memories of a broken heart.* She didn't know all the words to the song, but the melody sufficed. She hummed throughout the shower.

Nothing worked, not the song, the scrubbing, nor the cold rinse. Carisa was in love with Mitch Montero. The man she washed out of her hair was her father. Lock, stock, and barrel down the drain. *I've protected my heart long enough. It's time to love again, and Mitch is the man worthy to receive that love. Do I intend to play it safe for the rest of my life?*

No. She had chosen a career path that alienated her father, and so what? She loved her job, and dammit, she would pay him off and then buy herself a piano. And she would love a man who would love her back. She slipped on her silk pj's and marched back through the bathroom. She froze at the door on his side, hand poised to knock.

What if she was wrong about his feelings? She hadn't wanted a fling. She envisioned a true relationship, one full of love and ecstasy. She wanted to feel his muscles under her fingertips without clothes getting in the way, to gaze into his warm, tender eyes and taste the deliciousness of his skin. She longed to feel him inside her and have his babies. Above all, she wanted that man for the rest of her life, not just here and now.

Fear held her back, not the anxiety of another broken heart, but the apprehension of uncertainty. Her mind whirled with ideas about marriage and family, words that hadn't entered her thoughts before Mitch. What if he wanted none of it? She'd make a complete fool of herself and scurry back into a hole. She flopped onto the hamper, her confidence crushed.

Weak as water.

Her career involved blood and guts. Never once had she hesitated to act. And now…*oh, God. How can I feel so miserable so fast, so unsure*? Hell, the bathroom still held the steam from her shower.

Mitch hadn't said the words, but she wasn't wrong. He loved her. And listening to his speech at the restaurant, even with the booze flooding her brain, she grasped the meaning of his words. She looked at the man standing behind her, and she liked what she saw. She must make the move or forever live a life without him.

Still, she couldn't get her butt off the hamper.

The bathroom door swung open. Mitch stepped in and slammed on the light.

He wore a pair of black pajama bottoms, his magnificent chest bare. Carisa didn't hesitate to enjoy the view.

He snapped his head with a quick double take. "I'm sorry. You didn't lock the door." He narrowed his gaze. "Why are you sitting in the dark? Are you sick? Too much wine?"

She shook her head. "I'm sitting here because I'm a coward."

"Why?" He arched his brows. "Because you can't handle wine?"

"No." *Because I can't handle life.* She slid off the hamper and turned toward her bedroom. "Let me get out so you can use the bathroom."

"I came in for my aftershave. I heard you taking a shower so I ran down the hall to take mine. What's wrong, Carisa?"

"Nothing…and everything." *Oh, hell, what is wrong with me? Why can't I open my mouth and say the words?* She stopped in the doorway.

"Olivia took back the check."

So, he knew. That was one item off her mind. Slowly, she faced him and waited.

"I knew something bothered you. Even the wine didn't loosen your tongue. You must learn to talk to me."

"She's your sister, Mitch. The check was a bad idea, but I don't want you to hate your sister."

"When did she approach you?"

"When I had the icepack on my shoulder. She returned after you left." No acknowledgment. His face resembled granite with a gaze that seared into her soul. Not an encouraging sign.

"You chose me over the money. Because I'm worth more than the check?"

Those were Olivia's words flowing out of his mouth. "You're worth more than money, Mitch." Again, no acknowledgment. He hadn't moved since he stepped into the bathroom.

"Why label yourself a coward, Carisa?"

"Because I am. I'm afraid to take a chance, but you know what?" She straightened her back. "I can't fight this feeling anymore."

He gave her a slow, lingering look as he crossed his arms over his chest. "What feeling?"

She faced a now-or-never time. *I can do this.* She threw up her chin and took a deep breath. "You. Me. How wonderful you are. How you make me feel so…special." She swallowed hard. "I was coming to you, Mitch."

A veil fell over his gaze. "Is that a fact?"

He wasn't making this easy. *What if I'm wrong? I'll crawl into a hole and never come out.* Her shoulders tensed. "I want you." *Yeah, and you don't want me. I get it.*

"Is this a maintenance request?"

"No."

The visual analysis continued. She might experience a few ruptured nerves if she wasn't in his arms soon.

"I'm here for the long haul, Carisa. Are you sure?"

The words jarred her, and she felt her heart flutter in her chest. "More than you know."

A smile stretched onto his lips and his arms

extended outward.

Relieved, she flew into them and pressed kisses all over his face. He returned the assault by crushing her to his chest with enough force to make her puff into his mouth.

With a muttered growl, he carried her to his bed.

****

She wanted him. How Mitch had longed to hear the words, always with a prayer that she'd say them soon. The happiness rumbling in his veins felt good. No, the feeling was great, stupendous, marvelous, every word in the dictionary. He'd never experienced such an overwhelming bursting of joy.

So many times he'd taken a woman to bed, but the action was always mechanical, a primal urge, and he'd walk away empty of feeling. Love had lacked with those women. The women were never more than a pickup in a bar.

Carisa was different. This woman he craved, to taste, savor, and relish the beauty beneath the clothes. The vision had obsessed him. From the moment he'd stared into her startled face, he had struggled to get her out of his head. He convinced himself because he'd hurt her. His weight compared to hers put a lot of force into their collision. After he'd cuffed his suspect, he ran back to the spot. She was gone. A profound emptiness filled his gut that was hard to shake.

Then, she had walked in to stitch him up. The sun had come out again. Nothing seemed more important than to be with her. She created an unfamiliar spark deep inside his chest. He liked the feel of that spark, like a lit fuse buried deep within his gut ready to explode and splatter his emotions all over the wall. He fell for this blonde beauty, and he fell hard. What a fantastic feeling!

He held her on the bed in a tender embrace, tongues dancing, his desire rising into a heated frenzy as his hands rushed to explore every part about her. *Take it easy. Calm down.* He'd wanted this woman so badly. She haunted his dreams and forced him to lie awake at night, staring at the ceiling. And now, she was in his arms, in his bed.

I am a happy man.

Her hands slid over the muscles in his back raising goose bumps all over his skin until her fingers inched into his pajamas to grasp his butt cheeks. She had a wonderful touch, a woman's touch, sensual beyond belief. He groaned into her mouth.

But she pulled away. "Mitch, wait."

Doubt? Please, Lord, not now. He lifted his head with a cocked brow.

"We should lock the doors."

He nearly burst out laughing. "Already done. I locked yours while you slept."

He unfastened the buttons on her top with a slow, deliberate movement, mindful of the ache in his groin at the anticipation. Her exposed breasts were small and delicate. They fit perfectly in the palm of his hand while he brushed his thumb across the protruding nipple. Goose bumps sprang from her skin, and she shuddered. When he removed her top, he saw for the first time the ugly bruise of purple and green covering her shoulder. The injury that brought them together. He released a soft cry.

"It's all right." She touched his cheek. "The shoulder looks worse because of the blood pooling at the surface."

He stroked secondary bruises on her arm. Sal's grip had created distinctive finger marks, and his gut twisted. "I should have killed him." *And hung him from a tall tree.*

"Then they'd send you to prison, and I'd miss all of this."

She pressed those luscious lips onto his and sank her tongue in deep. Thoughts of Sal and her shoulder scattered as bare breasts brushed against his chest. He'd never thought that a woman could taste so wonderful. When he lifted his head, he gazed into soft, brown eyes, bedroom eyes that had floored him the first time they'd met. "I don't want to rush this night, Carisa. I've waited too long. You can protest, but I'm taking my time, and you can't say a word to change my mind."

Her mouth gaped. "Can you believe I'll protest?"

Her gaze was like soft pools of brown murky water, the kind he and his buddies jumped in as little boys. The murkiness had created a sense of mystery. He never knew what hid beneath the darkness. Even now. For once, he hoped the pool sucked him in.

"I love you, Mitch Montero."

His breath caught. She had indeed sucked him in. He lifted a lock of blonde hair from her face. "I'm already in love with you, have been since the emergency room. I'm glad my plan worked."

She pulled back, eyes wide. "Plan?"

"Getting you up here, hoping you'd fall in love. I was prepared to spend the next two weeks working on you."

Mitch crushed her against his chest and kissed her long and hard. He tasted the length of her neck then down to her hard nipples while his hand slipped into her pajama bottoms and caressed the smoothness of her butt. A feast, every inch of her body, one to relish for the rest of his life.

She struggled against him. Seconds passed before he realized she struggled to take off his pajamas, but he hardly gave her the room.

With flat palms, she shoved on his chest. "Look, damn you! If I don't get your help with those bottoms so I can see that gorgeous body of yours, I'll rip them off!"

He pulled back with a grin. "May I remind you that you still have on your bottoms, too?"

They simultaneously whipped off their remaining clothes.

Chapter Eighteen

I'm doomed. And loving every minute.

Mitch held her hands over her head with a feather touch of his fingers while his free hand traversed the curves of her body, his touch tickling every nerve along the way. His mouth suckled her breast, drawing the softness into his mouth with a force that drove her to distraction. She couldn't concentrate on anything except the sensations he created, astonishing and new. The man was a gentle giant, unlike any lover before him. However, she could go so long in the submissive role. She struggled to free her hands.

"Oh, no, you don't."

"I only want to feel your curls."

In answer, he licked her nipple and continued with whispered kisses across her abdomen then caressed lower to her pubic hair. He bit the flesh while strong fingers toyed with her moist heat, massaging until she lost her sense of place and time. She wanted to keep her eyes open and wanted to close them. She fought the urge to free her hands from his grip yet relished her tender captivity. Either way, she couldn't do anything since her brain concentrated on his roaming fingers, and all her nerves fired at once. "Mitch!"

"Not yet," he whispered.

Not yet? He wants to drive me insane. "Let me touch you."

"Nope." His finger slipped into her vagina.

"Oh—shit." An orgasm shook her core.

"My, my, I guess I'll have to start over."

Aggh! "Damn you. I'll get you for this."

"I sincerely hope so."

He released her hands, and she moved her fingers straight to his curls. She drew his head to hers and suckled his lips, kissing with everything she had.

He lifted his head. "One moment, beautiful." He reached across her to the nightstand drawer and withdrew a condom packet. "Better safe than sorry," he whispered. Condom on, he nestled her body beneath his then spread her legs wide.

At first, he teased with a gentle in-and-out motion, causing her heart to race with anticipation until a thrust came with the power to reel her into wonderful submission. Hard and rocking, he swelled within her. She cried out from sheer pleasure, and her climax hit with an uncontrollable shudder.

"My turn," he muttered and drove himself deeper.

His explosive release shattered her thoughts.

She had never experienced anything so powerful. No one in her life touched with such a profound physical and emotional connection. Love was the reason. She loved this big man, loved him with more than she believed possible.

"Carisa, you're mine."

Forever and ever.

The man never gave her a chance to recover. His exploration continued. With each swell of his appendage, he had entered and rocked, each thrust more powerful than the last. Words eluded her. She wanted to tell him how wonderful he was, but he'd never left her lips alone for her to speak. Instead, she used her kisses to tell him. She collapsed hours later, hot and sweaty, from breathtaking satiety.

She nestled under his arm with her face against his splendid chest. The scent of lovemaking filled the air along with the tingling afterglow of a body roused to new peaks. She wasn't sure how long she'd dozed, but when her eyes fluttered open, she rotated to see Mitch watching her. "We slept with the lights on?" She yawned.

"You slept. I consider myself the luckiest man alive to be holding you like this. You have terrific stamina."

Smiling at his praise, she kissed his nipple. "You did all the work, copper. I enjoyed the ride." *And damn, what a ride*. Her finger traced the curve of his chest muscle. "Were you anticipating this moment, or do you always carry so many condoms?"

"I anticipated. Hoped. Prayed. A good cop never walks into a situation unprepared." He kissed her hair. "Your stomach is rumbling."

"With all this activity, I worked off my dinner. If you're suggesting we get something to eat, no, thanks. I don't want to move."

"Neither do I, but I think some black cherry ice cream will be a marvelous treat right about now. That should give you enough energy to continue." He lifted her chin to kiss her nose. "I'm not done with you yet."

"Oh, dear. You're suggesting a little fat and carbohydrates to replenish our depleted energy levels. Smart move." She grinned as she slipped out of bed.

He followed by rotating his legs out the other side. He stood stationary, his gaze locked onto her face.

But her gaze wasn't on his face. The man had an extraordinary physique with defined chest muscles looking like rocks of various sizes. Tapered waist. Powerful legs with the same curly brown hair. He resembled a legendary Roman god, made more so when he assumed a body builder pose. Her gaze refused to stop wandering. "Very nice," she purred as she grabbed her pajamas.

"Carisa—" His erection sprang to life without an iota of hesitation. He looked at her with raised brows and a wave toward the bed.

Am I one to refuse? "The ice cream can wait, but only if you allow me to put on the condom."

Shaking his head, he groaned. "I'll die a slow death." He threw himself on the bed and tossed her a packet.

She'd always wanted to put a condom on a man's erection. Big deal, as a young resident, she'd learned how to insert a catheter into a man's penis. But really now, medical necessity and sex weren't the same thing. With Mitch, the man swelled in her hands, and her floodgates opened as she slowly rolled on the latex. He was hard and waiting. For her. She slipped on top of his body and guided him in.

Forty minutes later, they sat at the kitchen table, slurping big bowls of ice cream. Mitch had thrown on the tiny lights under the kitchen cabinets to create a cozy glow instead of the glaring overhead lights. She liked the look. *I should get them in my kitchen.*

Olivia strolled in, yawning, then stopped with a jerk. "I didn't expect to see anyone down here." Chin up, she turned to leave. "I'll come back."

Mitch waved her over. "No, Olivia, join us."

She stopped in the doorway. "Are you sure? I don't want to impose."

Carisa pulled out the chair next to her. "Sit down, Olivia. Are you hungry?"

"I came for something to drink, but I haven't had black cherry ice cream in ages. What possessed Emily to buy this flavor?" She grabbed a bowl from the cabinet.

Mitch used his spoon to point toward Carisa. "She's the reason. Want some coffee?"

"Coffee! In the middle of the night?" She joined them at the table. "You two will never get to sleep."

"Don't want to sleep," Carisa said before putting a spoonful in her mouth.

"You can guess why," Mitch added with a wink.

Olivia blushed. She guessed all right.

Even without makeup, the woman was beautiful. Her mussed black hair hung loose, but even so, a deep-seated sultry look surrounded her. She appeared relaxed and comfortable in her robe and pajamas, albeit the blush, which quickly subsided. Carisa had expected the woman to explode with rage at the idea of the two of them in bed, but she joined them at the table and helped herself to the ice cream.

She glanced from her brother to Carisa and back again. "You're a lucky man, Mitch."

Carisa nearly choked on a cherry.

Mitch smiled at his sister. "I'm even luckier with two gorgeous women at the same table."

What the hell is going on here? What changed to make Olivia normal? Carisa stared from one to the other.

Olivia curled her full lips into a shy grin as she

toyed with the ice cream. "Mitch and I had a discussion this evening. It seems my little brother is more of a man than I wanted to admit." She met Carisa's stare. "I behaved badly, Carisa, and I'm sorry. I took back my check."

Wide-eyed at the revelation, Carisa found her tongue. "So Mitch told me."

"I was furious when you and Mitch left for the day. I confronted him and...well, one word led to another. To make a long story short, we had a family discussion on the front porch." She took a spoonful of ice cream but watched the droplets melt over the sides.

"Looking back, I hadn't realized how much the death of my mother changed me. I didn't want to lose Mitch, too, so I clung and controlled every aspect of his life. I was wrong, of course, but this emptiness inside wouldn't go away. I lost touch with my painting and the career I wanted to pursue. Nothing appealed to me." She sighed heavily before continuing.

"Your mini-concert in the living room stirred quite a few memories. My mother would have applauded you, Carisa." She tasted the ice cream and rolled her dark eyes. "Yummy stuff."

Words eluded Carisa. She stared at Olivia as if the woman's head was falling off. *Is this for real? I missed the explosive argument while I slept?* She shot Mitch a questioning look. He looked back with a gentle smile.

Maybe she was upstairs dreaming. "Does this mean we can be friends, Olivia?"

Olivia chuckled. "Only if you introduce me to some tall, handsome doctors."

Carisa laughed. "You don't need my help. You're stunning."

Olivia blinked at Carisa, her spoon still in her mouth. She glanced at her brother.

"Told you," he said past a mouthful of ice cream.

Olivia's dark eyes misted. She nodded mostly to herself then stood. "I'll finish my ice cream upstairs. Good night, you two. And Mitch—" She leaned toward him. "Better watch your ice cream. She's stealing your cherries." She giggled on the way out.

Carisa stared at the kitchen entrance. "What happened here?"

"Your new friend reported you to the police, that's what happened. I knew you were stealing my cherries."

"I'm not talking about the ice cream."

Mitch sipped his coffee before answering. "My sister suffers from low self-esteem. She sprouted a lot faster than the boys at school, and they made fun of her. Until tonight, she never told me. Otherwise, I'd have busted a few noses. As usual, she protected her little brother by keeping quiet."

"She can't tell me that height is a factor now. Good Lord, Mitch, she's model perfect."

"Yeah, well, tell her that." He paused with his coffee near his lips, his gaze on the open doorway. "My mother's death affected her worse than she let on. If she cried, she did it in the privacy of her bedroom." He placed his cup on the table. "She wasted a large part of her life smothering me. She should have ten kids by now filling this house."

Yes, Olivia should get the house. Mitch lived too far away. Odd how the idea entered her mind. Odder still was the pang of envy that hit.

Mitch touched her hand. "I solved two annoying problems because of you. Leo and Olivia. For the first time in my life, I've cared about someone whom I want to keep around for a long time, and neither one of them will change my mind."

She squeezed his hand. "That's so nice to hear, Mitch."

He reached over, took her chin, and suckled her lips. Afterwards, she moved away while licking the corners of her mouth. "Coffee and ice cream. I should buy some of that flavor next time."

He eyed her through slits before standing to clear the table. "Time to work off the fat and carbohydrates." He set the dishes in the sink and returned to grab her hand.

"One moment, mister. That depends on how many condoms you have left."

"Enough," he growled. "Do I have to throw you over my shoulder?"

Not wanting to waste another moment, she beat him up the stairs.

Chapter Nineteen

A knock woke her, a hurried knock, determined, delivered in rapid succession.

"Mitch!"

Mitch leaped from the bed at the sound of his father's voice. He threw on his robe and opened the bedroom door.

Jack stood looking more ashen than usual. His gaze darted past his son but gave no reaction at the sight of Carisa's head popping from the bed sheets. "We can't find Willie. Emily's been down to his house. His car's still in the drive, and I checked the garage and winery."

Mitch suppressed a yawn. "Maybe he's with his buddy, Daniels. You know how they like to go into town for breakfast. Have you tried Willie's cell?"

"All I get is voicemail." Jack wrung his bony hands. "It's not like him to ignore me."

Mitch rubbed the back of his neck. "When did you see him last?"

"Yesterday evening. He wanted to dig up a dead vine before packing in for the day. Somewhere near the ridge, I think."

"Okay." Mitch suppressed another yawn and gave his head a fierce shake. "Give us a few minutes. Go wake Olivia. We'll meet in the living room and organize a search. Let's wake Tom, too. The more eyes, the better."

"Right." Jack turned away then quickly stopped. He glanced at Mitch with a cocked brow. "Tom wasn't in the winery."

"Then maybe he's in school. I recommended he kept up his studies." He touched his father's elbow. "Go get Olivia."

Carisa flew out of bed as soon as Mitch closed the door. "Does Willie have any medical conditions I should know about?" She grabbed her pajamas.

"A few mini strokes and diabetes. I haven't heard of anything else. But I'm not home enough to know for sure." He threw off his robe and yanked his clothes from the chair.

Carisa bolted to her bedroom. After speed-dressing into jeans, sweatshirt, and sneakers, she joined the others. Emily's complexion had a washed-out appearance, her hair in disarray while she stood in the middle of the living room, fingers intertwined tight enough to constrict blood flow. Jack acted as if he had ants in his pants and couldn't stand still. He shifted and fidgeted and even shook a leg as if to knock some of the ants down his pant leg. Olivia resembled a picture of calm between them. Their attention riveted on Mitch as he approached.

"Here's what we'll do," Mitch began. "Emily and Dad, search the perimeter of the buildings. Double-check inside the garage and winery. Stay together and make noise to attract Willie's attention. Olivia, Carisa, and I will head for the ridgeline, his last known destination." He pointed as he continued. "Carisa, you stay to the right, and Olivia, stay center. I'll hang left. Place at least six rows of vines between you. This will cover more territory. If we reach the ridge without success, we'll reorganize. Everyone have a cell phone? Good. Call immediately if you find him. Let's get started."

Carisa had no idea the width and depth of twenty acres, but even so, the task seemed daunting as they started in their assigned direction.

"Willie! Willie!" If he slipped into a diabetic coma or suffered a massive stroke, he wouldn't be able to answer. A half dozen other scenarios passed into her mind, all with outcomes where time was a factor.

She scanned for a body form or anything sprawled onto the dormant weeds. With scant leaves on the vines, the view allowed a visual inspection for quite a distance on both sides.

"Willie! Willie!"

Aged grapevines stood to her right. They were tall and gnarled to resemble trees. The trunks had wrapped around the stakes they no longer needed as support. To her left, newer vines stood, looking more delicate and fragile. No grapes though. Too late in the season, the harvest over and done for another year. The grapes probably looked cute hanging in their little bunches, vine-ripe and sweet.

"Willie! Willie!" The poor man was missing, and she wanted to taste vine-ripe grapes. *I should be ashamed of myself.*

The morning had a slight nip in the air, which was typical for October weather. A rising sun struggled to shine around a few drifting clouds to help evaporate the moisture covering the ground, but birds were everywhere, chirping in protest at the intruder in their midst. Philadelphia had an abundance of gray pigeons. At least here, a blue bird perched itself on a stake to wait for her to pass.

Eventually, she caught up to Mitch and Olivia on the ridgeline. Carisa looked around for ferret-face, but the vineyard showed no life. The shed sat alone, secured with a lock.

Olivia stepped in front of Mitch and held up her hand. "Look what I found." She dangled a gold necklace. "It's Sal's."

Mitch grabbed the chain for an inspection. "How do you know? The man's a walking jewelry store."

"I was with his wife when she bought it for his birthday two years ago. The link pattern is distinctive."

Lips pressed tight, he handed it back. "You hold it for him. The stupid shit probably doesn't know he's one less chain." He looked around with a heavy frown, eyes bright, jaw set. "All right, we need to expand our search. If we can't find him after this round, we call the police. Olivia, I want you to go back and start down the drive. Take your time and cover all the brush. Dad and Emily can help, but I don't want them too stressed out. Give them a section to cover, and you do the rest. After the drive, continue to Willie's house and look for evidence by the water line. I'm praying he didn't fall in. Call if his boat is missing. I'll get water rescue on the lake."

"Right." She ran toward the house.

"What now?" Carisa asked.

Mitch turned her away from his body and pointed. "Do you see that line of trees and brush? There's a stream running through about six to eight feet down an embankment. Search along the ridge while heading back to the house." He turned her the opposite way and pointed. "See that thick hedgerow on the other side of the garage? That's where I'll be." He turned her to face him and kissed her. "This was not how I wanted to wake up this morning." Another kiss. "Now, get going and don't fall into the stream."

What was her thought about a dull and mundane existence? Mitch had changed her life. Of all things, she was searching for the patient. An odd feeling. She had no life-support equipment, no drugs, needles, not even a gauze pad. Only her cell phone.

Cell phone! Willie couldn't possibly work on this size of a property without a phone in his pocket. Jack had said he called, and voicemail kicked in. The phone was either on him and he was unconscious, or it was lost somewhere in the weeds. Either way, she called Mitch and broached her question.

"Good thinking, Carisa. I'll tell Dad to keep calling. I think Willie used vibrate so we'll only hear the buzz."

She reached the embankment and looked up and down. The stream was perhaps four feet wide, its depth maybe five or six inches, no more. The water meandered downhill toward the Montero winery on its way to Seneca Lake. Thick brush and dead branches cluttered both sides of the embankment's incline, preventing a close inspection by human traffic. She walked along the ridge, her concentration on every shape, form, and shadow.

A cell phone buzzed. She snapped her head toward the sound, nearly throwing out her neck in the process. The buzz came from several rows in…somewhere. She searched for an opening along the vines and found one when the buzz stopped. She waited. *Call again, Jack. I'm close.* It buzzed again, and she zeroed in on the phone. She grabbed it, brushed off the wet grass and leaves, and answered, "Yes, Jack. I've got it. No sign of Willie yet. I'll call Mitch."

Mitch answered on the first ring. "Keep a sharp eye out, Carisa. I'll head over your way. He can't be far from the phone."

She was afraid he'd say that. Nerves prevented her from waiting. Willie had to be close by, hurt, possibly near death. Urgency pushed her forward, and she continued along the embankment.

"Willie! Willie!"

She might have several years of ER trauma under her belt, but search and rescue was a skill onto itself. Qualified personnel performed this sort of duty with trained dogs and high-tech equipment. They wore all kinds of gear, trudged through the worst conditions, and carried a backpack full of supplies. She at least needed a good pair of hiking boots. The morning dew had soaked through her sneakers and turned her feet into ice.

Nearly to the winery, she stopped and looked around. *Where in the world is he*? Was he somewhere on the other side of the embankment, among the brush and dead tree branches? She saw no way across except through the water. And why would he be on the other side? *Unless the stream isn't the property* line. No, she would continue toward the winery as ordered and ask Mitch later.

Roughly twenty feet downstream, she saw a boot connected to a leg. She couldn't move her legs fast enough to match the hammering of her heart against her rib cage. *It's Willie. I found him. Hurry*! She stomped on the thick brush to get a better view and promptly slipped on the wet slope, fell on her butt and slid down the incline. Gasping, she came to a stop against a log. *Ouch*!

"Carisa!"

"Over here."

Mitch cut through the brush and slid down the slope, his weight alone dragging mud and debris. He stopped short. "Aw, shit."

Willie was sprawled out like a broken toothpick, half in the water, half into the weeds. The top of his head was a bloodied mess, the result of a fatal blow.

Force of habit drew her fingers to his carotid artery. No pulse, of course. Brain matter had oozed from the hole in his skull, the blood around it congealed. Pieces of bone and scalp tissue covered the back of his neck, and blood saturated his jacket. "The wound looks like someone hit him more than once, Mitch." Why was the big question.

"Don't touch anything else, Carisa. This is a crime scene now." He helped her to her feet. "You may as well head back to the house."

Before climbing the incline, she hugged him. No more words had passed between them, no tears. As she moved away, she listened briefly as he alerted the authorities, his voice thick with emotion. She joined Jack, Emily, and Olivia on the patio.

No one spoke. An air of gloom hung over the group as one cop car after another pulled into the vineyard. Uniformed officers stretched yellow tape across several rows of vines, the stream, and downward toward the winery. CSI personnel drove in and stepped from a black SUV. They conversed with the medical examiner before grabbing cases from the trunk area. A short time later, a dark van rolled alongside the stream. A team of men hoisted an orange body bag up the embankment.

Jack refused to go inside. Willie was family, and family needed the attention of the patriarch. Emily and Olivia cried openly, dabbing tissues to their eyes. Carisa sat near them, feeling as useful as a broom without bristles. By late morning, Mitch trudged onto the patio and flopped into a chair. He looked tired with eyes drooping and the shadow of a beard darkening his face. Everyone watched Mitch and waited.

"Willie was murdered sometime late yesterday evening," he began. "His body shows evidence of a struggle. The motive wasn't robbery. He still has his wallet." He leaned forward on his knees while staring at the patio floor. "He was struck on the top of his head when he was down."

"But why?" Jack asked, his voice cracking. "He never hurt anyone."

Emily took Jack's ashen hand.

"My job involves that one word, Pop. We always try to understand why. Sometimes we don't get an answer." He turned to face Emily. "Am I asking too much if you and Dad stepped inside to make us some lunch? I don't know about Carisa and Olivia, but I'm starving."

"I can help," Olivia said, rising.

Mitch stopped her. "No, I need to talk to you for a minute. Stay put." His gaze locked onto Emily's. "Sandwiches maybe?" His head motioned toward Jack.

Emily nodded and stood. "Come on, Jack. These kids didn't eat breakfast. Help me put together a quick lunch."

Mitch waited for them to leave before turning to Olivia. "I need to know where you found the gold chain." He turned to Carisa. "And where you found the phone."

Olivia's mouth fell open. "You don't suspect Sal, do you?"

"It's not a question of suspects, Sis. We don't have a primary crime scene. Someone dumped Willie's body in the stream, and the lack of blood at the site means he was already dead. If we draw a line from the chain to the phone and then the body, we'll have a pretty good idea of direction."

"You mean if someone carried him and the items slipped from his pocket?" Carisa asked.

"Right. A dead man can't walk on his own. So, how about it, ladies? Do you think you can find the spot?"

"I'll try," Olivia said, standing.

"Mine's easy," Carisa said. "Three rows in from the stream, near a section of vines marked with a red flag."

Mitch slapped his knees and stood. "I know exactly where that is because I passed it on my way over. We'll start with Olivia."

The three of them walked side-by-side through the vineyard, and a tall, dark-haired man advanced from streamside. He towered over the staked vines as he made his way through the various openings. Carisa recognized him as the detective from the park.

He nodded acknowledgment toward Mitch and Carisa but his dark, gray eyes locked onto Olivia. A bright smile spread onto his lips. "I was hoping you'd be in town."

Olivia's face glowed. "Bob LeBeau! How have you been?" They hugged. "My word, I haven't seen you in ages. Mitch, you remember Bob, don't you? And this is Carisa, Mitch's girl."

Mitch's girl. And Olivia had said the words. Carisa glanced at Mitch who winked in response. Neither told Olivia they had already met in the park.

"I'm in charge," Bob explained. "Mitch, can I talk to you privately for a few minutes? Ladies, don't go anywhere." The two men moved out of earshot.

While chewing her lower lip, Olivia stared after them.

"Friend of yours?"

Olivia snapped from her trance. "We rode the same school bus every day. High school. He was a year ahead of me. I had a bit of a crush on him."

"I think you still do." She couldn't hold back a smile. "Your eyes brightened when he came into view. Did you date?"

"Oh, no. I was taller than him." A slow smile spread onto her lips. "Although he beat the crap out of a boy who teased me about my height. I never forgot that."

"Yet, you didn't date."

She dropped her gaze to the ground. "I wasn't the only one who suffered from height insecurity. I was too tall, and he was too short."

"Well, he's not short now. I guess he sprouted."

Glancing to the side, she watched him. "We lost touch after high school. He went to Rochester. A year later, I left for Cornell. A friend told me he returned to Geneva as a cop, but by then..." She let the sentence fade. "I regret a lot of my life now. Bob. Mitch." She

225

faced Carisa. "You. I won't be surprised if you hate me."

"I don't hate you, Olivia. I'm glad everything surfaced. I know Mitch loves you very much." She brushed the seat of her pants since she still felt the dampness from her tumble down the embankment. "On the lighter side, I never had a sister. I can't tell you how many times I tormented myself over whether a dress looked good on me or not."

Olivia stretched her lips into a beautiful smile. "I have the same problem."

The two men walked back, their footsteps crunching through leaves. Bob spoke. "All right, we have two people unaccounted for."

"Who's that?" Olivia asked.

Mitch explained about Tom and Rachel. "As of now, they are persons of interest."

Olivia gasped. "I saw Willie arguing with a young man yesterday morning. My room faces the winery. They were standing outside the door arguing, but I couldn't understand any of the words. Something to do with the boy's girlfriend. I meant to ask Dad about the boy but lost the thought when I discovered I was late for my lunch with Rosalie."

"I'll get a man on them now," Bob said and made the call on his cell phone. Afterwards, he turned to Olivia. "Let's see where you found the gold chain."

Carisa took Mitch by the arm to hold him back so that distance separated them from Bob and Olivia. Crime scene or not, she wanted those two to have a few moments together. Olivia still felt something for Bob. If Bob held similar feelings, he could ignite a few sparks, assuming he wasn't married already.

Mitch wrapped her arm in his. "I'm sorry this happened."

Mitch, being male, had no clue why she'd held him back. He took her maneuver as a personal one, and she smiled to herself. "It wasn't your fault."

A broad shoulder lifted in a shrug. "If I can, I'd like to help Bob on this. I owe Willie."

She had expected the comment and merely nodded in understanding.

For the first time since she'd left Philadelphia, she thought of her job. She wasn't on an extended leave. A ten-day stretch, if that. Enough to get over her shoulder injury. She'd have to return without Mitch if he stayed to solve the case.

They followed in silence until Olivia stopped at a place almost to the ridgeline.

"Around here," she said with a sweep of her hand.

Both men turned into hawks, scouring the ground for clues. Olivia retreated toward Carisa, her dark eyes clouded with tears. "Who'd want to hurt Willie? He was such a nice man. He minded his own business and kept to himself. And why out here of all places? There's nothing to steal. It's as if they deliberately went after him." A tear rolled down her cheek.

Carisa offered Olivia a tissue from her pocket. "Does Willie have family?"

"A daughter who lives in Chicago." After an acknowledging nod, she dabbed her eyes. "Natalie and I are the same age. She'll be devastated." She choked on a laugh. "I remember a time when we were being bad. Willie threatened to tie us to the vines until the grapes fell off."

Vines! Carisa grabbed Olivia's arm. "Wait a

minute, Olivia. Mitch!"

Both men turned simultaneously.

"Your dad said Willie went to dig up a vine late yesterday. Where's the shovel?"

Bob immediately got on his phone and barked out instructions.

Mitch ran over to kiss her. "Brilliant. I was half asleep when Dad said that. Why don't you two go back to the house and eat? Save me something. Actually, save me three of everything. We have a lot of ground to cover before I break away."

Carisa and Olivia agreed. They turned to head back.

"Olivia." Bob approached. "Can I talk to you before I leave?"

"Sure." She cocked a brow. "I don't know how much more I can tell you."

"It's not about the case."

"Oh." Her lips stayed in the "o" position until she shook herself. "Meet me in the kitchen then. I'll make coffee."

"Great." A smile flashed before he ran back toward Mitch.

Olivia stared after him, her mouth half-opened, eyes wide.

This from a woman who dictated in a corporate boardroom. Carisa nudged her arm. "Sounds to me like he wants to get reacquainted."

For a few seconds longer, Olivia frowned in Bob's direction. "I doubt it." She turned toward the house.

Carisa followed. "I think you should give yourself some credit, Olivia. You're not wearing any makeup, and trust me, dear, you don't need it. You can't look any more natural to a man."

Olivia stopped short and stared.

"Not all men want a glamour doll, you know. Men want to see the woman as she should be, relaxed and beautiful. And you, dear girl, are very beautiful."

Olivia continued to stare. Then, she shook herself. "Yeah, well, he's probably married with a load of kids."

Chapter Twenty

Geneva had its own communication system above and beyond what the big phone companies could provide. Word had spread like a fire through a dry forest regarding Willie's death. One neighbor called another, and before the police could stop them, they hurried through Jack's front door like open house day with their casseroles and cakes, offering condolences.

Carisa met so many people at once, her head spun. Theories flowed. Everyone played CSI. In truth, no one understood anything at all. Willie was dead. Who killed him and why caused far-fetched speculations.

And poor Tom Ewing. Where was he? Had he struck Willie in anger? *Yes, the boy had a temper,* one neighbor declared with a hard shake of her finger. *Can't trust him around chickens or a hen house.* Even Tom's father hurried in looking for answers. No one had any answers.

Carisa escaped to the exercise room, hoping for some quiet time alone. And to hide. For the ultimate in privacy, she'd prefer her bedroom, but the activity in the vineyard was a constant reminder of a nice man's early demise. She hadn't wanted to sit with the drapes drawn either. She liked the view too much.

The view…*the lights*! *Good grief, what a dumb ass*! She called Mitch. "Two lights, Mitch, one stationary, one moving. I hardly had a chance to pinpoint their location before they snapped off. Not stream side, but your bedroom light came on, and theirs went out."

"A nice bit of observation, sweetheart. Harvey's shed maybe?" Silence. "You've given us a good reason to question Fergus. I'll make a detective out of you yet. Where are you now?"

"In the exercise room. A lot of neighbors are now upstairs."

"Great. Just what we need. But before I do anything else, I've got to eat something. I'm about to pass out from hunger. Bob's coming along with me. We'll sneak in the back way. See you in ten."

Olivia needed private time with Bob. How with all those people gathered? Carisa ran up the stairs and into the living room. She grabbed hold of Olivia and dragged her toward the foyer.

Olivia gasped from the sudden movement. "What are you doing?"

"Bob and Mitch are coming. Neither wants to confront the neighbors."

"Oh—right—yes, I promised Bob some coffee. He's probably hungry, too." She gave a smile. "Thanks, Carisa."

"Do you have a private place to talk?"

Olivia bit her lip. "Not with all these people. Oh, God, what am I going to do?" She shook herself and brushed at her hair. "I'll think of something." She ran toward the kitchen.

Carisa retreated to the exercise room.

A short time later, Mitch hurried down the stairs. He carried one sandwich in his mouth, another in his hand along with two bottles of water. With a jerk of his head, he motioned for her to join him on the bench by the wall. He handed one bottle to her, his brows crunched together in a deep frown as he swallowed one sandwich and then started on the other.

"Is this the homicide detective look?" She opened her water bottle.

His head jerked back. "No, it's the get-out-of-here-because-I'm-in-the-way look. The kitchen for one. Too many people hanging around. I told Olivia and Bob to go to the picnic table alongside the garage if they want to talk privately. I think Bob was very eager to get her alone." He stared at the staircase. "Bob asked if Olivia was married. He's been in love with her since high school and actually asked my permission to court her."

After only a few chews, he swallowed. "He thought I'd feel awkward. I told him Olivia made up her own mind." He stuffed the remainder of the sandwich into his mouth and took her hand. "I love you, you know that."

"Don't try to sweet-talk me." She puckered her brow in a mock frown. "I know you're itching to work this case."

He squeezed her hand before releasing. "The truth is Bob is overwhelmed. Geneva PD isn't like Philly. They don't have the manpower." Mitch opened his water bottle and took a swig. "Another child was abducted yesterday. They pulled Bob off that case for this one. He wasn't too pleased until he spotted Olivia. She made him forget how mad he was." He swallowed the water in four gulps and stared at the empty container before continuing.

"Bob's like me. He hates to give up a case. He wants to catch the son of a bitch who's taking these kids." With a sigh, he rested his back against the wall. "I know from experience kidnappers plan thoroughly. We could have a mountain of suspects, but without proof, our hands are tied."

He leaned over to kiss her. His lips were full of tension, giving none of the tenderness of earlier. He couldn't hide the distress or the determination emanating from his gaze. He wanted to solve Willie's murder and probably kill the bastard in the process. She grabbed the front of his T-shirt and kissed him back, suckling his mouth until the tension disappeared. The stubble on his face pinched her lips, and she stroked his skin to feel the growth.

His head lifted. A tender gaze watched her. "I wanted to spend every second with you while we were here, Carisa, but my loyalty to Willie makes me determined to find his killer. I'll go back to Geneva PD with Bob and concentrate on Willie's murder while he pursues the child murders." With one finger, he touched her chin. "I hope you don't mind."

What could she say? *No, don't go. Stay here and screw me.* She kissed the finger that strayed to her lips. "Aren't there legalities to consider?"

He dropped his hand. "Bob talked to his captain already. We only have a forty-eight hour window on a case. After that, the trail normally goes cold. Bob needs to find the little girl before she turns up dead. To drag him off that case for Willie is crazy. I'll make sure they don't switch him because of my father." Again, he sat back against the wall, his expression grim.

She turned slightly to face him. "And if you can't solve Willie's murder before we head home?"

He looked at her, his gaze intense. "I'll solve the

case, Carisa. It's who I am."

She hadn't a doubt in her mind about the statement. She also believed he would stay in Geneva until he finished the job. She patted his leg and leaned against the wall. "Have you found the shovel?"

"No." He gritted his teeth. "He uses this red-handled one."

"I know the one. He carried it the day I met him. What about Sal's gold chain?"

"Circumstantial. As a member of the family, he's always here. I've seen him plenty of times playing with the kids out back." He crushed his water bottle and lobbed it into a trash bin. "Tom Ewing wasn't in school today. We can't find him or Rachel so we put a pick-up-and-hold on them. I'm praying Tom didn't kill Willie. I'm also hoping Rachel took off without Tom."

"Ha!" Carisa swallowed the last of her water. "Rachel doesn't strike me as a woman who will let Tom go. She might get rid of the baby, but I doubt she'll stay away from Tom." She handed Mitch her empty water bottle, and he promptly lobbed for another two points.

Mitch rubbed his palms on his thighs as if they itched. "Right now, Tom's a viable suspect. If Willie was killed with his own shovel, then the scenario suggests a weapon of opportunity. Tom and Willie argued. Tempers got out of control. It happens every day." He slapped his knees and stood. "I'll take a quick shower before I go. Will you be all right?"

"I'll be fine." She stood also and stretched while suppressing a yawn. "I'll take a nap since you kept me up all night. And Mitch—" She touched his arm. "Not too quick a shower, please. Give Olivia and Bob a chance to get reacquainted."

"Good idea." He grabbed the front of her T-shirt and pulled her close. His lips captured her mouth, roughly at first until the kiss softened into an easy probe. When he lifted his head, he gave her a playful bite on her nose. "While I'm in town, I'll pick up another box of condoms."

"Why, are you out?"

"I will be."

He grabbed her hand and hurried her up the stairs.

****

Dinner with the Montero family without Mitch wasn't as awkward as Carisa had anticipated. They treated her as one of their own with the same duties of getting supper ready. A nice feeling, despite the melancholy air hovering over the table. After a time, the conversation shifted to an awakening of memories.

The group reminisced about Willie and his wife, how they had become so much a part of the Montero household. Olivia lightened the mood even further with a comical story about the chaos of getting Willie's daughter to the airport on time in the middle of a torrential downpour. By the end of dinner, Carisa understood Mitch's motivation to solve Willie's murder. Willie was another uncle to him, a man he admired because everyone at the table felt the same.

Carisa and Olivia stayed for cleanup while shooing Jack and Emily out of the kitchen. The two older folks had looked a little too drawn. Jack hadn't recovered any color, and Emily looked plain tired. Carisa tried to talk them into an early bedtime, but they wanted nothing to do with sleep. The news was on—Willie's murder and the kidnapped child were the leading stories.

"Dad's not looking well," Olivia said with a furtive

glance at the entrance. "Has he said anything to you?"

"Yes, and I suggest you pressure him to talk."

Their gazes locked.

"Does Mitch know?"

Friggin' secrets. A part of my job I'd give up in a second. Carisa's jaw tightened as she shook her head.

"All right. I'll see what I can find out after he's rested." She put the dishes into a sink of sudsy water.

The back door opened. Sal poked in his head and gave a cursory glance around the kitchen.

"He's at the police station." Olivia turned from the sink and glared. "You have your nerve showing up."

Sal stepped inside. "I'm here to apologize to Carisa."

Carisa threw back her shoulders, felt her right shoulder twinge, and silently cursed Sal. "Apology not accepted. You were forcing me to the wine cellar. I'm surprised Mitch didn't beat the crap out of you."

"All right, I'm sorry. I should have known better." He limped over to the table and flopped onto a chair.

"What's with the limp?" Olivia asked.

"Pulled calf muscle. No biggie." He stretched long legs out in front of him. "I heard about Willie. Tough luck."

Olivia snorted. "Luck isn't the right word, Sal. Willie was murdered, plain and simple. The police are still searching for the murder weapon."

He nodded, his face an emotionless mask while his fingers drummed the table in an annoying, erratic rhythm. "Do they know what hit him?"

Holding it close, she inspected a dinner plate. "Probably his own shovel. You know, the red-handled one." To Carisa, she said, "Dish towels are in the drawer behind you, if you want to start drying." She placed the plate on the drying rack.

"What's the matter with the dishwasher?" Sal asked, waving a hand toward the machine.

"We're trying to keep occupied," Carisa said as she grabbed a towel. "Acting normal with the police wandering all over the place isn't easy."

"By the way—" Olivia turned from the sink to face Sal. "I found one of your gold chains."

His dark brows shot upward. "Mine? How do you know?"

"Because I was with your wife when she bought it. Move your arm." She leaned over and wiped the table.

Looking at his chest, Sal checked the chains around his neck. "Oh, yeah, that one. I lost it some time ago. Where was it?"

"At the far end of the vineyard. A link broke."

He shrugged. "Probably one of those times while Michael and I tossed around a football."

Shaking her head, Olivia peered at him. "I found the chain a little too far back for tossing around a football, Sal. Dad would ream your ass if he caught you playing catch around the vines. You should know better than that." She returned to the sink. "The police think Willie found it."

"That makes sense. He's always puttering out there. Well, hand it over, and I'll see if the link can be fixed." He held out his hand.

She lifted the drain plug then glanced over her shoulder. "The police took it. Murder scene, dear. I'm sure they'll be at your house soon."

He dropped his hand and stood hurriedly then winced. "I better get home then."

Carisa studied him. His complexion was a little too pale for such a minor injury. "Are you sure that isn't more than a pulled muscle?"

His head snapped up. "What are you, a doctor?"

"As a matter of fact, I am. Not that I have the slightest desire to help *you*." She didn't give a damn if his leg fell off.

"If you—"

Olivia flipped the switch to the garbage disposal, drowning out the words coming from Sal's mouth. After a couple seconds, she flipped it off. "Don't run away like you're guilty, Sal. The police already have a person of interest."

"They do?" His dark eyes grew wide, and he darted his gaze between the women. "Who?"

"A boy working with Willie. They're looking for him now."

"Wow, that was quick work. Good for them." He adjusted his jacket. "Who's the boy?"

"Frank Ewing's son. He's been living in the winery with his girlfriend. They're both missing and probably drove off into the sunset."

"Too bad, but I've no interest in them. I'm leaving. I don't want to be here if Mitch returns. When do you think the cops will finish?"

Olivia faced him while wiping her hands on a towel. "We don't know. Harvey Fergus won't let them extend the search onto his property without a search warrant. With old man Fergus away, Harvey's on guard, and you know what that means. Unfortunately, Harvey's usual behavior will seem unusual to the police."

He studied his cousin. "Why do they need to

extend the search?"

"They can't find a primary crime scene. Willie's body was dumped."

Sal cocked his head, his face returning to the emotionless mask. "They need probable cause for a search warrant."

"Harvey's obstinate behavior is probable cause," Olivia said. "The guy's so weird. Oh, and Sal—" Her gaze narrowed to a slit.

Sal stopped with his hand on the doorknob.

"Your Uncle Jack's handling Willie's death like a trouper. Thanks for asking."

Sal shot her a sharp, penetrating glare and left without another word.

Olivia turned to Carisa with a lift to one brow. "If he hit on you while his wife was in the other room, he must have a hell of a routine on his mail route."

A regular Don Juan, no doubt. "I don't like men who wear a lot of jewelry."

"Neither do I."

Something on the floor by the table caught Carisa's eye. She reached down to retrieve it. "Oh, dear. Another of Rags's teeth. What a shame." She rolled it in her palm. *A tooth full of holes. The poor dog.* "Soon he'll be slurping pabulum."

Jack wandered in. "Has anyone seen Rags? With all the excitement today, he hasn't been around."

"Maybe he's hiding," Olivia suggested. "He's a little too old for all the commotion. If you want, I'll check outside."

"Yes, you do that. In the meantime, I'll put some food in his bowl to see if he comes in to eat. I won't be surprised if he stays hidden 'til morning."

"Right." Olivia threw off her apron and left by the back door.

"I'll go with her." Carisa hurried after her.

The sun had set hours ago. As October progressed, so did the weather. She and Olivia were outside without jackets, and the air had turned a little too nippy.

Olivia rotated as Carisa caught up. "You don't have to come."

"Sure I do. I don't want you wandering in the dark alone."

They searched around the perimeter of the house, calling the dog's name before continuing down the drive.

"He often hides in the bushes." Olivia stopped and caught Carisa's arm. "We should have a flashlight. Let's head back to the garage. Dad keeps one in the tool box."

The garage exterior had the floodlights on full, illuminating the patio and one side of the house. Olivia hit a button to raise the bay doors. Of the four bays, only two had cars. Boxes and junk crowded the other two, a throw-all place for stuff that belonged in the trash but no one wanted to throw away.

Olivia flipped on the interior lights, and tumbling boxes greeted them.

In unison, Carisa and Olivia jumped backward.

Olivia clutched Carisa's hand. "Who's in here? This property is swarming with cops. All we have to do is scream."

A teenager crept out from a pile of boxes.

Carisa let out a long breath as she tugged on Olivia's hand. "That's Tom Ewing."

Tom approached. "Didn't mean to frighten you,

ma'am. Hi, Dr. MacDowell."

Carisa stepped toward him. "Where have you been? The police are looking everywhere for you." She scanned the garage. "Is Rachel here?"

"I can't find her." He bit his lip. "I think she ran away."

Lousy timing on Rachel's part. "Did you kill Willie, Tom? You were seen arguing with him."

Mouth half ajar, he stepped back. "Gosh, Doc, I can't kill anyone."

"Do you know where his shovel is?"

"No, ma'am." He jerked. "Is that what killed him?"

Olivia stepped forward. "The police think so, but they can't find it. Why were you hiding in here? I understand you were living in the winery office."

"Yeah, but the police are everywhere. I'm hiding 'til they're finished. I guess they're waiting for me to walk into their arms."

Tom stood before them, fidgeting from one foot to the other, gaze darting in all directions. He had declared himself a man earlier, but right now, he acted every ounce like a nervous fifteen-year-old.

Carisa stepped toward him. "The cops want to question you. If you didn't kill him, you have no reason to hide."

"Yeah, right. I watch cop shows. They'll pin the crime on me to close the case."

Carisa touched his arm. "Mitch is in charge of Willie's murder. Talk to him so the cops don't waste precious time searching."

"She's right," Olivia chimed in. "Let Mitch do his job. He's good, and I've never known him to take shortcuts."

Tom studied them, standing frightened and rigid.

"You told me you came here to become a man," Carisa said, keeping her voice at an even tone. "Real men do not run from responsibility. You need to talk to Mitch."

Tom nodded and followed the women out of the garage.

Chapter Twenty-One

Carisa lounged in her usual position on the balcony rail, contemplating the changes in her life since colliding with Mitch. Love was a part of her again. She felt light, her mind clear, and her future not so uncertain—a huge void filled to overflow because of one man. The Montero house, the vineyards, the entire Finger Lakes region were permanently imbedded into her memory as the most beautiful and serene location in the world...despite Willie's murder.

The police had finally packed up and left, taking along their floodlights. The vineyard had returned to its familiar blackness with a quarter moon obscured by drifting clouds. Was she wrong to feel the peaceful tranquility when the murder of a nice man took place somewhere among the vines? She had ached along with the family, even though she'd hardly known Willie. Years of dealing with death had a way of erecting a shield around her emotions. *One of these days, I'll lose it in front of everyone.*

A light illuminated Mitch's half of the balcony to create shadows among the chairs. A few minutes later, he stepped out still fully dressed. "You're in the wrong bedroom." He approached.

She'd left on her bedroom light so he wouldn't miss her in the darkness. "I assumed you'd need some quiet time." She slipped off the rail to meet him halfway. He wrapped his arms around her and held tight. A flow of warmth passed through her robe to take away the chill of the night air. Everything about the man lifted her into a world of comfort. After a day like today, she needed him. She suspected he felt the same. She held tight. "I missed you."

"I'm glad." With a finger, he lifted her chin for a kiss.

The kiss intensified, and desire grew in her gut. *The man has a way of turning me into a puddle of goo.* She rested her head on his chest to listen to his heartbeat. A nice steady rhythm for a heart that belonged to her. "Any luck?"

He sighed heavily into her hair. "We can't find the weapon, can't find the primary murder scene, and can't find a motive. My job is never easy."

"Rags is missing. Olivia and I made a quick check outside, but he never answered our calls. I hope he's not hurt."

"He's an old dog, Carisa. He's way past his life expectancy." Squeezing a bit tighter, he kissed her hair. "We'll search for him tomorrow."

She lifted her head to meet his gaze. "No, you have enough work to do. Olivia and I will wander around. We'll spot his fur better in daylight." She returned her head to his chest and savored the comfort of his embrace. Would this comfort continue? How long before he said adios to a woman who'd interfere with his quest to reach captain? She'd never thought beyond this trip to New York. *Actually, he has jumbled my thoughts from the first kiss.* She'd like to have more than a friendship with the man, but reality had a nasty habit of slapping her in the face.

"I talked to Tom about his argument with Willie," Mitch said. "Willie insulted his manhood by saying Rachel deserved a better place than the cold office. Unfortunately, Tom flared up in front of everyone, and that kind of temper puts him high on the suspect list. The police are holding him for twenty-four hours."

Leaning back, she met his gaze. "Do you think he's guilty?"

He shook his head. "Willie's body showed evidence of a struggle. Tom does not. Willie might be in his seventies, but he won't take a beating without fighting back. The coroner confirmed a metal object cracked his skull, something flat and heavy. His shovel fits the description."

She wrapped her arms around his neck and gazed into his tired eyes. "Sounds to me like you need a bit of cheering up."

"Having you in my arms does the trick." He flashed her a quick smile then kissed her nose. "Do you think you could marry a cop?"

Mouth agape, she pulled back. "Is this a proposal?"

"I guess so since I don't want to let you go. You can think about it." He touched her chin, his gaze searching her face. "A homicide detective works long hours, Carisa, sometimes for days on end. I need you to know that."

A marriage proposal? So soon? Was he crazy? *Be still my heart.* Obviously, Mitch had wanted more than friendship. *And here I was worried.* "You sure know how to spring surprises on me. We hardly know each other."

He took her face into his hands and stroked her cheeks, his gaze tender. "I know I love you very much."

"I love you, too."

"Then your answer must be yes?"

Was it? Should she? *I'm as crazy in love as a storybook heroine. How can I possibly refuse?* She smiled at him. "It's a yes."

He lunged at her mouth, crushing her against his chest with a grip strong enough to force the air out of her lungs. When he lifted his head, he stretched his lips from ear to ear with the brightest smile she'd ever seen.

"You've just made me a happy man, Carisa." He loosened his hold. "If I undress you out here, I'll have you on the floor of this balcony."

"Then I guess we'll head inside…oh!" Squinting, she riveted her attention on a light in the darkness and pointed. "There's one of the lights from last night."

He dropped his arms and moved closer to the rail. "That's over the ridgeline. The Fergus property. Probably Harvey's shed."

"Olivia said Harvey demands a search warrant."

"Yeah. Bob and I talked to him. He's as weird as ever." He peered into the darkness. "I didn't see any electrical wires to the shed so we're seeing a flashlight or lantern, maybe a light powered by a generator." His face grew thoughtful. "No one should be working in a vineyard at this time of night, especially after the harvest."

"Maybe someone's stealing something, but that will be two nights in a row."

"Yes, unlikely. What was Harvey doing when you saw him?"

"Stepping out. The second person stayed in the shed."

Shaking his head, Mitch stared into the darkness.

"The shed's a far cry from the house, and Harvey has never been known to work the vines." The stare intensified. "I wonder if Harvey is doing something illegal."

"Like growing his own weed?" She grabbed his arm and tugged. "You don't need another case, copper. Come on. You need rest."

The man continued to stare at the light, unmoving, his gaze peering through narrowed lids. "There's a reason why Harvey insisted on a warrant. He knows we'll have a hard time getting one. If we had found Willie's body closer to the ridge, we'd have no choice but to extend our search onto the Fergus property."

"Maybe his murderer figured that out, and that's why Willie was found so far downstream." She shuddered at the reality of her words. How some humans could be so cold and calculating was beyond her comprehension. To fend off a chill, she slipped her hands into her robe pockets. "Willie's a big man. Someone with strength had to carry him unless—"

Mitch snapped his fingers. "He used an electric cart. Every winery has several on hand, Fergus included." He chewed on his lip and raked a hand through his hair.

"What are you thinking?"

He took a few moments to answer. "What if Willie witnessed something he shouldn't have while he was on the ridge?" He faced her. "What if he needed to be silenced?"

She gasped and grabbed his arm. "You described motive."

"Yes, I know." He headed back into his bedroom. "I've got to be sure, Carisa."

"Oh, God! Shouldn't you call Bob?" She followed him.

"And what if someone's working in the shed? I can go in as a concerned neighbor. I'll call Bob when or if I find anything."

"I'll go with you." She tore off her robe and ran toward her bedroom.

"You're staying here."

"Like hell, I am. I won't let you go alone." She slipped out of her pajamas, threw on a sweatshirt and jeans, sneakers and jacket, and rushed into his room. Empty. Carisa ran down the staircase through the dining room and out onto the patio as Mitch whirled around the corner driving an electric cart. She jumped in his path.

He braked with a frown. "I suppose you'll run alongside me despite any argument I give."

"Right. I'm coming with you." She hopped in. "Since you refuse to call for backup, you're stuck with me."

He grunted. "Some backup. You probably couldn't punch your way out of a paper bag."

Probably not. She punched his arm anyway. *Like hitting a rock.*

He handed her a flashlight to hold. She clamped it between her knees while she put up her hair in a ponytail. A faint curl of a smile touched the corner of his mouth. "Do you realize how sexy you are with that ponytail?"

She met his gaze and smiled. "No, but you can tell me any time."

Am I out of my mind? Was Willie silenced for a reason? What if we are driving straight into disaster?

Her life had never included cloak-and-dagger stuff. Blood and guts, of course, but never without good lighting. She and Mitch hurried into the black vineyards to investigate a lone moving light. *How foolish is that, and what does Mitch expect to find? Harvey counting his weed pots? Or worse, building cute little bird houses? Now, that would be embarrassing.*

"Is the light still on in your bedroom?" he asked.

"I never thought to turn it off."

The cart hit a bump. *Ouch! That rut nearly dropped us to China.*

"Good. I'll use your room as a reference point since we can't see Harvey's light down here. Hang tight. The road is bumpy."

An understatement. The cart's suspension had died eons ago, and the wheels felt as if they rolled on squares, not to mention the seat had a paper-thin sheet of foam that had dried up into tiny balls. She swore the tip of her spinal column broke off and stuck sideways into her butt cheek after one bounce too many. She almost told him to stop so she could run the rest of the way.

He hit the brakes.

The force yanked her forward, and then shot her back with the ponytail slapping her face.

"Give me the flashlight." He aimed the beam into a thick wall of brush.

A mound of fur shone in the light. *Rags!* They jumped out and ran to him.

Blood and mud covered his head and body, his tongue dangling useless from an open mouth. No breaths. No sign of life. Alongside his body was Willie's shovel.

Carisa wanted to cry, scream, anything to let out the anguish. Instead, she dropped to her knees. "Who would do such a thing?"

Mitch stood with his fists clenched, his face like granite. He swung the beam into the brush. "I'm guessing whoever killed Willie also killed Rags. The forensics team combed this area earlier. Someone dumped him after they left."

Rage surged within her. She fought to suppress it as she had done so often in the emergency room. *It isn't often I feel like strangling someone, but I do now. Is there no place on this earth safe from violence?* "I don't like this, Mitch."

He helped her to her feet and held her close. "Neither do I." He scanned the area. "I want you to take the cart and head back."

She tensed in his arms and lifted her head from his chest to see tight lips accompanied by a sharp gaze staring into the darkness. "I'll leave but only if you call Bob. I won't let you go alone."

His gaze drifted to her face, and he studied her long and hard. "I'm a police officer, Carisa. If you can't handle the danger of my job, say so now."

"You're also the man who proposed to me. I can't help feeling protective. You have to break me in a little slower."

The granite face softened. "You're blackmailing me."

"I have a lot of experience with men and blackmail." She jumped into the cart and grabbed the handrail. "Let's go. We're wasting time. We either head back to the house, or we continue."

With little choice, he jumped into the cart and

threw it in gear. They sped off.

As he approached the ridgeline, Mitch clicked off the cart's lone headlight and coasted up and over, boldly trespassing onto the Fergus property.

She cringed with the possibility of activating strobe lights with bells and whistles to indicate intruder alert. Nothing. All quiet.

"We should be close," he whispered. The cart rolled to a stop. "No light."

He had damn good eyesight. Her vision took a few seconds to distinguish the outline of the shed, and even then, she wasn't sure. *Mental note: eat more carrots.*

Indeed, no light. No sign of life or movement. Just a lone shed sitting in the middle of a vineyard.

Mitch took the flashlight and stepped out of the cart.

She expected an order to stay put, but he simply walked up to the shed and yanked on the padlock securing the door.

"Harvey's not taking chances. This is a heavy duty lock." He swung the light beam up and down the wood sides. "Awful big shed for no windows." He stepped back to see the roof. "No skylights either."

The shed was a good twelve-by-ten-foot structure built on cinder blocks to keep it off the ground. A solid building, not cheap by any means. Taking cautious steps, she approached the door.

"What are you two doing here?"

They whirled into a bright flashlight.

Mitch directed his beam at the voice. "Well, hi, Harvey. Aren't you out a little late?"

"Mitch?" The other man's light shook. "What are you doing here? I told you I won't let you on my property without a warrant."

"I came to borrow a rake."

The little man staggered. "What the hell are you doing with a rake at this hour? Get off my property!"

"Your property? Your old man owns this."

"Well, he does, but he's away. So, get out before I call your superiors."

Mitch's brows burrowed into a frown. "We're here to investigate a light, Harvey. We thought someone was stealing from your shed."

"That was me. I was working." Frowning, he glanced toward their cart. "You should go."

"Working on what?"

"None of your business." A tic lifted the corner of his mouth. He stood rigid, yet slightly lopsided as if the ground beneath his feet was uneven.

Mitch banged on the shed wall. "Nice shed, Harvey. Can I see the inside?"

"Not without a warrant. Get out, Mitch, before I do something nasty."

Oh, yeah, big threat, Harvey Fergus. She'd like to see him take on Mitch Montero. She could use a good laugh.

Mitch's frown lightened. "Nasty, Harvey? Tsk, tsk, how un-neighborly of you. And here we wanted to see if everything was all right." He shook his head sadly. "I guess we'll have to make this another crime scene." Without warning, he swung a foot into the side of the shed and splintered the wood plank into two separate pieces.

"Aggh! What are you doing?" Harvey shot forward, hesitated with ever-widening eyes, and stepped back. He swallowed hard. The man wasn't a fool. Mitch outweighed him, had more height, and would use Harvey like an inflated roly-poly.

Mitch stared down at the broken plank. "You'll have to call the cops now, Harvey."

Clever man. With that move, Mitch bypassed the warrant. Carisa studied the shed. A sturdy structure. Big enough for all kinds of equipment. A workshop even. Mitch was right. The shed was too big to not have windows. She grabbed the padlock and pulled.

"Get away from the door, Blondie! And didn't I tell you to wear a hat?"

Mitch jerked, his gaze shifting from Harvey to her. "What's with the hat?"

"She needs to cover that head of bright hair."

"Why? I like it."

"Well, I don't. It's too glaring."

Glaring? Carisa gasped. "He's xanthophobic!"

Mitch stared. "What's that mean?"

"He has a fear of yellow."

Harvey pointed to the cart. "Go over there, Blondie. Your hair will be out of the light."

Mitch stopped her. "She's not going anywhere. How long has this fear of yellow been going on, Harvey?"

"Forever." Harvey shifted on his tiny feet. "I'm also chromophobic. I've been that way my entire life. The doctors tell me the two phobias go together."

Mitch looked at Carisa, lifting a puzzled brow.

"Chromophobia is a fear of color," she answered. "That's why he wears black and white clothes. He wore them the first time we met; he's wearing them now. I'm sorry, Harvey. You should have said something."

"Wow, all these years and I never knew," Mitch

said. "Not like I care. Anyway, let's get back to the shed." He tapped the wall. "What are you hiding, Harvey? Weeds? Poppy seeds?"

"Look, she has to cover her hair first."

"No, she's doesn't because I happen to love every little strand. Nice and bright yellow with waves and a few curls here and there, wouldn't you agree? Now, what's in the shed?"

"I don't have to tell you nothing. Get out!"

Mitch swung his foot again and splintered another plank. Then another.

"Stop it! Stop it!" Harvey turned red.

She expected him to stroke out right in front of her.

"You have to call the cops," Mitch said. "We're not leaving. In fact, I'll call them for you." He reached for his cell phone.

Harvey screamed and lunged forward, flashlight poised to strike. Mitch lobbed his flashlight to Carisa and, in one swift move, grabbed Harvey's light and wrenched it from his hand.

The little man swung fists like a rotating windmill. Mitch threw one punch that connected with a crack. Harvey cried out and staggered but recoiled with the windmill moving faster. Mitch rolled his eyes before grabbing him in a headlock.

Carisa used the light to inspect the padlock securing a windowless door. A thick plank fastened the lock hinge to the shed wall. No windows, no sunroof. So, no weeds. A meth lab maybe? Although—

An odd odor touched her nose. No, a familiar odor. She bent down where the smell grew stronger and sniffed. Acrid and sharp. She gasped and pulled back. "Mitch, I smell urine!"

He responded with a comical lift to his brow, his headlock on Harvey unyielding.

Well, all right, he didn't know what it meant either. Harvey had every right to urinate on his own property. Lazy, but nonetheless, a privilege. Still…

A bad feeling surfaced. Harvey dressed a little too prim and proper to drop his pants in the middle of a vineyard. *He could have prostate problems.*

The answer was behind the door. "Mitch, will you stop toying with Harvey and get the damn key!"

Mitch glanced at her and sighed. Obviously, the big man was having fun. He threw a punch that put Harvey down with a groan. A quick search of Harvey's pockets. Successful, he tossed her a key ring.

She didn't want to do this. The man had fought to keep them away from the shed, and she was about to find out why. She tried one key after another until one clicked and released the lock. With a shove, she threw open the door.

Chapter Twenty-Two

A little girl lay so still on a cold wooden floor. She couldn't be more than three years old, hardly out of diapers with dark curly hair matted to her head. She wore no trousers or underpants, a T-shirt showed food stains, and urine and feces surrounded her. A strip of duct tape sealed her small mouth while another strip secured her tiny hands together. A wide choker collar was clamped around her thin neck, like an animal chained to a wooden post. The sight turned Carisa's stomach along with the stench of concentrated urine and feces assaulting her nose. She had entered a torture chamber. Cooing nonsense words to alert the little girl to her presence, she knelt alongside.

The child was nearly lifeless, eyes shut, skin cold and white, pulse thready and barely palpable. Her pupils were dilated but responsive to the flashlight. Her breaths puffed rapid and short through a nose half plugged with secretions. With a two-finger touch, Carisa removed the tape from the little mouth, cringing at the possibility of lips stuck to the other side.

Once done, the little girl gasped to suck in much-needed air. The hands were next, like flaccid pieces of meat.

Physical palpation revealed an abdomen swollen to the size of a melon, hard and round. Carisa lifted the filthy shirt to scan for the bruise she knew was the cause. She turned to Mitch who stood behind her with nostrils flaring. "The bastard kicked her, Mitch. She's bleeding internally. We've got to get her to a hospital."

Again, Carisa fumbled with the key ring, her hands shaking so badly she dropped it twice onto the floor. She tried one after the other to unlock the collar around the small neck, frustration building with each unsuccessful attempt. Finally, one key clicked open the lock. With an audible curse, she threw the collar against the shed wall.

Out of nowhere, Harvey leaped into the shed, pushing past Mitch. He tripped over his own feet, collided into Carisa's back, and reached for the child.

Mitch grabbed him by the scruff of the neck and hauled him back.

"She's mine!" Harvey screamed. "I paid good money for her." He struggled to free himself from Mitch's grasp.

Paid for her? Like a sale at a meat market? I'll kill the bastard. Carisa glared.

"Willie ruined everything. We had a great arrangement, and he ruined the best setup ever." Harvey choked on a sob, swung his arms wildly at Mitch, but hit nothing but air.

Mitch narrowed his gaze. "We? Who is *we*?"

Harvey sobbed like a baby. "We had to kill him, Mitch. Willie caught the delivery, but I couldn't enjoy her. Police were everywhere."

"You didn't have to kick her," Carisa argued. She rubbed the child's arms and hands to generate some heat. "You probably ruptured her spleen."

"She wouldn't stop crying. I had to do something to shut her up with all the cops wandering everywhere."

Gripping Harvey with both hands, Mitch shook him. "Who delivered her?"

Harvey struggled to break free. "I didn't kill Willie, Mitch. You gotta believe me, but he was gonna call the cops." The tears rolled down his fat cheeks.

Mitch slapped him several times across the face. "Stop crying, you bastard. Who delivered the little girl?"

"Your stupid cousin, Sal. If he had a brain in his head, he'd look around first. Willie was near the ridgeline working with his shovel. But no, Sal couldn't wait. He wanted the friggin' money, always the friggin' money. The ass never stopped for a second to think. Everything's ruined." He hung his head and bawled.

Mitch stood rigid, his eyes shooting out flames. "What about Rags?"

"That dumb dog tried to be a hero. He charged after us and bit Sal. The shovel was nearby, and Sal killed him. I know how much Jack loved that dog."

Sal's limp. Pulled muscle, my ass.

Mitch responded with one violent swing at the man's face.

Harvey hit the ground in a cloud of dust and moaned.

Carisa whipped off her jacket and wrapped the little girl inside.

Mitch grabbed a rope off a hook. He showed no mercy toward Harvey Fergus and tied him up like meat on a skewer. "That should hold him 'til I get back." He kicked Harvey for good measure.

She swept up the near-lifeless body and ran for the cart.

Mitch used his cell phone as he drove, calling for

an ambulance then Bob LeBeau. His voice spoke with a controlled professionalism, but the fury emanated from his eyes.

She struggled to maintain her own level of standards. Hard as hell. The little girl's life ebbed from her body, and Carisa hadn't a damn piece of medical equipment to help the child. "Her breathing is labored, Mitch. I'll go to the hospital with her. She doesn't have much time."

He nodded his approval. "I'll pick you up after I get that son-of-a-bitch locked in a cell." After glancing at the still child, he gritted his teeth. "I noticed blood in the shed. We may have our primary crime scene. If we find Sal's prints, we'll have concrete evidence to substantiate Harvey's story." He slowed to maneuver around a deep rut. "Sal probably picked out the little girls on his mail route, became friendly so that taking them was easy. I'll kill him."

Carisa stared down at the still body in her arms and fought back tears. "We live in a cruel world." People paid for sex. They paid for children. Where would it end?

Mitch stared straight ahead. "I'll torture Sal first. Then I'll kill him."

Carisa touched his arm. "Please don't. We're just getting our life started."

He softened his gaze and nodded.

An ambulance with wailing sirens and flashing lights raced up the drive. Mitch steered the cart onto the asphalt and pulled up behind them. Carisa jumped out and met the two male crewmembers hurrying to open the rear doors.

One stopped her from jumping in. "We'll handle

the child from here, ma'am." He reached forward.

Ambulance protocol be damned. She'd worked the ER long enough to know the rules governed by insurance companies. The body in her arms had only minutes to live and to hell with anyone who threatened to stop her.

"I'm Dr. Carisa MacDowell. I'm a certified emergency care physician. This child is dying, and we're going to save her!"

****

The ambulance activated its sirens as it pulled onto the main roadway, echoing over the countryside loud enough to wake the dead. Pride intermingled with regret swelled within Mitch as the sound faded. Regret because he wasn't on the ambulance with Carisa. Pride because that woman had agreed to marry him. *Damn, I love her.* Such a profound feeling. Words weren't enough to describe the depth of his love for Carisa MacDowell.

His hands hurt. He looked down to see his fists clenched with nails digging into the flesh of his palms. He had never liked Harvey Fergus. Something about the man had always raised the hairs on the back of his neck. Even in high school, he had acted weird, prissy— to use Carisa's word. Now, he understood why. The son-of-a-bitch was a pedophile, the scum of the human race. Harvey used his substantial inheritance to buy little girls.

Mitch glanced at the porch to see his dad, Emily, and Olivia standing in their robes, faces full of questions. "Later," he said. "When LeBeau arrives, send him over the ridge to the Fergus property. I'll be near the shed." He hopped into the electric cart and sped off.

He should kill Harvey. What jury would convict him? Load the jury box with locals and boom! Acquittal. With his method, he'd receive their thanks for saving the state a ton of money. *Calm down. I'm a seasoned professional, expected to act with certain standards, follow the rules.* Unfortunately, he was so angry he could spit rust.

Sal was another matter. If he was involved in the abductions as Harvey claimed... *I should beat the crap out of both of them, mix them together, and make stew meat.* Mitch reached the ridgeline to hear Harvey yelling his head off.

"Help, help, help!"

Is he joking? In the middle of acres of grapevines, he expects someone to hear him? Maybe a bug crawled up his leg, the friggin' priss. Mitch pulled alongside the shed and left the cart's lone headlight on for illumination.

Harvey looked like a walrus attempting to flop all the way to his house. He saw Mitch and changed his direction toward him. "You took your damn time! He's going to kill me!"

Sal stepped out of the shed, a crowbar in his hand. He spotted Mitch and took a striking pose, dark eyes blazing.

His cousin had the advantage. He had a weapon and a damn good one. Mitch had only his bare hands— no service weapon, no backup. "Put down the crowbar, Sal. Harvey already gave you up. The child is on the way to the hospital with Carisa, and the police will arrive any second. You're done."

Crowbar shaking over his head, Sal stood frozen.

His gaze darted in every direction, frantic.

Mitch wouldn't mind beating the bastard, but a crowbar had a long reach. He didn't fancy a cracked skull. "Give it up, Sal. Don't make matters worse."

Sal's face contorted with indecision. The crowbar lowered. "I had to get rid of Willie. Fergus and I had a good business going, and I didn't want it ruined. That pesky old man followed me into the shed. He should have minded his own business." He ran a hand through his hair, twice. "I'm sorry about Rags, though. I didn't think the old dog had any fight left in him."

"Who dumped the girls' bodies, you or Fergus?"

He motioned toward Harvey. "That was fatso's responsibility. He pays me to deliver. I fill the order and leave."

"This is Willie's fault," Harvey cried, jerking his chin as he spoke. "If he hadn't been so damn nosy, he'd be alive right now." He struggled against his restraints. "Loosen me a little. I can't breathe."

Mitch rolled his eyes. "Poor baby. Lose some weight." To Sal, Mitch said, "How much was Harvey's payment?"

Sal threw up his chin. "Ten grand apiece. He paid a nice sum of money, Mitch." He slumped. "The extra coins help me make a better life for my wife and kids."

Mitch staggered, not certain he'd heard right. "You sacrificed the life of a child to pad your wallet? Are you out of your mind? You have kids of your own, you jackass."

Fire flashed in Sal's dark eyes. And more. Hate poured out. Sal raised the crowbar and stepped forward. "I didn't have life handed to me on a platter, Cousin. My father wasn't a successful winemaker like his younger brother. No, he worked for your father, making a pittance of a salary like mine from the postal service. Fergus made me an offer I couldn't refuse. Now, it's ruined." He approached with short steps.

Mitch stood his ground. "I recall the story differently, Sal. Your father laughed when my dad made him an offer to go into partnership. Your father didn't believe his brother had the guts to make the business work. As the winery thrived, your old man cried to get in the door. You inherited your father's stupid genes." Well, that wasn't a smart point to make. Sal's gaze changed from fiery to glacial.

"He wants to frame some kid," Harvey yelled. "After he kills me, he's gonna hide the crowbar in the winery."

"Shut up." Sal moved sideways and kicked him.

"Why didn't you put Rags with Willie's body?" Mitch asked. *May as well stall him for as long as possible.*

"Because Harvey's cheap-ass electric cart sputtered with the weight of both so I only dumped Willie. I returned for Rags but by then, the light in your bedroom had clicked on. Olivia's old room followed. I thought someone spotted me for sure."

"Doesn't matter, Sal. For your info, the boy has been in police custody since eight this evening. Your stupid genes are still intact." If that didn't make him swing, nothing would. Mitch pushed his luck. "So, you intend to kill me now? Then Harvey? And after that? You can run and hide, but the FBI will be breathing down your neck every step of the way. You'll be on the ten most-wanted list and never get a decent night's sleep. Hell, you won't be able to take a crap without worrying about the guy in the next stall. You have a choice, Sal. Make it."

"I'll pay!" Harvey squealed. "I'll pay both of you. Untie me, and I'll get my checkbook." Contorting his body with a grunt and a groan, he struggled to free himself.

Flashing lights raced up the old access road. *About time*. Of course, Mitch shouldn't have told LeBeau everything was under control.

Sal's face lost its color.

As the cop cars approached, Mitch stepped toward his cousin. "It's over, Sal. And yes, I'm sorry, too. There's nothing I'd like more than to beat you to a pulp, but for Dad's sake, I won't rearrange your face. Drop the crowbar."

Sal stood frozen. He shifted frantic eyes from Mitch to the approaching headlights.

"You're done, Sal. Drop the weapon."

Sal's arms fell. The crowbar dangled by his side until his grip loosened, and the metal fell to the ground.

Mitch grabbed Sal's right wrist and twisted it behind Sal's back in the traditional suspect lock as uniformed officers ran toward them.

Sal glanced over his shoulder at Mitch. "Will you help me?"

Mitch's mouth fell open with surprise. "Help you with what?"

"Through this. We're cousins, man. You have connections. Help me out."

Mitch sneered as one cop handed him a set of wrist restraints. He took the cuffs and slapped the first one onto Sal's right wrist. "It gives me great pleasure to do this, Sal." He yanked Sal's left wrist into the second cuff. "Salvatore Montero, you are under arrest for murder." He whirled Sal to face him and put his face close. "Yeah, I'll help you. I'll help you change your name, because you certainly disgraced the Monteros." Mitch shoved Sal toward the waiting officers and then turned to Bob LeBeau as the officers hauled away Sal.

Chapter Twenty-Three

Carisa bossed the two crewmembers as if they were her own ER staff. In reality, one was the driver. The other had hopped in the back with her. The child's fate rested in their hands because time was not on her side. "Are we meeting with a life support unit?"

"This is the life support unit, ma'am. We're a man short because of a call-out."

Carisa ripped open the sterile pack and started an IV.

The medic slapped on an oxygen mask to the small face and hooked up a monitor to the chest and a child-size blood pressure cuff to the thin arm. The BP barely registered. The heart rhythm was erratic and weak at two hundred beats per minute and climbing. Bruises covered the girl's body from the top of her head down to her toes.

Carisa refused to check for sexual assault, although the bruises on her legs were a telltale sign. Best to leave the actual diagnosis to the ER staff. She already wanted to kill the bastard, maybe hang him naked from the nearest tree and flog him to death. Her focus had to be on the waning life on the stretcher. "How far to the hospital?"

"Twenty minutes, ma'am."

"She won't make twenty minutes. We've got to decrease her heart rate. Give me the biggest needle and

syringe you've got and that wastebasket by your foot."
She pointed to the abdominal swelling. "My guess is
the bastard ruptured the spleen. All the leaking blood is
compromising her cardiac output."

The medic fumbled through his case to get the
requested supplies. Successful, he handed her the
needle and syringe, and then grabbed the wastebasket to
place it by her foot. He watched Carisa stick the needle
into the swollen abdomen and gasped. "The syringe is
filling on its own!"

*Small wonder the blood isn't squirting out like a
faucet.* "The abdominal pressure is too high, infringing
on the diaphragm. Keep an eye on her heart rate and let
me know when it decreases. I want it under one fifty."
She refilled and then emptied the syringe into the
wastebasket four times until the heart rate reached the
desired level. *Best not to overdo it.* "Put up the heat,
will you? Her skin feels like an ice cube." She taped a
gauze pad over the needle hole.

"Her temp is ninety-three degrees, ma'am."
Twisting, he adjusted the cabin controls behind his
head.

Carisa doubled a blanket and covered the cold little
body. *Is this how Harvey treats all his victims? A toy to
be discarded once broken? Had he fed her food or
water?*

No. According to the autopsy reports, all the girls
were malnourished and dehydrated. The food stains on
her shirt were every mother's challenge. Harvey hadn't
fed them, hadn't kept them warm. He treated his
victims without a thought about comfort.

Carisa forced back tears and clenched her jaw tight.
She wanted to twitch her nose and make everything

right, turn the world into a happy place where children were safe. She had seen enough children enter the ER as victims of violence, little innocents who viewed the world without prejudice. *Stay calm. Stay professional.* Yeah, a damn difficult achievement considering the circumstances. *I will kill that bastard first chance I get.*

"We appreciate your help on this," the crewman said. "The others were already dead when we arrived. This little girl is getting one lucky break because of you."

"Thank you."

He hung the IV bag on an overhead hook. "How many drips per minute should I set?"

"Follow protocol as long as it's not wide open." She looked into his concerned expression. "We don't want to put her in pulmonary edema. Twenty is good."

"That's our protocol, ma'am."

She had questioned Mitch about being out of his jurisdiction, and here, she was in the same boat. But to hell with legalities. *I won't sit back and watch when I can do so much.*

Moments later, the ambulance pulled into the unloading dock. The ER staff met them at the door and whisked the stretcher through the doors with Carisa closely behind.

The media had already assembled with cameras and microphones ready. The little girl was big news in the community. She was alive, the perpetrators caught. Everyone wanted to be part of the moment.

Carisa relayed her findings to the attending physician but stood behind as they wheeled the stretcher into a curtained bay. Her job was done, and for that, she was grateful. The night's events swept through her like a dam opening its gates. Her knees wobbled, and she placed a hand on the wall to steady herself. *A chair…yes, a chair.* She flopped onto the nearest seat, feeling exhausted and alone despite the patients occupying nearby chairs. She observed with a blank mind the activity around her, the stretchers and walk-ins hurrying through the doors, the security guard looking ready to shoot the first person who challenged him. Familiar activity of a job she loved.

Time passed. The patients sitting alongside came and went—new faces with new problems but the same moaning and groaning.

The media crowded the ER entrance, barely moving aside to let a patient through. Extra security had arrived to push them toward the other end of the dock. Live coverage. Reporters striving to make a name for themselves. Thankfully, no one pointed to her as being with the girl. She had become another indistinguishable body waiting in the emergency room.

The attending physician called her over. Surgeons had rushed the child to the OR for a possible splenectomy. Liver contusions plus partial pneumothorax were seen on the CT scan. No semen but sexual assault confirmed.

A tear fell down her cheek as the physician hurried away. No sooner had she wiped it when Mitch hurried through the entrance. As if on cue, the tears rolled free. She threw herself into his arms and cried. Her rock held her in his strong embrace, the man she loved, the man who had helped save a child tonight. Then, she cried some more when the parents rushed over to thank them. Afterwards, Mitch guided her to the car.

The night's emotional toll had sapped all her

remaining energy and left her empty of feeling. She moved like an automaton, staring straight ahead, too exhausted to blink. The drive home was a blur.

Jack, Emily, and Olivia stood inside the front door, waiting. They asked nothing. They merely hugged her then Mitch before Mitch guided her up the stairs to his room.

He undressed her then undressed himself. He placed her in the shower and stepped in behind her. She gave no protest when he lathered soap all over her body, his movements slow and meticulous. His skilled hands emptied her mind of the horrors of the night. He kissed and suckled—her lips, her eyes, her breasts—and he lathered again.

Finally, she gave herself to him completely, allowing him the freedom to explore her body as no man had ever done, relishing the tenderness of his touch, until every nerve threatened to explode from sheer pleasure. "Mitch—" The word choked in her throat. He heard anyway and carried her dripping to his bed and entered her body. Their climax hit with a furious shudder, and she fell asleep in his arms.

In no hurry to face daylight, she slept late. A noise in the bedroom alerted her to movement, and she opened her eyes to see Mitch fully dressed and smiling downward. The bed sheets were still damp.

"I can't think of a prettier sight to help start my day." He bent to kiss her. "I told Bob I'd stop by the station to make a full report. I'll also get an update on the little girl. Will you be all right?"

With a yawn, she nodded and grabbed onto his shirt collar. She wanted his warm lips on hers for more than a quick kiss. He sat alongside and lifted her in his arms, his strength intoxicating her with an overwhelming sense of joy while his mouth tingled hers with the taste of minty toothpaste. She couldn't imagine waking every morning to such a wonderful man. She sighed into his mouth. "I could do this all day."

"Me, too, if I didn't have to work."

She lifted a curl from his forehead. "What about Sal?"

He lowered her to the pillow and covered her nakedness with a sheet. "He confessed to everything, how he singled out dark-haired little girls and how easy a prey they were. The FBI had Sal on their radar but, like I thought, had no proof. They have their proof now. Sal and Harvey won't see the outside of a prison for a long time."

Carisa shook her head sadly. "Sal never considered the pain to his family."

"Actually, his family was his argument. The money kept his wife and kids living like royalty." He took her hand and caressed. "I wonder what his wife will say when she finds out how he obtained the money?" He leaned over to tease her lips with his breath. "I can't believe how much I love you, Carisa MacDowell. Everyday will be a struggle to get out of bed and onto work." He kissed her tenderly before standing. "I'll see you in a little while."

Carisa slept another hour. Maybe two. She lost track of time then eventually made her way downstairs toward the kitchen and the smell of coffee. The kitchen was empty. A note propped against salt and pepper shakers informed her Emily and Olivia left to console Sal's wife. Carisa filled a cup with coffee and headed to the front porch.

A cool breeze tousled her loose hair and blew the steam from the coffee toward her nose. Overhead, high-altitude cirrus clouds stretched across the sky, forcing the sun to peek around them as they passed. A wave of peaceful serenity filled her heart, despite the blue jay squawking at her intrusion. The big bird hopped onto the porch rail, squawking, then down to the asphalt drive before a loud tractor-trailer on the road scared him off.

Jack wasn't in his usual chair. She was about to sit and enjoy the view alone when a car meandered up the drive. Tom Ewing rode in the passenger seat. An older man was driving but no sign of Rachel.

Tom stepped out first. "Hi, Dr. MacDowell. This is my dad, Frank Ewing." He turned to his father who had just closed his car door. "I'll get my stuff." He ran toward the winery.

Frank Ewing was a man in his late forties, no gray in his brown hair yet, but he had the beginnings of a beer belly. Carisa had met him briefly on the day of Willie's murder, but that day blurred one face into another.

He approached the steps. "Jack around?"

Carisa leaned against a post. "I haven't seen him yet. He must be in the house somewhere. Do you want me to find him?"

"No. Tell him thank you for taking care of Tommy. He's coming home."

"I hope matters work out."

"They won't. Rachel's on the run." He tugged on a pants belt partially hidden by the beer belly. "She left word with her parents that she's moved out of state. She's in a lot of trouble."

The inevitable conclusion. At least, Rachel was smart enough not to take Tom with her. Statutory rape plus kidnapping would keep her in a cell for a long time. "How's Tom taking it?"

He ran a hand through thinning hair. "Not well. Thankfully, he doesn't have a driver's license so he can't go chasing after her." He put one foot on the step and looked up at her with a pair of tired brown eyes. "Do you think she was pregnant?"

"Yes, sir, I do."

"Damn." He thumped a shoe against the step riser while stuffing both hands into his jacket pockets. "That's our grandchild she's carrying."

Carisa sipped her coffee before responding. "She can never come after Tom for support. Simple math will tell the judge she seduced a minor. She may show up after Tom turns eighteen, but I'm not familiar with the statute of limitations on this sort of crime. Does Tom know she's carrying his child?"

He chewed on his inner lip as he stared into the distance. "I don't think he does, and I'm not about to tell him." He snapped his gaze back to her, anger flashing. "She was the school bus driver, damn her, the perfect environment to seduce a young man with dancing hormones."

Tom returned with a backpack, which he threw into the rear seat. "I'm ready, Dad. Thanks for everything, Dr. MacDowell."

Frank Ewing shot her a quick glance before stepping away from the porch. With a nod in her direction, he slipped behind the steering wheel. The car drove off with hands waving out both windows.

She put her mug to her lips only to discover it

empty. Turning, she returned to the kitchen for a second cup.

An inner voice spoke. A warning of sorts. Why or how it popped into her mind wasn't clear, but the feeling was about Jack. Age had its disadvantages when combined with stress-related events. The deaths of Willie and Rags, the discovery of the little girl, the involvement of his nephew. All three incidents increased the probability of serious consequences to an ailing old man. She wandered through the house to rule out he hadn't fallen-and-couldn't-get-up routine.

The wine cellar yielded nothing. Same for the weight room. One door lead to the library with two walls of floor-to-ceiling books. *Mitch, the librarian.* She smiled at the thought.

She strolled to the foyer and stared up the staircase, nerves tingling with uncertainty. Was he in his room? Hell, what if he simply soaked in the tub?

"Jack!" She wasn't sure how good his hearing was, but what the hey? She headed onto the patio and spotted Jack's long legs sticking out of a lounge chair. One leg twitched as she approached, and she let out a long breath in relief. "I hope I'm not disturbing you."

She stopped short when he turned his head toward her. His skin was gray ash. His dark eyes were glazed and vacant as he struggled to focus. She put her mug on a side table and dropped on the lounge chair next to him. "Jack?" She tugged on his jacket sleeve to feel his radial pulse. It beat slow and weak. Too slow. Cardiac arrest was imminent.

His pale lips spread into a thin smile. "I'm glad you're here."

No, this isn't happening. Why here? Why now? She

clutched his hand. "What do you want me to do, Jack? Can I call someone? Your kids? Emily? No one's home but you and me."

He shook his head. "Best not to get them upset. I always wanted to go peacefully, and with your pretty face to look at, I can't get any more peaceful than that."

Tears welled in her eyes. After last night's adventure, she wasn't sure she could handle this alone. *Stay calm.* "I can still call an ambulance."

"No, don't let anyone make a fuss. I'm sitting here because the vineyards are what I want to see before I go. I picked a beautiful day to die, don't you think?" He paused to catch his breath. "I don't want a long death, Carisa. I'm ready."

Since he struggled to put the words into a sentence coupled with skin starving for oxygen, the man would get his wish. Her tears rolled. She made no attempt to brush them away because she simply wanted to hold his hand. "You don't have long at all, Jack."

"Good...good." He closed his eyes.

She bowed her head, awaiting his last breath.

But he grabbed her hand with a grip like ice. "I had a good life, Carisa. I'm sorry you weren't in it longer."

Oh, God! Someone please come home! She desperately wanted that person to be Mitch. "I'm in love with your son, Jack. He asked me to marry him."

"Yes, he told me this morning. I'm glad." He released her hand and pointed a shaking finger toward the sky. "My wife's calling me, Carisa. She's here with me now, waiting." He opened his eyes and stared upward. His gaze was unfocused, distant. "One last request, Carisa." He rotated his head to look at her. "Play some Brahms for us."

She inwardly gasped. *Please don't ask me to do this.* "I don't know if I can."

"Try, Carisa. And please, don't call anyone until I'm gone."

A brave man and a proud one. What possessed some people to fight tooth and nail for that last valued breath, and others, like Jack, let death come without the least bit of resistance? God had a special place in heaven for people like him.

Shaken, she fought the urge to run and call someone. She shouldn't be the one to see him take his last breath. His family should be by his side, holding his hands. Instead, she opted to honor a dying man's wishes. She kissed his cold forehead and headed into the house.

She wasn't sure how she accomplished the concerto, but she played with the heart of a seasoned pianist. Tears dripped onto the keys with every accented note. The music sheet was a blur, and constant blinking failed to clear her vision. Death was a part of her career, but the patients were strangers, met only when they passed through the ER doors. Jack, she knew, however brief an acquaintance. He was Mitch's father, and Mitch had no idea this visit with his father was the last.

Please come home, Mitch.

After an hour, she wiped her eyes and returned to Jack. He lay motionless on the lounge chair, arms at his side with his head tilted slightly to the side. Oddly enough, a faint smile touched his thin lips. She checked for a carotid pulse on both sides of his neck and examined pupil response by shading his eye and then exposing it to the sun. Full dilation with no change.

Jack died as he wanted, peaceful and without fanfare. She stepped inside to make the necessary phone calls.

"Hello?" Mitch yelled from the foyer. He caught sight of her entering the dining room and approached. "I wondered where you were." He froze at the sight of her tear-stained face. "What happened?"

Moving her head, she motioned toward the patio since words wouldn't come from her clogged throat.

Mitch ran out, took one look at his father, and fire rose in his eyes. "Why aren't you working on him?" He grabbed the lifeless body and lowered him to the ground. "Call 911!"

She stared wide-eyed as he listened and felt for breaths. "Mitch, stop. He's gone."

"Not if I can help it. I've too much to tell him." He intertwined his fingers and positioned his palm over Jack's sternum. He pumped on the old man's chest. "Help me!"

"Mitch, please stop. Let him be. He doesn't want this."

"How the hell do you know what he wants? He's my father. Call 911, dammit!" He blew air into his father's mouth.

This is a dream. I'm still upstairs sleeping. She squared her shoulders and placed a hand on his shoulder. In her sternest doctor voice, she leaned down to force him to look up. "Mitch, enough. He wanted to go in peace. Please let him."

He shrugged off her hand. "Are you going to call 911?" He pumped harder, his speed fueled by his anger.

Ribs cracked, and she cringed. She grabbed his arm. "Mitch, stop!"

He pushed her away. "If you're not here to help,

then get the hell out." Pumping with one hand, he used the other to reach into his pants pocket for his cell phone. He fumbled, caught it, and dialed. He glanced up at her with a glare. "Out! Get out of this house!"

His words hit like a sledgehammer. The same words were spoken with the same fierceness by her father. Was this destiny? Would her entire life involve men who tossed her aside when they didn't get their way?

But Jack was the issue now. She promised him and pushed her own feelings aside. She squatted on Jack's opposite side and clutched Mitch's shirt, forcing him to meet her steady gaze. "If your dad comes back, he'll be brain dead. You've got to stop."

"Out!"

Hatred flashed from his eyes, the pain, the disappointment—all directed at her. In the hospital, she had an obligation to act. Here, she merely followed a dying man's last request. Heart sick, she could do nothing more but let history repeat itself.

Chapter Twenty-Four

Mitch worked feverishly on his father. He had used the life-saving technique many times in his career—pump, pump, pump. The CPR pattern had changed over the years, but the principle remained the same—breath, breath. On other occasions, he'd brought back people. He could return his father to the world of the living. *Come on, Pop*!

Ambulance sirens wailed on their way up the drive. *Hurry, dammit*! Three crewmembers rushed in, plunked down heavy cases, and took out an array of apparatus. A woman inserted an IV line; a man stuck white adhesive pads to his father's chest and attached heart monitor wires. Another man slipped a tube down his father's throat and hooked a resuscitator bag to the tube to push air into his father's lungs. All three recruited Mitch to remain on the chest.

Anything to help bring back his dad—pump, pump, pump—to tell him the words his old man had waited so long to hear. "What about the defibrillator?"

The medic pointed to a small monitor displaying numbers and lines. "Flat line, sir. Useless. But we'll try anyway. Clear!"

The old man's body bounced off the floor. Everyone stared at the monitor, expecting the flat line to show life.

The woman turned to Mitch. "How long was he

down?"

"I don't know. I walked in and found him like this."

Carisa would know. She had let him die, probably walked away as his old man took his last breath. *Oh, God help me.* The words had the effect of broken glass sliding down his throat, every piece cutting the tissue and settling in his stomach like molten lava.

He rode with them to the hospital, still pumping on the chest. One medic pushed the air in. The other medic injected medication. The third—the driver—notified the hospital of their estimated time of arrival. Mitch had no experience doing chest compressions in a moving vehicle, and he struggled to maintain his balance. The constant rocking and jerks inched his hands toward his father's neck. He repositioned only to repeat the process at the next curve.

"We stabilize ourselves with the overhead bar." The medic pointed.

"Good idea." Mitch grabbed the bar and pumped with one hand, stabilizing his sway as the ambulance zipped through traffic. "I think I broke my father's breastbone."

"Yes, sir, I heard. More normal than you think. Keep pumping."

Come on, Pop. Come back.

He tried not to think of Carisa's lack of action. She had saved a child without hesitation. For his father, she'd done nothing. How could he possibly love a woman like that? He pumped harder and cracked a few more bones along the way. He winced. *Sorry, Dad.*

The problem was he loved Carisa MacDowell. He had proposed marriage to the woman. What had possessed her to ignore her oath? Did she believe she was God and picked who should live or die? Hell, he'd never had the privilege, and he carried a gun.

They arrived at the hospital. As soon as the stretcher touched the tarmac, a young man in hospital scrubs took over chest compressions. The medics hurried the stretcher through the entrance with Mitch closely behind. They whizzed past several gurneys lined against the wall and a woman mopping a spill on the floor before rushing into a room with two double doors. A team of ER personal waited, one with a resuscitator bag in her hand, another readying needles and IV bags.

"You have to stay here, sir."

Mitch started at the medic's voice and glanced around the area. "Yes, of course."

The team set to work with chest compressions and breaths. Nurses inserted more IV lines and emptied syringes full of medication. Still, only a flat line showed on the monitor.

Mitch surveyed the activity with a helplessness he'd never experienced. If Carisa had only done something, anything—

The vision of Carisa running into his arms last night twisted his heart. She had become a local hero by putting life back into a child because of her quick action in the back of the ambulance. Yet, she had let his father slip away. Why? Because he was an old man?

"You should wait outside," a nurse told him, motioning toward the door.

He didn't want to, but with little choice, he inched backward toward the door. Confusion clouded his mind—followed by anger and pain. All three emotions gripped his heart like a vise. With a sigh, he stepped from the room.

The nurse closed the door in his face.

His affair with Carisa was over. He couldn't love her anymore, not after this. He activated his cell phone and made a call, knowing this last action would finalize their breakup.

The minutes passed. Minutes changed into an hour of sheer torture. He paced about the crowded waiting room, ignoring the annoyed glares from the people he passed. His father *had* to live. Pop *had* to wake up to hear the good news.

His heart told him he was too late.

"Mitch!"

He whirled to see Olivia and Emily rush through the ER doors, eyes red and swollen. All three hugged and cried.

"Can we see him?" Olivia asked.

"They're still working to revive him."

Both women gasped. Olivia yanked his arm, her eyes wide. "Dad didn't want this!"

He snapped up his head. "How do you know?"

"Dad told me last night while we waited for you and Carisa to return. He's been sick, Mitch. He told me about the living hell he went through over the past year. He knew he was dying and never said anything." She tightened her grip.

Emily stepped close. "We would still be in the dark if Carisa hadn't talked some sense into him. He arranged with the lawyer and the undertaker, yet he kept his family in the dark. Carisa made him see the danger of that behavior."

A flush of anger rose from his gut. "Why didn't she

tell me?"

"Because your father wouldn't let her." Emily touched his arm. "He made me promise, too. I don't like keeping secrets so I can imagine how Carisa felt. I can tell you for a fact that a flood of relief hit last night when he told Olivia. Now, stop this ridiculous shit and let your father go!"

His gut clenching, Mitch stared at Emily, then Olivia, and back to the housekeeper again. He alone was responsible for keeping his father in a living hell. But he hadn't known. He had asked Carisa to find out, and she'd warned him about the doctor/patient privilege. She had accomplished what he asked and got his father to talk. Yet, he had refused to listen. Anger closed his ears. Pain clouded his logic. What if his father survived? Would he be brain dead as Carisa said? Then what? *Oh, dear God, what have I done*? Not only with his father but with Carisa, as well.

A doctor lumbered toward him, looking a little worse for wear in a stained lab coat.

Mitch made quick introductions.

After acknowledging the women, the doctor directed his words at Mitch. "Your father's heart returned several times, but the electrical impulse is too weak to pump effectively. I've consulted cardiology for a pacemaker placement. He'll need your permission to insert one." He studied Mitch through a pair of black-rimmed glasses. "Your father's brain is anoxic, Mr. Montero. In other words, the oxygen we're pumping into him is not reviving his brain. His pupils are fixed and dilated. That's not a good sign. The pacemaker may keep the heart beating, but at this point, we don't know what we're saving."

The doctor waited for a response, a confirmation…a reaction. Mitch merely blinked, unsure what to do. He looked at Olivia's grave expression.

After a quick nod, she took his hand. "Let him go, Mitch."

She was right. He had to face reality, his father's age, his illness, and most of all, his wishes. Selfishness drove him, and selfishness pushed away Carisa.

Mitch dropped his chin to his chest, and in words hardly audible to his own ears, he told the doctor to stop. He turned to embrace Olivia and Emily and then cried like he'd never cried before, sobbing on his sister's shoulder as if he was five years old again.

Olivia and Emily joined with their tears until no more tears remained.

The rest of the day was a blur. Olivia handled the details of the body transfer to the funeral home. She handled the hospital bill and set up an appointment to arrange the burial ceremony. His brain stayed numb. Like his heart. He'd lost his father. Even worse, he'd lost the woman who made his life feel right.

How will I ever fix this? He had no answer. Even as he trudged up the porch steps and into the house, he stood in the foyer feeling about as helpless as a schoolboy.

A strange eeriness greeted them. The rooms sounded hollow and empty from too many deaths in too short a time. Mitch stared up the marble staircase.

"Go on. Talk to Carisa," Olivia urged with a wave.

I feel like the biggest idiot in the world. "I treated her badly. She'll never forgive me."

"She's the one who called us, Mitch. She knows you were upset."

He faced his sister. "I was angry, not upset. I didn't listen when she told me to stop."

"She explained everything to us. Go and apologize." With hands braced on his shoulders, she nudged him toward the staircase. "I'll help Emily get some dinner ready."

But Carisa was not upstairs. She was gone, and he had only himself to blame.

Hoping he was wrong and she forgave every stupid word out of his mouth, he climbed the stairs and entered his room. But the room was empty, the bed neatly made. He stepped onto the balcony and looked toward her favorite spot. Empty as well. The two bathroom doors stood wide open so he hurried straight through to her room.

The barrenness struck him first. No hand cream on the bedside table. No watch and rings along with a brush on the dresser. No makeup on the vanity. Knowing what he'd find, he opened the closet anyway. No suitcase or clothes. No note either. He didn't deserve one.

His own fault. He wouldn't listen. He had shouted words that were cruel, and then, of course, the phone call…

With a heavy heart, he headed down to the kitchen.

Emily and Olivia stood by the counter, waiting.

"She left," he said, forcing out the words through a tight throat.

"We know." Emily stepped forward. Her blue eyes were misty behind the glasses. "She left me a note to say goodbye." She showed it to him.

Mitch snatched the paper out of her hand and read.

"Did she leave you a note?" Olivia asked. "I

noticed she didn't say goodbye to you in that one." She stepped in front of him, her posture challenging. "What did you say to her, Mitch?"

"I told her to get out." He stared at the note, searching for a hidden message, but the wording was a simple goodbye with condolences. "I told her to get out of this house." He swallowed hard. Were his words the same spoken by her father? If so, the memory must have torn her to shreds. He'd sworn never to hurt her, yet he had done just that. He handed the note back to Emily before he crushed it into a ball.

"She knew you were upset," Olivia continued. "She's a doctor. She probably hears all kinds of words spoken in emergencies." She cocked her head. "What else, Mitch? What aren't you telling us?"

Something he hated to admit. He felt his heart fall out of his chest. "I made the most asinine phone call because I was so angry. I called her a cab from the hospital. I gave them specific instructions to wait for her to pack."

Olivia gasped and backed away. "That was definitely a wrong move. What possessed you to do such a thing?"

"I wasn't thinking straight, all right?" He stood before judge and jury, and dammit, guilty as charged. He ran a hand through his hair. "Maybe she's still in Geneva." He took out his cell phone and dialed. Voicemail activated. "Call me." She won't call. Only an idiot would leave a message like that.

In desperation, he telephoned the airport. After identifying himself in an official capacity, he asked what flights were scheduled for Philadelphia. Only one flight and the man confirmed Carisa MacDowell as one of the passengers. The plane had departed three hours earlier.

"What now?" Olivia asked as she paced. "You can't leave us to return to Philly. We have a dual funeral to arrange and Rags to bury." She stopped to rub her forehead. "Natalie's flying in tomorrow. She'll stay with us because I don't want her to stay in her father's house alone." She pointed to the housekeeper. "Emily will notify the family. I have to contact the lawyer and start with the estate." She faced him. "I need you here, Mitch."

Undecided, Mitch fidgeted. He wanted to run after Carisa, hell, leave the car and take a jet, but Olivia was right. Too many responsibilities existed that needed handling. He nodded. "Before I start anything, let me try something." He sent Carisa a text message. *Please tell me you're home safe.* A message returned twenty seconds later. *Home safe.*

Assuming someone hadn't stolen her phone and only returned the message to pacify him, he sent another. *How do I know it's you?*

Ponytail is up.

He smiled at that. Maybe she wasn't so mad after all. "Dad should have told me," he grumbled. "This could have been avoided. Instead, I ruined the best relationship I've ever had." The *only* one he ever had.

Olivia opened the refrigerator. "You haven't lost her forever. You may have to crawl on your hands and knees after the cab stunt. What you said can be corrected."

Damn right. Mitch Montero was not Carisa's father. He planned to get that woman back into his life whatever the cost.

Chapter Twenty-Five

Mitch entered the large waiting room, expecting to see the obvious: a room full of pregnant women in various degrees of expansion. A few looked ready to explode. Several others shifted in their seats, their faces contorting with the discomfort of an ever-growing abdomen. Only one other male sat among them, and he was about four years old.

The little boy stared at Mitch with round, wondering eyes.

Yes, another male in a female world. A world of pastels and flowers, of vanilla air fresheners and soap operas on the television screen. Pictures of babies hung on the walls, most pudgy and cute. The magazine racks showed covers of mothers cuddling newborns. Pamphlets for first-time mothers were on every table.

Mitch felt too big for the room. Regardless, he had chosen this way, no beating around the bush, no waiting until office hours were over. *Get it done and get it done right* was his motto. Because of that saying, he'd become a police lieutenant at the ripe old age of thirty-three.

He approached the check-in window.

The receptionist looked up from her writing with widening eyes. She slid aside the glass partition. "Can I help you? The doctor isn't seeing any sales reps today so if you have free samples, you can leave them with me."

"I'm Lieutenant Mitch Montero from the Philadelphia Police Department. I need to see Dr. Anthony MacDowell."

"Do you have an appointment?" Glancing down, she scanned her appointment book. "He's very busy."

Mitch leaned halfway through the window. He kept his voice low but firm. "You will tell Dr. MacDowell that Mitch Montero is here to talk about his daughter."

Her wide eyes grew wider. She rolled her chair backwards and stood. "Wait here, Lieutenant. He's with a patient." She returned thirty seconds later with another woman.

Mitch staggered back a few inches. Carisa's double followed the receptionist, older perhaps with a lackluster style to her blond hair, but Carisa nonetheless. She opened a side door. "Come with me, Lieutenant. I'm Carisa's mother. Is she okay?"

The resemblance was phenomenal. Mrs. MacDowell had a few more wrinkles around the eyelids, but they were the same brown bedroom eyes. Unfortunately, this was the woman with no backbone, the one who hadn't stood up to defend her child. In a way, he should thank her. If Carisa had stayed in Ohio, she'd never have been out jogging on that fateful day. "Let's find a place to talk, Mrs. MacDowell, along with your husband. Tell him what I have to say won't take long."

"Are you sure you don't want to tell me instead? I can write him a note so we won't waste his time."

What the frig—His body tensed, and he gave her a stern look. "My visit concerns his daughter. I think he can take a few minutes from his precious schedule to hear what I have to say."

Waving toward a doorway, she ushered him into an office. "Wait here. I'll get Anthony. He's with a patient and might be a little while." Frowning, she hesitated with her hand on the doorknob. "Please tell me Carisa is all right."

The woman showed genuine concern. He smiled gently. "Yes, Mrs. MacDowell, your daughter is all right, and no, she has not been arrested."

The woman's face changed from worry to puzzlement with a simple shift of her brows upward. She stifled her words and left the office.

For a man who had tossed his daughter out of the house, MacDowell had an office loaded with family photos. Carisa as a little girl smiling alongside her mother. Carisa as a teenager hugging her father. All three smiling brightly at Carisa's graduation. Mitch leaned closer. *Yes, med school.* She looked beautiful, no matter what age.

Mrs. MacDowell returned a short time later followed by the man Mitch came to confront.

Dr. Anthony MacDowell wore a lab coat in place of a suit jacket, his tie clipped at the bottom to hold it tight against his shirt. A deep frown wrinkled his face as brown eyes, sharp and critical, traveled the length of Mitch in one sweep. He merely nodded at Mitch's presence, walked directly to the chair behind the desk, and dropped into the leather without as much as a hello or handshake.

Mrs. MacDowell placed herself off to the side, biting her lower lip, her gaze riveted on Mitch, hands straight by her side. She stood stiff, like a soldier waiting for the next command.

The doctor looked boldly at his watch. "I'm a busy man, Lieutenant. Why are you here?"

"I'm here to meet the man who threw his only daughter out of his life, the man who chastised her because she chose to build a life of her own." He threw the newspaper that was tucked under his arm onto the desk. "Open it."

Dr. MacDowell obeyed and the paper crinkled.

Mrs. MacDowell shrieked as she bent over the desk to see. "It's Carisa!"

"You're damn right, it's Carisa. She saved a little girl's life because of her quick thinking. The town of Geneva, New York, has declared her a local hero."

The doctor broke his gaze from the photo and looked up, one brow arched. "What was she doing in Geneva?"

"Visiting my family." Mitch leaned over the desk, fighting to hold onto his temper and the urge to grab the man by the scruff of his neck. "*My* family, Doctor. She couldn't introduce me to hers because of a father who won't allow her to come home."

Mrs. MacDowell again shrieked. She rushed around the desk and grabbed Mitch's arm. "You're in love with Carisa?"

Mitch smiled at the suddenly animated woman. "Yes, Mrs. MacDowell, I am in love with your daughter. She has agreed to marry me. *You* will be welcomed at any time to stay in our house and play with your grandchildren, but this gentleman must do some serious apologizing if he wants to see any grandkids."

Dr. MacDowell grunted and pushed aside the newspaper. He swiveled in his chair, his air nonchalant.

"You obviously aren't here to ask for my daughter's hand."

"No, sir, I'm not. I'm here to pay the debt you placed on her head." He took out his checkbook from his jacket pocket. "Tell me the total amount." He waited, pen poised.

Dr. MacDowell studied him. "I don't want your money."

"I insist, Doctor. I know she's been saving to give you that one big check you demanded. She doesn't have the full amount yet, but I do." He again poised his pen over the check and glared. "I'm waiting, sir."

MacDowell drummed his fingers on the desk, his gaze critical. "You're only a police lieutenant. You can't possibly have that much money."

Mitch flashed a crooked smile. "I am the son of a successful winemaker. My father accepted my choice of career. He wasn't happy at first because neither my sister nor I had any interest in the wine business. He never disowned us nor put a price on our heads—" He leaned over the desk for emphasis. "—like you did with your daughter." He straightened, pen again poised. "The amount, Doctor. I will not allow Carisa to delay our wedding because of this outstanding debt."

Despite MacDowell pushing aside the paper, he glanced down, his gaze drifting back to the photo. Someone had snapped Carisa as she worked on the little girl in the back of the ambulance. Her ponytail dangled and two strands escaped, but she looked gorgeous.

Mrs. MacDowell stood beside the desk, crying into a tissue. "Our daughter's getting married, Anthony. And look at the man she chose! You should be proud." She stiffened her back and sniffed. "I've had enough of your stubbornness. You must forgive her, or I will visit our grandchildren alone."

Well, well. Carisa's mother has a backbone, after all.

Anthony MacDowell glanced from Mitch to his wife and back again. Then his gaze strayed to the photo. He touched it. "Carisa always made me proud. She had a mind of her own, even as a little girl. My own self-centered stubbornness got in the way."

"She needs to hear those words from you, sir, and you need to take that debt off her head. Either let me pay or forget it."

MacDowell nodded and stood while extending his hand. "Forget it. She met a good man, and one I'd be proud to call a son-in-law."

Mitch took the doctor's hand. "I'm heading back to Philadelphia now. She's on night shift so I won't see her until tomorrow afternoon. You'll have ample time to call." He replaced the checkbook into his suit jacket. A new suit. For two funerals.

"My daughter knows nothing of your visit?" Mrs. MacDowell asked.

"No, ma'am. My father passed away while we were visiting. Carisa returned to Philly. I stayed for my father's estate settlement." He met Anthony MacDowell's steady gaze. "Carisa sat at the piano and, at his request, played like a concert pianist. She brought my father to tears, and he died a happy man."

MacDowell nodded. "That's another one of my regrets. She plays very well. I never told her that either." He stepped around to the front of the desk. "One question, Lieutenant. Why did you refuse your father's business?"

Mitch gave him a wry smile. "I hate the taste of wine."

Startled, MacDowell stepped back. Then he laughed, a loud belly laugh that vibrated the walls. "I'll call her," he said.

Mitch took Mrs. MacDowell's hand and kissed it. "Your daughter is as beautiful as you. Now, I'll know how she'll look as she ages."

At which, the woman blushed. "You take care of her."

Three weeks had passed since he gazed into Carisa's beautiful eyes, three long weeks where nothing seemed to go right without her. He, Olivia, and Emily had worked together to pack and donate his father's possessions. Clothes mostly were picked up by the Geneva shelter. The estate itself would take time, and that was Olivia's job. They had worked out the details before he left. Bob LeBeau had attended both funerals and was a constant presence in the house ever since.

But three weeks without Carisa had passed like a decade. She still wouldn't answer his calls. Text messages had gone unanswered. He wasn't sure she'd speak to him again, but with the debt problem out of the way and hopefully, a convincing apology from her father, Mitch intended to move in and conquer.

"I'd like to see her get off shift work," MacDowell said as he led Mitch toward the door.

"I'll work on it." Since his calls went unanswered, he had his cohorts at headquarters check on her. They, in turn, had advised him what shift she worked. He didn't want to waltz up to say hello when she was trying to get much-needed rest.

Mitch paused at the door and faced MacDowell.

"When you threw out Carisa, did you call her a cab?"

The man's eyes misted. "Worse mistake of my life. The action finalized the separation."

The older man's words stabbed him in the heart. Mitch Montero had some serious ass-kissing to do.

Chapter Twenty-Six

Dull and mundane. Back to normal. Somehow, the words created an odd pace to her jogging, throwing her a tad out of synch. Carisa felt as if she stumbled over her own two feet.

Maybe she'd taken too long a vacation.

Oh, who the hell am I kidding? She had spent an amazing week where nothing was normal. Mitch had changed her life. She became part of a family again—at least temporarily, experienced rage at a child predator, witnessed first-hand police procedure in their hunt to find Willie's murderer, and love had touched her heart, an organ she'd sworn had died because of her father.

A yearning had developed because of Mitch, one greedy for love and family, full of the contentment it offered, and most of all, belonging. Everything involved Mitch, a man who gave her a terrific sense of security. Whenever thoughts of that week surfaced, memories of his love, his passion, had poured into her mind and wouldn't go away. He was the best thing to happen to her in a long time.

Now, it was over. Three weeks had passed since she'd left. Lonely, empty weeks. Leaving a lot of time to think. She'd made a decision to move on. Not just with Mitch, but the house, her job, and her life. She was tired of the dull and mundane. Mitch had awakened a side of her that she relished, a happy, fun side, full of passion and adventure. Time to forget the past and start new. Even though winter wasn't a good season to put a house on the market, she'd signed the papers anyway. *Get started. Make the final commitment.* She'd use any profit to pay off her father once and for all.

"Hi, Carisa!"

Little Harriet again. She played on her own front lawn these days. Mrs. Schubert had installed a small garden fence to protect her precious blades of grass, which right now were blades of stiff straw. The old woman had even hammered in a Keep Off The Lawn sign. Like Harriet had the ability to read. Unfortunately, Harriet's curly dark hair stirred images of a near-lifeless body gasping for breath. Every day, Carisa scrutinized the mail carrier as if he had a child tucked in his big leather pouch.

And what about the little girl? Was she okay? If Mitch called with an update, well, too bad. She had let all his calls go to voicemail, ignored the text messages, and the mixed emotions every time his name appeared. Why, she wondered, when she loved him so much? She missed him, dammit, yet, she couldn't bring herself to answer his calls. Only the first text message. Nothing after. And all because of the friggin' cab. Fighting back a tear, Carisa waved to Harriet and kept up her pace.

How could Mitch say the same words that her father had seared into her heart? She had never wanted to leave Dayton, but her father gave her no choice. She hadn't wanted to leave Geneva either because a week in that lovely house felt like home and hadn't been enough. Only Mitch had asked her to leave.

All right, he was upset. A lot of people said nasty words and made ridiculous accusations during the stress of a horrific moment. *Human nature.* She'd taken it in stride, let herself calm down, and called Olivia. Not too long after, the cab pulled in. For the second time in her life, she stared stunned at a cab driver who had been instructed to wait.

A twist of fate, without a doubt.

Her cell phone rang. She ignored the irritating shrill until she remembered her request for overtime. A crisis would take her mind off her troubles. Caller ID showed *Mom.* Surprised, she slowed to a walk and activated the phone. "Hi, Mom."

"Carisa?"

She stopped dead. The voice was one she recognized from so long ago.

"It's your father, Carisa."

Her mind raced. What could he want that broke four years of silence? "Is Mom okay?"

"Yes, your mother is fine."

Who else died? Did she even care? She wasn't close to anyone back in Dayton. So, that meant Anthony MacDowell called for one reason. "I don't have the money yet, Dad."

"I don't want the money anymore, cupcake. I want you."

Tears filled her eyes, and she swallowed hard. Her father hadn't used that nickname in years. "I don't understand." Her voice trembled. She collapsed onto the curb.

"I want my daughter back. I want you to forgive me for abandoning you. I was selfish to think you'd follow in my field. I'm proud of you, cupcake, proud of what you do and who you've become. You've made a good life for yourself despite the pain I've caused. I want you home."

Apologies had never come easily from her father, if he attempted to make one at all. Was he stringing her along with an ulterior motive in the wings? "Are you dying?" She heard his breath suck in like a vacuum. Then, a nervous chuckle escaped from his throat.

"A logical assumption, daughter. Nor is your mother standing with a gun to my head. I love you, Carisa. I don't want to live my life without you anymore."

She wanted to believe him, but four years of silence grew into a pain she couldn't squelch. Was he serious? Did he expect her to forgive and forget so easily?

"I'm sorry, Carisa. I should have said this a long time ago."

The tears rolled. She couldn't avoid what she had known from day one. "I always loved you, Dad." Her love for her father had stayed in her heart, despite everything he'd done. She had buried it deep in the crevice of the ventricle and surrounded it with a protective shield. But a special man was needed to break the shield, and for that, she would forever be grateful to the man who'd taught her to love again.

A soft sob resonated over the phone. After several long minutes, he cleared his throat. "Your mother and I want you home for Thanksgiving. She said she needs practice making your favorite cupcakes. And we want you to invite that police lieutenant. Think you can make it?"

She started, not certain if she'd heard right. "You met Mitch?"

"Yes, he stopped by. He talked some sense into

your old dad. He's a good man, Carisa. He's made quite an impression on us. So, how about Thanksgiving?"

Words eluded her. Mitch stopped by? From Geneva? Had he returned to Philly? *Breathe, dammit.* She shook herself. "I'll check my schedule and get back to you. I don't know about Mitch."

"Do what you can, cupcake. We have a lot to catch up on. Your mother sends her love."

Carisa stared at her phone after disconnecting. For four years, she had volunteered to work every holiday because she hadn't any place to go, no family to worry about, nor any desire to celebrate alone. What magic spell had Mitch cast to get her father to apologize? And when? She wiped her eyes with her sweatshirt sleeve and stood.

What now? Should she call Mitch to find out why he had traveled all the way to Dayton? *I know why, for the same reason I stopped breathing. Maybe it isn't over between us.* Not since Geneva had she felt such a surge of hope flooding her core, but she still hadn't a clue what to do.

Her phone chirped, indicating a text message that read, *Turn around.*

She whirled.

Half a block away, Mitch sat on her doorstep watching her. Her heart skipped a few beats at the sight of him filling the small stoop with his bulk. He wore a suit and tie and looked as handsome as ever. She wanted to run into his arms and forget everything that had happened, but pride stopped her. Pride intermingled with hurt. Her feelings toward him hadn't changed, but what about him? Would he forgive her for not saving his father? Perhaps he had already moved on while she remained in limbo.

Don't jump to conclusions. Find out why he's here.

Famous last words. She was thrilled to see him…and scared, afraid the shield wrapped around her heart wouldn't hold, and she'd break down like a fool. With measured steps, she approached.

Mitch stood. "I said a lot of words I regret, but I will tell you for a fact, I am not your father. I will not wait four years to say I'm sorry." Smiling, he stretched out his arms.

No, he was a man who pulled her from her cold medical world and filled her heart with love. He had given so much, and she'd taken it without hesitation because more than anything, he was the man she loved and wanted to marry.

In an instant, she flew into his arms. Every emotion swept through her at once, like an avalanche of snow, impossible to stop. She loved this man, the strength he offered, the comfort, his smile, his voice. *An endless list.* He held tight as if afraid to let go. The feeling was overwhelming, and she could no longer contain the flood of tears rising to the surface. She placed her head on his chest and cried. Joy. Love. Relief. First, her father. Now, Mitch, the man she wanted to spend eternity with. Was this a happy day or what?

After a time, he kissed her hair and whispered, "Give me your door key." He carried her over her own threshold and settled on the sofa cradling her in his lap. "I wasn't sure you'd see me again." His voice cracked. "I missed you so much. You don't know how many times I kicked myself because I acted like an idiot."

"Is that why you stopped to see my dad?"

"Yes. It was time to meet the other idiot in your

life. We both used words that were ridiculous and cruel. And then to find out I called a cab just like your old man. I understood why you wouldn't answer my phone calls after that." He paused.

She lifted her head from his shoulder to see a tear roll down his cheek. Her finger wiped the tear then touched his lips. With a movement as gentle as a caress, he took her hand and kissed each fingertip, his gaze tender but tired, with shadows below the lashes.

"I convinced your father it was time to stop and forgive." With one finger, he stroked her cheek. "Forgive me?"

"God, yes!" She clung to him, and his arms wrapped tightly around her. The tears returned. Buckets of tears for a man she hadn't stopped loving. Her lips sought his, and his kiss tasted sweeter than black cherry ice cream. She heard a sob. Whether from her own throat or his, she wasn't sure. She lifted her head to wipe the tears streaming down her cheeks.

He cleared his throat. "You need to see something." Blinking fast, he reached into his suit jacket and extracted a folded newspaper.

She gasped at the front-page photo and grabbed the paper from his hand. "Who took this?"

"An orderly on a smoke break. He sold the snap to the paper and created a celebrity. You photograph well."

"What are you talking about? I'm a mess!" As an afterthought, she tucked a loose strand of hair behind her ear.

He grinned broadly. "The mayor wants to give you a medal."

"I don't want a medal. We gave a team effort. You

should get the medal for beating up the bastard." She threw the paper onto the coffee table. "Is the little girl okay?"

"She's recovering, but I imagine the psychological scars will remain for a while. Carisa—"

The seriousness of the tone surprised her. She met his gaze. "What?"

He toyed with her sweatshirt sleeve. "If we hadn't gone to see my dad, and if you hadn't loved sitting out on the balcony, we'd never have uncovered Harvey and Sal's enterprise. On that choker collar was DNA evidence of two other victims."

The words turned her stomach. She lowered her head to his shoulder and fingered his jacket lapel. "What happened to Harvey?"

"He hung himself in the jail cell. No one tried to revive him. In his deposition, he explained how he placed his order with Sal every time his father planned one of his trips. The little girls were usually dead and disposed of by the time his father returned."

"He should have been strung up and quartered," she said bitterly. Then she lifted her head. "What happened to Sal?"

Mitch sighed heavily. "They're throwing the book at him. He's going away for a long time. His wife already placed the house on the market, and she's taking herself and the kids back to Vermont where her family is." With a gentle tug, he eased her head back onto his shoulder.

Carisa toyed with Mitch's tie. Memories of her little hands on her father's tie came to mind. She'd play with it as he read her a bedtime story, always on his lap. She had loved those moments. And now, she had

Mitch. *I'll play with more than just a tie with this man.* She slipped her hand inside Mitch's suit jacket to feel the muscles under his shirt. "Any news about Rachel?"

"None. So far, she hasn't contacted Tom. He's sulking, and his grades have plummeted. He'll have to screw his head on better if he doesn't want to repeat his sophomore year."

They fell silent. She listened to the heartbeat in his chest while her head moved with the rise and fall of his lungs. She hoped they spent many nights like this. Two lovers enjoying the silence, embraced in each other's arms, a sharing of love and comfort. After a time, she lifted her head to look at him.

His gaze was focused on the newspaper photo.

"It's not that great a shot."

A sad smile spread onto his lips. "I stared at that paper every day after you left. I hurt the most beautiful woman in the world because I refused to listen." He took her hand and kissed the palm. "I got angry because I didn't get the chance to tell my dad I was coming home for good."

What? She pulled back, eyes wide. "I thought your ambition was to reach captain here in Philly?"

"I want to reach captain but not necessarily in Philly. Geneva PD offered me a position, and I accepted. I came home to tell you and Dad and…well, you know the rest. I had a lengthy discussion with Olivia and took possession of the house. Emily will stay on. The only missing detail is you."

I'm going to live in that house? "Mitch, are you serious?"

"Very serious, love."

He lowered her onto the sofa and kissed her.

Memories of Geneva and a king-size bed floated into her mind. For weeks, she'd fooled herself into thinking her feelings for him would pass. She made up excuses, which were as asinine as denying her feelings. She loved this man, dammit. Case closed.

Mitch reached into his breast pocket and pulled out a small, black felt box. A ring box. "This has been burning a hole in my pocket since Geneva. I want you to marry me, Carisa."

Heart pounding in her ears, she stared at the box. "You asked already. I haven't changed my mind."

"I'm asking again. Marry me."

With shaky fingers, she took the box. "Well, if you insist. My grandmother always said to let a man ask twice to make sure he's serious. So yes, Mitchell, I will marry you." She opened the ring box and gasped at the size of the diamond, a four carat at least, sparkling from the sunlight through the front windows. She sat up. "This is huge, Mitch." She choked on a sob as he slipped the ring on her finger. "I can't believe this." She stared at her hand, moving it to let the light glint on the stone. "I've never had anything so gorgeous." She lunged and pinned him down on the sofa, planting kisses all over his face.

He chuckled softly. "You really are good at wrestling."

She looked at him with a grin. "I'm so much in love with you. I don't know why it happened so fast, but I like how I feel around you." She sat up and wiped a stray tear from her cheek, a happy tear, one that blurred her vision as she stared at the ring. "I can't go to Geneva yet. I'm under contract at the hospital."

"How long?"

"To the end of the year…six weeks." *Way too far away*. She wanted to be with him forever and always. She touched his cheek and met his warm gaze. So much love poured from them, and the sensation filled her chest with indescribable happiness. "I already told my boss I wouldn't renew my contract. Plus, the house is going up for sale next week."

"Oh?" He pecked at her lips. "Time for a community hospital where people say thank you? Like Geneva?" He loosened the ponytail to allow her hair to fall about her shoulders. "Actually, six weeks will work out well. I already gave notice at headquarters. We both need to clear out our homes. Maybe by the time we return, Olivia and Bob will be engaged."

Her mouth fell open, and she faced him. "Really?"

He slipped his arms around her. "Maybe we'll have two weddings for the price of one. Oh, and by the way, Bob likes to make his own beer. We might have use for the winery, after all."

Her nerves got the better of her. Too much information too fast, too many emotions fighting for control. She broke free of his arms and jumped to her feet. "My God, Mitch, there's a ton of stuff to do. We gotta get our belongings packed and moved out; we need to plan a wedding. We have to talk about finances and planning a family. Plus, my father invited us to Thanksgiving dinner, and then Christmas is coming— wait a minute." She narrowed her gaze, suddenly needing to know one very important fact. "What did you say to change my father's mind?"

He stood, removed his suit jacket and tie, and tossed both onto the sofa. "I told him he won't see his grandchildren. This time, your mother didn't stand passively by. She told him she will visit alone if he didn't apologize."

Her mouth gaped. "No kidding?"

"She finally put down her foot." He swept her in his arms and headed for the staircase. "I don't know about you, but we have a lot of time to address your concerns. For now, I have one activity on my mind. Your bedroom's on the second floor?"

He muffled her answer with his lips as he headed for the staircase.

A word about the author...

Jane Drager has an extensive medical background honed from years in an emergency room setting. She is an amateur astronomer, an amateur ham radio operator, and an avid people watcher. When she isn't writing, she enjoys her keyboard and occasional pounding on the drums, two skills learned from her stage mother. Unlike her mother, Jane will only sing in the car with the windows rolled up.

~*~

Other Titles by This Author

Secrets By Necessity
Ask Nothing In Return